DATE DUE			
OC 0 8 '09			
MR 0 8 '10			
SE 2 0 '10			
DE 0 2 '10			
2-7-11			
8.12.19			

THE ALMOST
ARCHER SISTERS

**Center Point
Large Print**

**This Large Print Book carries the
Seal of Approval of N.A.V.H.**

THE ALMOST ARCHER SISTERS

Lisa Gabriele

CENTER POINT PUBLISHING
THORNDIKE, MAINE

This Center Point Large Print edition
is published in the year 2009 by
arrangement with Simon & Schuster, Inc.

Copyright © 2008 by Lisa Gabriele

The text of this Large Print edition is unabridged.
In other aspects, this book may vary
from the original edition.
Printed in the United States of America.
Set in 16-point Times New Roman type.

ISBN: 978-1-60285-479-6

09-1493
S+S
(Ch. Pt.)
6/09
$31.95

Library of Congress Cataloging-in-Publication Data

Gabriele, Lisa.
    The almost Archer sisters / Lisa Gabriele.
        p. cm.
    ISBN 978-1-60285-479-6 (lib. bdg. : alk. paper)
    1. Sisters—Fiction. 2. Large type books. I. Title.
PR9199.4.G324A79 2009
    813'.6—dc22
                                        2009004901

acknowledgments

Much thanks to Marysue Rucci, Virginia Smith, Helen Heller, Maya Mavjee, and for the generosity of the Ontario Arts Council. I would also like to thank Susan Gabriele, Lisa Laborde, Jenn Goodwin, and Ola Pelka for their support, advice, and encouragement on the early drafts. And a special thank you to Adam Nicholls.

For my sister, Sue

chapter one

Until she left the farm for good, I never thought much about what made me different from my sister, what set me apart from her beyond our looks, beyond her hair color (unnatural blond) and mine (unremarkable brown), her body type (tall, thin) and mine (neither). She had always been fickle where I had been firm—mean to my kind. She shone brighter than me, for sure, but sometimes painfully so, like the way the sun hurts to look at when you have a head cold.

But it wasn't until I left the farm years later that another difference made itself clear: unlike with Beth, men had mostly been good to me; it was women who broke my heart. First our mother, then Beth.

I was almost sixteen the morning she left Lou and me for school in New York, her packing so purposeful that the whole house seemed windy with her escape. As I watched her, my slippered feet swinging off the side of her bed, I don't remember thinking that I'd never leave myself. I hadn't planned to stay forever in the same house, town, and country in which I was born. Do stayers do that? Do we toddle around as babies, then children, then teenagers, fingering the chipped Formica, the cat-mangled armchairs, the muggy drapes, thinking, I'm pretty sure this old house and these burnt fields are as good as it's ever going to get for me, think I'll stay? I didn't do that. That's not how it happened.

"Throw me that belt, Peach," Beth said, half-awake, sipping coffee Lou had carried upstairs on a tray. "Dammit, I hate my clothes. I'm gonna have to steal some new outfits."

"Go ahead. Dad says you're old enough to go to jail now and he won't bail you out this time."

She gave me an arch look.

"Want these?" She excavated her roller skates from the bowels of her closet and was holding them up in her clothespinned fingers. "Can't be bombing around campus in these. Or can I? Maybe that could be a cool way of getting around. Short shorts. Maybe a little felt cap?"

I could picture it too, Beth on the way to class roller-skating backward, wearing her Walkman.

"Nah, on second thought, they're stinky and old. You have them," she said, gently tossing them with the rest of her castoffs engulfing me on the bed. That's how Beth parted with things. Even then, I was aware that in order for Beth to let go of something she had to convince herself that she had never wanted it to begin with.

"How about this?" she asked, pressing her

long silver prom dress to my shoulders. It was an unsettlingly grown-up gown, a mermaid-style confection she had daringly paired with hippy-type sandals and rows of leather bracelets on her upper arms. Beth had also brought an actual grown-up to the gala, a twenty-four-year-old professional hockey player with a drinking problem and an ex-wife. "Maybe someone will ask you next year if you put down a book and put on some lipstick. And if they do, Peachy, go, okay?"

Prom night had turned into a lost weekend for Beth, during which time we received no fewer than a dozen phone calls from her date's ex, threatening murder. As for me, I'd spend my own prom night with Lou, coaxing a wounded raccoon out from underneath the porch. We had seen it get hit by a car on the highway, had watched it quickly amble to the farmhouse, ducking under a break in the lattice. For days Lou hunkered under the house to move the flashlight across its face to see if the raccoon's eyes reflected back at him. I would periodically place sardines on the end of my field hockey stick and wave it in front of its nose, pleading with it to take a bite, *Just a bite, come on, please?*

Poor thing took four days to die. We buried it in a laundry bag by the willow stump that served as the farm's morbidly crowded animal cemetery. Maybe because of the encroaching subdivisions and widening highways, the farm became a kind of last-stop refuge for these luckless creatures, a place where the wounded could get a bit of comfort before dying. And I became, like Lou, a talented cheerleader for those who'd arrive at our doorstep on their last legs.

Beth took a dusty, unframed picture of our mother off a high shelf, its edges curled from resting slumped in a corner. In it Nell's on a beach shielding her eyes from the sun, the other hand holding up three fingers—the number of months she was pregnant with Beth. On the back someone had scribbled "Santa Cruz '71." I wish I could say Beth became mournfully reflective. I would like to have remembered that moment as one infused with tender sadness over our mother's death, one of the few things we shared. But instead Beth flung it in my direction like a Frisbee.

"Want this?"

Before I could answer, Lou struck a knuckle on her doorjamb, the dog peeking around his legs with endearing curiosity. Scoots had long given up entering Beth's room alone. It had been off-limits to him since he was introduced to us a year earlier, when even he seemed to sense Beth's ambivalence toward anything cute or kind. She wasn't a cooer or a petter, so Lou's attempt to use a puppy to keep his errant oldest closer to home had failed miserably. In fact, that's how he got his name, from Beth kicking him away from her, saying, "Scoot, dog. Get out of here. Stop licking my feet."

"Your ride called," Lou said. "I'm gonna go meet them."

At orientation a month earlier Beth had met a girl from Leamington whose parents were also sending her to school in New York to study fashion and design. They offered to bring Beth over the border with them in their big pickup truck with the passenger cab, but it meant she'd be limited to two boxes and two suitcases. The rest Lou and I would have to ship.

Beth gave them directions to the Starlite, the convenience store in the center of town. It was easy to find; the farm wasn't. We knew how to get ourselves home, but when we had trouble guiding people over the train tracks, past the highway, over two county roads and several concessions, it was best to just send them to the store, where one of us would drive the ten minutes to fetch them. The store used to dazzle Beth. Its clean neon sign and plain white stucco exterior belied a busy inside; narrow aisles with saggy metal shelves were stuffed with loud metallic bags of junk food, sewing supplies, kitchen utensils, and cheap games and toys made in foreign countries. It was a place crowded with choices and Beth loved it. And for a long time our mother could use a trip to the Starlite to get her to behave in a hurry. But after our mother died, the toys began to look used and poor to Beth, the doll's hair plugs apparent through the dusty plastic, their stenciled eyes and mouths misaligned and kind of menacing. Soon after, Lou's own promises to stop at the Starlite were greeted by bored sighs and blank stares out the car window.

Lou moved sheepishly about the house looking for his keys, all of us aware that political stubbornness was the only thing preventing him from driving Beth to New York himself.

Lou hadn't stepped foot in the United States in almost eighteen years, not since arriving on Canadian shores as a welcome draft dodger and proud coward. But Beth didn't seem to mind that morning. I had often wondered if her love affair with America wasn't partly fueled by the knowledge that her shabby kin couldn't, or in my case, wouldn't, follow her there.

"Okay, gals, be back in ten!" he yelled, the front door slamming behind him.

"I think that's it," Beth said, surveying the room, fists at her hips. Then she plopped down next to me on a bed piled high with her past. "Peachy, I need to tell you something, okay?"

"Yeah," I said, shrugging my shoulders up to my ears, bracing myself against potential poignancy. It wasn't that we weren't close, but her adolescence had left me battle-weary. Discussions about periods, orgasms, heartbreaks, and hangovers had always been completely one-sided and uncomfortably forthcoming.

Beth took a deep breath.

"Okay. In that box," she said, pointing to one of four we'd be shipping, "is several thousand dollars' worth of high-grade marijuana. A kind of mix between local skunk and Holland white widow that I've been growing out back behind the barn all summer. It's been properly dried and wrapped in plastic. Then I sealed the bundles in some coffee tins I've been hoarding. If the border police find it, you *could* go to jail. But I'm ninety-*five* percent certain that they won't. So no worries. And I'll take the rap. That is, if they find me. But just make sure those boxes are completely sealed, okay? And make sure you ship them after me as soon as possible, today even, because I know how you and Lou procrastinate about going into town for errands. You guys put things off. I don't want to wait two weeks for them. I need that box, Peachy. You understand what I'm telling you, right?"

During the cruel five seconds that passed before she burst into her wicked laughter—the kind that bent her completely forward onto her hands and knees on the floor of a bedroom we'd leave exactly as she left it—I actually pictured a SWAT team pulling up our long gravel drive-way, brandishing rifles.

"Holy shit, Peachy, you should have seen your

face! Oh my God, you kill me you are so fucking naïve."

I punched the side of her arm hard.

"Ow!"

"Jesus, Beth. You are such a bitch! Why do you do that to me?"

"Oh my God," she said, panting for air and rubbing the spot where I hit her. "Because I *can*."

We heard Lou's Jeep turn into the driveway, followed by the Leamington family's tires hitting the gravel. At a honk we sprang up and began to gather her things. Beth giggled as she loaded my shoulders with her carry-on and her knapsack. Lou appeared in the doorway with his sleeves rolled up over his downy white forearms. Beth hoisted one of the two smaller boxes she was bringing with her and pointed with a foot to the other one. Lou and I formed the not-so-reluctant caravan following her down the stairs, out the front door, across the porch, and into the cool August dawn.

Introductions were short and vague. The rich girl's father began to ask Lou about the kind of crops growing on the acres that lushly surrounded our farmhouse. Before Lou could tell him they weren't our crops, that much of the remaining land was leased after the outside acres had been sold to pay for Beth's tuition, Beth swatted us back and away, far from the truck to make our private, awkward goodbye.

14

"Okay. So. I guess this is it," she said, hooking an arm around Lou's broad shoulders then mine. They were exactly the same height, both a full head taller than I. "I'll call you when I get settled, Lou. And I'll see you at Thanksgiving. The American one."

"Well, my love," Lou said, his blue eyes watered down with genuine tears. "We will miss you oh so much, you know?"

"Aw," she said, cocking her head as though Lou had merely been her kindly landlord for seventeen years and not the man whose last name she shared, who had sold most of his property to pay for her dreams.

"I'll miss you too, Beth. A little," I said, still bruiséd by her prank. I tried hard to catch up to Lou's emotions, to muster up at least a hint of something sad around my eyes, but I couldn't. It's not that I wouldn't miss her, but in the weeks and months before her departure I was becoming curious about what life would be like on a Beth-less farm and in what direction I might grow if I ever got out from under her dense shadow. I had plans. University, and then the purchase of a car perhaps. I wanted to grow out my bangs, read in peace without Beth snatching my books and lobbing them across the room if she wanted my attention. Perhaps I'd visit Nana Beecher in Florida. Nothing dramatic. But plans nonetheless.

"Oh, you will miss me. Believe me, Peach. You just don't know it yet," she said.

And that was it. She was gone. I did the walk and wave, following the heavy truck backing out of the driveway, later joining Lou on the porch, where we watched the sun come all the way out, the two of us sipping coffees on Nana Beecher's wicker chairs. It was so quiet the air felt tinged with religion. Still, we wasted no time in reminiscing, both of us laughing loud and hard at Beth's pot prank.

"Oh, man," Lou said, exhaling with a whistle, "you can call Beth Ann Archer a lot of things, but you can't say she isn't funny. That's *funny,* Peach."

"I know. I walked right into it too," I said, shaking my head.

"Always do."

"I know it."

We took in some more silence.

"You need to check that box though," Lou said, taking a sip of coffee, "before we send it."

"Already did," I said, leaning back to click his cup with mine. I left out the part about cutting open the box and finding a sealed envelope resting on top of a pile of sweaters, my real name, "Georgia," printed in Beth's neat scroll. Inside was a note.

Gotcha! I suppose I deserve it. I haven't been all that trustworthy lately. Anyway, Miss Georgia

Peach, I just wanted to tell you that I love you more than monkeys, mountains, or the moon, because I probably won't be able to say it to you in person before I go. Be good. Or at least be gooder than me. XXOO Beth.

I placed the picture of Nell in the envelope and resealed the box. Later, Lou and I drove into town to ship them.

Over the next few years, while Beth pledged passionate allegiance to a flag he hated, Lou refurbished a silver Airstream trailer and turned it into a hair salon he parked out back near the river. While Beth made out with strapping models in crimson darkrooms, married instructors in dim hotel rooms, and one Korean lesbian on a dare, I lost my virginity to seedy Dougie Beauchamp after a high school rock concert and some beer in a parked car. While Beth financed her first trip to the couture shows in Milan by taking a summer job selling ecstasy for an over-leveraged bond trader, I began studying for a glamorous career in social work, chosen because Beth always said I was a good listener, a great helper, her favorite sidekick, and, like her, I should try to make a living at whatever came naturally to me.

So I began the daily commute to the university to study the art and science of helping people help themselves. There I would learn how to

17

negotiate the psychological landmines of longing and loathing, and to dissect how families can easily fall into the throes of violence, poverty, and addiction. It was hard work, but I often felt like I'd be embarking upon something necessary, noble even, after graduation. So I acted smug rather than jealous when Beth called to say she had landed a high-paying job dressing vapid celebrities for national television. Sure, I would have liked to have gone to Rome or Paris on a press junket, and I wouldn't have said no to meeting a movie star or eating a five-hundred-dollar meal. But I comforted myself with the knowledge that it was more important to help people be good than look good. Unlike several of my classmates, I actually read my expensive textbooks cover to cover, highlighting the parts I would later memorize, making it a priority to put a dent in the suggested readings list between the extra courses taken in an attempt to graduate a little earlier. Because Lou was right—managing the lives of the less fortunate felt like a thing I was born to do. I saw my name, Georgia Archer, before it was caboosed by Laliberté, with a B.S.W. on the end, followed perhaps by an M.S.W., and still later a Ph.D., because you never know. And I wanted it—really meant it—all the way up to the day I quit school, six credits shy of my degree, and a few months after the nicest guy in town knocked me up and married me at twenty.

chapter two

I once read that prime hours for break-ins were between four and six in the morning, when occupants, if they were home, would be too deeply asleep to notice any commotion. But the boys were five and eight now, so it had been years since I'd been up before daybreak, years since I'd breast-fed my sons while watching the sun come up over the Rosarios' farm across the way.

But now the morning sky was becoming so bright it hurt my eyes to look up, partly because I was slightly hungover for the first time in months, partly because tears were pooling in the corners of my eyes, which was partly due to the smoke from my first cigarette in eight years. But mostly it was due to the crying. Still, you could tell that it was going to be a beautiful day. Made me less afraid to leave.

We had arrived at the park a couple of hours earlier, I'd say about four-thirty in the morning. I had thrown the car blanket over Jake, who fell easily back to sleep in the grass. Sam had stayed up with me for a while, slightly confused and beyond exhausted. Then he too dropped at my feet at the foot of the slide. I watched him get

19

hit by his invisible lightning. You could tell the difference between sleep and a seizure by the way his feet would whip back and forth like tiny windshield wipers gone awry. I'd grown so blithe about his epilepsy by then, I actually petted his hair with my toes while he seized.

The dawn finally stirred Jake awake. He jumped up to tug on my pajamas like a teething lion cub.

"Mom, we have to go home now," he said, knuckling the sleep from his eyes.

Why wouldn't joggers stare? I'd gape too if I saw me sitting in the dark on the edge of the slide, looking as battered as a blow-up doll with a slow leak. I had a wad of balled-up Kleenex shoved in a nostril to stop the blood, and one hand down my eight-year-old's pants patting around his little penis to see if he'd wet himself again. Jake began circling me in an orbital blur of impatience and confusion. It occurred to me that it was the first time he'd ever seen me smoke.

"Nasty sagrits!" he said, expelling big fake coughs.

"That's right, baby, cigarettes are nasty," I said, blowing the smoke skyward, watching Sam start to stir in the grass.

"I wanna go home!" Jake yelped. "Why do we gotta not go home."

Watching his adorable anger, I suddenly wished I'd had a camera. If not for Beth, who flew in from New York six times a year to get her hair expertly touched up by Lou and to take me out on the town, I'd probably have no pictures of my boys. At the end of every visit, she'd pose us on the porch of the house in which she also grew up, sometimes on the wooden swing, sometimes on the paint-peeled stairs, sometimes by the mailbox, BEECHER scratched out and replaced by ARCHER, which was scratched out and replaced by CHEZ LOU which had been professionally stenciled beneath LALIBERTÉ FARMS, the name I took when I married Beau.

Whenever the farmhouse felt like it would collapse under the weight of another new repair or addition, or another argument over how to pay for it, Beau would threaten to move us into town, into one of these bland model homes, on an even blander street. When he entertained these tangents, I'd feign deafness. Though nothing farmy remained about the farm, with 325 acres long sold to put Beth through college, another 80 leased to the bachelor brothers' organic tomato concern, which now paid for Sam's treatments in Detroit, I couldn't imagine living anywhere else. I never thought much about how a town becomes a city, but I suppose it had something to do with the evolution of our farm, how its outer acres were quickly sprouting subdivisions, its breeding inhabitants flourishing on the fringes of our remaining 20.

"For godsakes, smile, Peachy," Beth would yell over the top of an impossibly small digital contraption, which no doubt cost more than Beau made as a mechanic in a week. "Be hap-hap-happy like me!"

But there'd be no commemorating this visit. Hours earlier, I had walked in on my husband Beau having sex with Beth from behind, the default position, I suppose, of people who can't bear to look each other in the eye. Beth screamed, "Peachy!" And for the first time since our Roman Catholic wedding, my entrance inspired Beau and me to invoke the name of our Lord Jesus Christ in unison.

"Alrighty then," I gently added, closing the door to the walk-in pantry. It killed me that even at the apex of my family's apocalypse I was still polite. How I had willed my legs back upstairs to wake the boys in the middle of the night, I'll never know. But I was grateful that I had Beth's rented convertible as the draw.

"Sam, get up. We're going for a drive in Auntie Beth's fancy car. Get your brother."

"What time is it?" he said, still surrounded by darkness.

"Time to go."

Beth had promised them a ride that morning, not necessarily at four in the morning, but the hour didn't dampen their enthusiasm. Sam ran downstairs bypassing the kitchen where his aunt and dad were now yelling at each other and furiously dressing. Jake trailed behind him. I grabbed my housecoat from the downstairs bathroom and calmly joined the boys in the carport where Sam was acting like a game-show model highlighting the convertible's features.

"Is Dad coming?"

"Not anymore, Sam."

I noticed the keys had been left in the ignition. Beth not only didn't want children, I thought, she wanted mine dead. An exaggeration, sure, but when people asked her if she wanted kids, her standard reply was that she was too selfish to be a mother. She'd sometimes glance toward me for a contradiction I never offered. Instead, I'd nod away as she'd explain how much travel is involved with her work, how being the host of a popular style show meant being away from home at least a third of the year. She came up with the idea for *Clothing for Cavemen* while working as a stylist at MTV, a job that seemed to involve a lot of sex and shopping. But after she'd told a famous country singer that his hat made him look like an ass, an executive who fell in love with her frank manner put her on TV. Thus *Cavemen* was born, a show that involved bossy Beth telling hick boys and blue-collar men how to dress like rock stars, for success—or just plain sex—a skill she had honed as a teen in our small town.

"Sam, you buckle your brother in, okay?"

He yanked the strap across Jake's hip bones.

"Mum. I have to pee bad," Jake said.

"That's okay, sweetheart," I said, throwing Beth's rental into hard reverse. The tires spit a very specific hailstorm of gravel at the back of Beau's Jeep. "You can pee in the car."

Of all the idiot things to wake me. It wasn't the sound of Beau and Beth wrestling in the pantry. It was forgotten meat. I had made a mental note to pick up steaks on our way back from the hospital. But my mental notes seemed to be written on blackboards left in the rain. I wasn't new to the twin jobs of stay-at-home mom and full-time housewife, but I had always been lousy at them. I wasn't a rememberer, a darner, a scrimper, a time saver, a coupon cutter (my sister-in-law, Lucy, kept a little file folio. She alphabetized the damn things!). I didn't clean as I cooked. I watched too much TV, listened to the radio too heartily, pacing back and forth between the rooms in which they were left blaring: kitchen, living room, kitchen, living room, I paced, trying not to smoke, even though I had quit on our honeymoon eight years earlier, not for Beau, but for Sam who was five months old in my belly and already starting to swing from my bottom ribs. And even though I had the time, I didn't volunteer to bring complicated platters to potlucks, smug upon my arrival. I was not the woman who said to the marvelers, *Oh, it was really nothing,* when, in fact, I had given it everything I had. Nothing I'd ever done turned out exactly the way it looked like in the picture. Not my dinners, not my house, not my marriage, not my education, not even the boys.

We had stopped at the Starlite Variety, now open twenty-four hours to compete with the 7-Eleven and the all-night grocery. I poured myself some stale coffee, bought licorice for the boys and an extra box of Kleenex for me. Sam was still out cold under the decrepit slide, the same one Beth and I played on as children. A lurid smear of my blood started at his wrists and petered out at the tip of his thumb. I felt inside his pants again. Still dry, thank God. I'd grown immune to the mute stares a person would naturally attract when openly molesting a passed-out eight-year-old in a public park. I continued to ignore the morning joggers and dog walkers while I lit another cigarette. This used to be a small town. We used to know everyone. Then came the subdivisions and the monster homes and all these well-dressed strangers with their silver minivans and their skateboarding kids who never played in rivers or built forts like we did when we were kids. Instead, they hung out in menacing clusters in town, outside the doughnut shop or the diner, wherever they sold things kids could afford to buy.

Usually, I'd usher Sam home so he could seize in familiar surroundings. Peeing his pants was a constant concern with his condition, and now that he was noticing girls, the potential for permanent mortification was becoming difficult to stave off. After his diagnosis, we were given pamphlets on antiseizure medications and an awful helmet, a horrible boxer-looking contraption that made our already odd boy look like an insulated freak. Since he rarely wore the helmet, I added full-time head catcher to my résumé. We were also given pep talks by teachers and neighbors about what an "old soul" Sam was and how his so-called wisdom, his seeming maturity, would pull him through. But I knew Sam's soul was the same age as his body; that he still believed his parents were omnipotent and that bogeymen lived under the bed. He could occupy himself with a stick and some dirt for longer than it takes me to finish with the soaps. He was so supportive of Jake's imaginary friends you'd think he saw them himself. He was no more an old soul than I was. Yes, he was the quieter of our two boys, but if told a time bomb was embedded in your brain, you'd keep activity to a minimum too. It didn't mean he was thinking deeper thoughts than the other kids. In fact, quite the opposite. When asked, "What are you thinking, buddy?" during one of those faraway looks, he'd more likely have said chocolate cake or kittens than anything rueful, shocking, or sad.

After our mother died, people used to whisper these things about Beth and me. They granted us the same lofty wisdoms cultivated by adults transformed by the terrific blows of random tragedy. ("The girls are strong. They'll survive this. They have old souls.") But it was Lou who had deepened and aged; Lou's hair turned white in one year. And now Sam's condition was something we experienced, we witnessed, we feared, not Sam.

While Sam stirred in the grass, I tried to engage Jake.

"Would you look at that sunrise. Beautiful, isn't it, Jake?"

"I hate the sun."

"Me too."

Sam opened and shut his hands, studying the blood on his fist, my blood.

"Welcome back, buddy," I said. Convertibles had always infuriated me, how they commit such cheery violence on a driver's head. The ride had spun his hair into a cotton candy Afro. It reminded me of the way home perms used to make Beth and me look like masculine soccer moms until our hair would finally relax. My dad loved the chemical precision of administering perms, so we had had a lot of them as kids. Beth still flew home for the odd touch-up at Salon Chez Lou, because it cost the same, if not less, she said, to fly home on points and to rent a car at the airport, than for her to get her streaks done at a top Manhattan salon. Also Lou took his time, booking the entire day to do his daughter's head.

Chez Lou was parked behind the farmhouse along the river, the silver tube topped by an enormous upside-down sombrero of a satellite dish, the only truly "Ugly American" thing left about a man born in East Texas who still retained a slanty Southern accent even after almost three decades in Canada. Beau and I never intended to shove my father out of the house my mother had been born in, the one Lou fixed and adored. There was plenty of room, and I would have been happy with us all under one roof. But Lou said he had always wanted to drop anchor closer to water, that he had always dreamed of living in a Airstream. He had driven a truck for almost ten years, which had happily prepared him for living in the miniature.

I pulled the wadded Kleenex out of my nose.

"Did I hit you?" Sam asked.

"You did, bud. You socked me clear in the schnozzola. We didn't see it coming."

"Jeez," he muttered into his lap. I could tell he was thinking that if he could almost break his mother's nose at eight, eventually he might kill me as his condition overtook a growing body.

Jake pointed in the general direction of our house out on the highway and stomped a foot, a stunt he picked up from Sam.

"Why do we gotta *not* go home?" he whined. "It's forty-five thousand o'clock. I wanna see Auntie Beth before you guys go to New York. And I want to see Grandpa too, and Dad."

"We can't right now, Jake. I'm mad at your daddy," I said.

"Why?"

"Because."

"Because why?"

"Because he did something stupid, that's why."

"Well, tell him to stop it," Sam said, picking grass off his T-shirt.

"Too late."

"Then tell him to say sorry for it," said Jake.

"Too late, too."

"Are you going to get a divorce? Annalisa's parents are," Sam said, perking up. We all knew that, and though I was sad for the Morrows, more so for their three kids, without their epic arguments, to whom would the rest of the town's couples compare themselves? When things between Beau and me would get a little sour, I too thought, At least we are not like the Sorrowful Morrows, at least we don't make a public display, at least Beau's not drunk at the tavern like Scott, at least I didn't put on sixty pounds after the kids like Jean did, so no wonder Scott messes around with Trina Leblanc, because Jean had just let herself go. I said these things, out loud, to other assholes in town, and now perhaps I was paying for it.

"We're not getting a divorce," I said. "I just need a time-out from Daddy."

"Are you going to get another husband? Annalisa's mom said she's going to," Sam said.

"How's your head feel?"

"Okay."

"What's going on in your ears."

"A little ringy."

"Lemme feel your fingers."

He handed me his hands. They were cold.

After the diagnosis, the last remaining plans for Beau to finish renovating the farmhouse, or for me to finish my degree, or for the both of us to do any of the things young couples were supposed to do when their kids were old enough to be left with relatives, were completely scrapped. Life was all Sam: Sam's symptoms before a spell; Sam's diet and whether what I fed him had a positive or negative effect; Sam's sleep patterns; Sam's stools. I'd pull him to me, almost ardently, in order to smell his skin. Metallic? Putty? Grassy? Fishy? It was hard to think of anything but his ceaseless metabolism; how often he peed and pooed, the color and consistency of both, his stomach size, weight, height, his bruises and how long they took to heal; how dirty he was, or how smelly were his feet.

Jake, however, I began to handle as though he was formed from rubber, shoving him down into tubs, unraveling his limbs from bikes, wrapping forks around his filthy fists, lifting, dragging, and dropping him, tugging his shirt over his nose too hard, tying his shoes too tight, all the while watching Sam walk, saunter, canter, run, scanning his movements for flaws, for tilts, for clues to impending spells, clearing his path before certain accidents. Admittedly, around the time Sam started to faint and seize with daily ferocity, the part of my brain that had previously stored Big Plans for the Future, was suddenly flooded by relentless thoughts of adultery—just thoughts. Though it was miraculous how just thinking about sex with another man could take my mind off the tests and CAT scans doctors administered to Sam after they told us his epilepsy would get worse before he was old enough for an operation that might make him better.

"That's so fucked," Beau aptly responded, grabbing Dr. Best's chart as though what was written there might make better sense than what he was saying. "So like my kid might get worse before we can have an operation to make him better?"

"Or he might not get worse," said Dr. Best. "Or timing could be perfect. The condition could worsen just as he needs the operation. Then again, there's no guarantee of the efficacy of the operation."

"Fuck," said Beau.

All the while I'd be imagining that Dr. Best, homely, brown-toothed, British Dr. Best, was falling madly in love with me. Beau would ask if he could use the bathroom, and in his absence, Dr. Best would clench his fist and quietly hammer at his desk, whispering, "Dammit, Peachy, why don't you leave him and come live with me. I'll take care of you and the boys. You can all live in my mansion on the lake with that ridiculous heated garage. You can go back to school if you want to. I'll pay for everything. Beau doesn't need you, but by God, Peachy, I do. And so do all those sorry people who are dying for you to keep a file on them, to tell them how to live their lives. To be better people. Don't you see?"

I, of course, would say no, I couldn't leave Beau. I could never break the boys' hearts like that, especially Sam's. He was devoted to his father. My imaginary career would have to wait. Besides, leaving could worsen Sam's symptoms, I'd say. And there's more to marriage than sex and intimacy. It didn't help that quality time with my husband was usually spent at the brain clinic where we would watch a nurse finagle the demonstration dummy so roughly it seemed almost sexual. Then my body began to reject Beau, maybe because he constituted half of whatever formed our damaged little boy and my womb was having none of him. Around that time I had become afraid of relaxing, of unraveling nerves fully stiffened with hypervigilance.

My adulterous thoughts had started out common: soap operas would fuel them, then I'd masturbate in the bathtub. But because Dr. Best was about the only man I saw on a regular basis who was roughly my age, I began conjuring a fantasy lover, someone who would surprise me on a rambling walk through the brush, like a kinder type of rapist might. I'd imagine myself strolling alone (alone being the most impossible part), and this lover would leap out and grab me. Take me far away from our rueful home. Pin me down hard to the ground. I would fight at first. And then I wouldn't. That's it. That was the extent of my fantasies. Maybe we'd make weepy eye contact. He might gently unbuckle his belt; take off his pants. Fold his pants. Dammit, fold *my* pants. I'd watch myself lying still beneath him like that marble-eyed demonstration dummy as he desperately worked to revive me, to fuck me fully alive again. These fantasies seemed stupid, but they were important. An imaginary lover gave me the sense of being beautifully unworthy of my family, even just for a moment. It became a way of breaking free from the people

I loved so desperately that leaving them in my mind was my only respite from this exhausting vigilance.

I had no one in mind. No face. No body type. But the fantasy had the effect of an aspirin swallowed at exactly the right time, just before the headache took hold. Beau could sense something rancid brewing in the dark corners of my mind. It made him open and close drawers, check and recheck phone messages, wash and brush extra hard.

The only person I had told about my adulterous fantasies was Beth. In fact, though I stopped sleeping with my husband and started treating my father like a sitter, and herding the boys like sheep, Beth I began to need more than ever. Our biweekly phone conversations provided a kind of tonic of distraction and drama. It was satisfying to talk to someone who seemed to have chosen her own life out of some mysterious catalogue stored on a high shelf that had always been out of my reach: *I'll take that career, this city, those shoes, these dates, that past and this future.*

"Got anyone in mind?" she asked. "Has anything happened? Is that what you're saying?"

"No. Haven't gotten that far."

This was a tricky prospect in a place like Belle River. Beau and I knew everyone. Plus, I had married the only person in town I had ever really wanted to have sex with. So far. I told her I was waiting until summer to find a hot little tourist. Or maybe some hipster-type punk they hired at the marina. Someone kind of just passing through.

"And you think this will help?"

"No, Beth. I am really hoping it will *hurt*."

"I think I'm a little bombed right now," Beth said, acting surprised, like, *Hey, how did this happen?* But I knew it was a preemptive move in case she couldn't recall bits of our conversation the next time we spoke. I had mentioned her drinking to Lou, told him that I was worried about its frequency, but he always shrugged it off, saying, "If she has a problem, it's not like she doesn't know where to go."

"Oh yeah? What'd you do tonight? Did you go out? Tell me, tell me," I asked, yawning. It was 9 P.M.

"Nothing yet," she said. "I'm going to Jeb and Nadia's for dinner. Kate came over for a while."

Jeb was one of Beth's oldest friends. She met him when she worked at MTV, before she started her own production company and stole Jeb as her director. The way Beth had described Jeb always made him seem a little gay to me, the way they'd shop, and trade scintillating gossip about singers and stars they'd known and dressed. But then a few years ago, Beth spoke at Jeb's wedding to a woman named Nadia.

"Hey, Beth. Tell me something. How many guys have you slept with?"

"Is that why you called? To lecture me?"

"No. Seriously. I'm just wondering."

I had always gathered distracting information from Beth the way little birds tugged shiny string out of bushes, her confessions padding my anxious nest.

"What do you mean, 'slept with'? 'Slept' as in *sleep* with, or 'slept with' as in *fucked?* There is a difference," Beth said, drawing on a cigarette. I could hear her wine bottle clacking against a glass. "Why do you suddenly want to know the exact number?"

"I don't know. I lost track."

"Maybe so did I."

I slid open the back door and quietly shut it behind me. I was careful to bunch my nightgown between my legs before crouching on the cool stairs, because God forbid should anyone see my underwear. Who did I think was watching me? Waiting to get a peek? Raccoons?

"I've only slept with two guys, Dougie and Beau. I don't think that's right, Beth. I wish I could do something about it, but who'd want me? Two kids and I got tits that point down now like a Snoopy's nose."

"Plenty. Beau still does. And why are you talking this shit? How're things?"

"They're okay, you know. Nothing big. Just . . .

being married . . . and now with Sam . . ."

I admitted to Beth that it had been almost two months since we had had sex.

"Jee-zuzz," she said. "I'm getting you a hooker next time I'm home."

Suddenly, probably to make her bored married sister jealous, and for reasons that had more to do with accuracy than Beth would really admit, she let the number "fifty" fall out of her mouth.

"D'you just say *fifty?*"

"Yeah."

"Bloody hell, Beth! You slept with fifty?"

"*No.* I'm kidding. I was kidding."

"Ahh, I *heard* you."

"Ahh, it was a *joke.* Anyway, why are you whispering?"

"Because, Beth Ann Archer, my youngest son is just learning how to count past forty and maybe I don't want him to use Auntie Bethy's sex life as practice."

"Fuck you."

"*—and how many fingers does Jakey have? Ten! And how many toes does Jakey have? Ten! And how many men has Auntie Beth slept with? FIFTY!* Eww, Beth, is that not kind of *skanky?*"

Lawyerly, slowly, Beth explained that actually it was not skanky. It was normal for New York. Then, sounding too defensive, she added, "And don't forget, Georgia Peach, I am thirty. And I have been having sex for almost fifteen years, so if I *had* slept with about fifty men, that would really only be about three a year."

"Guess when you put it that way."

"Not that I'd ever tell Marcus."

"No. Not a good idea. Hey, Beth. Are we going to meet this one?"

"Maybe. Maybe," she said, sounding more doubtful than she had a month earlier. "But listen, I gotta go. Marcus is supposed to call when he lands in Phoenix."

"Okay."

"Okay. So I'll call you later this week, okay?" she said.

"Okay! Good night, you cheap, filthy whore."

She laughed a hollow little laugh and hung up. I instantly regretted the jokey taunt. Something was changing in Beth. Where she should be happy now that she had met someone special-sounding and clearly smitten, she acted doomed and moody, like her spirit had begun down-gearing in anticipation of a rapid descent.

Beth had been dating a new man, Marcus Edward Street, for close to seven months. Right away he sounded like a completely different species than any of Beth's other significant boyfriends, a category that included any man who had ever made her cry. There was the don't-ask-don't-tell deal she had with this married guy, Terry, a boat maker from Jersey City, and father of four by three wives. I told her he'd never leave the third wife, and when Beth pressed the point, he naturally fled. Then there was the one-year fight-fest with John-O the comedy writer, a man who seemed addicted to the adrenaline of a good argument. But in the last few years, her time off the market grew increasingly shorter. A mere six months with Kevin the junkie journalist, a textbook codependent relationship, diagnosed straight from one of my old textbooks, in fact. That was followed by four months with a video-game designer called the Other Kevin, his nick-name later changed to ADD Kevin, because he couldn't commit to a TV channel, let alone a woman. But ever since she'd begun dating Marcus, her calls home had dropped off dramati-cally. I was the one who initiated contact, an issue Beau brought up when it came time for him to pay the bill. Not that he minded playing the role of breadwinner, but it was just a role. The mortgage on the farm had long been paid for, and the land-lease arrangement with the bachelor brothers not only covered the taxes, but also generated a tidy income in my name. Surely no broken home or recent refugee needed me more than my own son, I'd say, to anyone wondering why I still wandered the farm while the boys were at school. And because I believed I was needed at home, Beau and Lou believed it too. But no matter how I couched my excuse, Beth wasn't buying any of it.

"You stay at home because you're afraid of a lot more than Sam splitting open his skull, and you know it" . . . *and I was talking to Marcus about this and he said he'd break up with me if I wasn't passionate about my career. He said one of the things he likes most about me is that I'm a successful entrepreneur . . . I'm not trying to brag, Peach . . . but I think you're too smart to sit on the porch all day wearing sundresses and hosing off your kids and blah blah blah . . . and you can't run around holding a net under Sam all your life . . . and it's not like I'm plan- ning the wedding or anything like that . . . but Marcus is so funny, so smart, so sexy . . . and Marcus says the situation in Afghanistan is a fricken joke and that we should be bombing the Saudis instead . . . and Marcus was saying, just the other day, that the real estate bubble isn't a bubble, but something that's here to stay, and did I ever tell you Marcus only has one nipple because the other one got torn off in a bass fishing incident when he was around seven . . . ? Did I? Oh, I did. Oh well, he still has the scar . . .*

At first it didn't bother me that Beth insinuated Marcus into every discussion, because I figured it wouldn't last past three months. And I'll admit I was jealous when she sent me his picture (sun-

gingered hair!), more so when she told me how much money he made, how good he was in bed, and that he was an avid ass man—though for the life of me I couldn't imagine how he'd managed to locate one on Beth. Still, she always seemed one temper tantrum shy of losing him.

But then this Marcus fellow did the oddest thing. He kept sticking around, even after Beth had to have an ovary removed, further hobbling her chances of having the babies she had never really longed for anyway. He stayed, even after she confessed she'd put unnecessary Botox injections on her already extended credit card, and that she had never, would never, cook a chicken, pork loin, or pot roast, in her life. He kept her fish when she went away on extended trips, and then just held onto them under the assumption that when they lived together it would just continue to be his job to tend to the tank. When he sent her flowers on her thirtieth birthday, ensuring there were no carnations, and later told her he actually thought she was too skinny, which, indeed, she was, I began to worry. I began to imagine Beth as the happy wife of a wealthy lawyer, managing a busy social calendar, a woman who'd begin to screen my calls, because why would she want to talk to me, her uneducated, put-upon sister, living in Nowheresville, heading toward Sadland, accompanied by an aging hippy of a dad, two sweaty boys, one getting sicker, an old smelly dog, all trailed by the nicest guy in town? I began to imagine all of her past boyfriends knotted at the bottom of a faraway lake, like a pile of rusty bikes, me eventually joining them.

chapter three

"It's weird we're in the park so early. Can we go home now?"

Sam was fully awake by 6 A.M., still three hours before Beth and I were due at the Detroit Metro airport. I noticed that he had Beau's feminine features, his upturned nose, dark freckles, and long eyelashes.

"Can we go home?" he asked again.

"Soon, bud."

I wish I could say this wasn't supposed to happen, but it was always supposed to happen. And though Beth had not planned for it to happen this weekend, its inevitability was written on both of their bodies. She and Beau had a past, one full of regret and sorrow, so there was no other postscript to their story than one also full of regret and sorrow. I thought of Beth's naked, bendy body, her foothill of a butt, her manicured hands grasping the sides of our utility shelf, her legs so thin she could register them as a font.

Even Beau's staccato banging didn't jiggle her ass flesh, or the canned goods, which made me feel more like my name than ever before; something that bruised too easily, something fuzzy and round, fleshy and bursting. I often wondered what my mother, who had never shaved her legs or armpits, would have thought had I grown up to follow the Southern debutante feel of my name. (In fact, both our parents were hippies of the first order; Lou remained so, with his long white ponytail, drawling all political about the hell of war, the miracle of universal health care, and the gift of gay marriage, while snipping split ends and darkening roots.)

They had named me Georgia Peach Archer after the state in which I was conceived. They'd been driving north so my father could dodge the draft with the help of his new Canadian bride and her "imperious little one-year-old," Beth, as Lou described his first impression of the baby who sat up front, back when infant car seats gathered dust in garages, if you owned one at all. But the "Georgia" part never took, the state giving way to the fruit of my middle name. I had always hated Peach. To me it better suited a girl who was raised to chase county pageants, with sequin dresses and dubious talents trailing behind her. Admittedly, Peach would have been easier had I been blessed with Beth's ass. But I dented the cheap seats at the Detroit Children's Hospital. Bag boys likely

43

rubbed one off in my wake. I wasn't fat by any stretch mark of the imagination, but the body wasn't a friend anymore. The body cracked in half giving birth the hard way. Twice. No detours through the tummy for these boys. They took the bloody scenic route and half my innards along with them. And now my body felt like a room-mate, one I used to let my husband fuck now and again.

I was focused on the investigation in the park, trying to unearth where this visit had gone wrong. Beth had arrived the day before, ostensibly for Lou's birthday barbecue, an event she never missed. But I had caught an email Beth had sent to the family account coordinating dates and flights with Beau about my surprise trip to New York, which was to be my first. He had deleted the email but he hadn't emptied the trash, which I regularly checked after reading in a magazine how to retrace your kids' steps to make sure perverts weren't trying to seduce them online. In the email Beau had explained to Beth that I'd never go to New York on my own, that I wouldn't leave Sam, let alone Jake. He wrote that she'd have to come to town to "physically escort Peachy over the border, physically carry her on that plane." I was touched when I read that, felt a bit smug too, imagining how the martyrdom of delaying my return to school must have been terribly apparent to all. Now I was trying to remember if there'd been seduction in their exchange, some menace to their messages.

For days I tried to pretend I didn't know about the trip, meanwhile taking the boys aside to prepare them, telling them that it was our secret and that they should act more surprised than me when their aunt announced she was taking me to New York. Beth didn't have children, so she didn't know that mothers rarely took surprise trips unless they were addicts or adulteresses, or seriously depressed.

"When Auntie Beth says she's taking you to New York, I'm gonna go, *Wow! Oh my gosh!* You are going to New York and I can't believe it!" Sam screamed, slapping his face with his palms.

"And then I'm gonna go like this," Jake said, spazzing all over the kitchen, yelping and clapping.

"That's perfect, guys, no one will know," I said. Not that it registered for them that I would, in fact, be leaving, but I would deal with that later.

Though he never crossed the border himself, Lou was still sad that no one met Beth at the airport anymore. Jimmy Carter had long pardoned draft dodgers, but Lou refused to step foot in his home country. Not a day went by without Lou openly railing against war and the price of gas, which he thought should be prohibitively higher, along with the price of cigarettes, alcohol, fast food, bad movies, video games, highway tolls, and city living for the rich. But I knew he missed America more than he'd ever admit, the imperial system, the miles, inches, gallons, and Fahrenheit of it all. When I used to greet Beth off the plane, Lou would sometimes come as far as the McDonald's in Windsor by the border crossing. He'd bring a thermos of coffee, practically daring the pimpled teenagers to tell him to vacate his seat for a paying customer. There I'd fetch him after fetching Beth. Lou would give her a big hug, make a comment about how thin she was, and then he'd use the drive home as an opportunity to discuss American peculiarities with Beth, such as urban blight, extreme poverty, litter, and modern segregation, a subtle, therefore more insidious, foe. His caravan of criticism was an important part of the cheerful trip to and from Detroit.

"Sometimes, Beth Ann, I just don't know how you can live in that country," he'd invariably cluck at the end of a diatribe.

"Lou, darling, I am an American. I make a lot of money in the television industry. I have friends who are unboring, an adorable Mexican boy who delivers my vodka and cigarettes to my door, a view of the Hudson River, more than eleven hundred square feet of high-end parquet that another Mexican, a lady, polishes once a week. And I have a second home, on a river, in a cheaper country, that costs me a few hundred dollars to get to every six to eight weeks, where I get my hair perfectly streaked, *for free,* where no one wakes me up before noon, and where I am surrounded by the people I love. And on the way *home,* to America, where I live, there's the duty-free, the cherry on the top of the whole dang deal. Now my sex life could improve, but it's doubtful Belle River could help me remedy that."

"Not that you haven't tried," I said.

"Right. Otherwise, I've nothing to complain about."

"Buckle up," I'd say to Beth in the rearview mirror, watching her light another cigarette.

"Can't," she'd say, blowing smoke through the window crack, appearing more famous than the minor cable celebrity that she was. "Jacket's linen." Or she'd say, "These pants are crushed velvet," or, "I'm not feeling right in the middle. Must have been something I ate." Her explanation was that if she never wore a seat belt in a New York taxi and lived this long, surely she was safe with me behind the wheel.

Sometimes, if she knew she'd be arriving in a particularly foul mood, some drama trailing behind her, she'd ask me not to bring Beau or the boys, because they made it impossible for her to smoke in the car. But I missed the part when Beth would head, head-first, into the Beth-sized space we would open between us. She'd duck into our huddle like a shy quarterback, or maybe

47

like someone hiding, not wanting anyone to see that these were her folk. But the boys didn't care about appearances. When she pulled into the gravel drive in the fancy convertible, they unselfconsciously bolted from the house, desperate to make contact with her and her car.

Beau noticed right away that the rental was a foreign make.

"Hope no one eggs it," he said, winking at me. It was a protective county. Too many auto jobs in Windsor were reliant on the domestic market, even though a lot of the foreign ones were assembled in North America, I reminded him.

"Doesn't matter," he said. "The profits go to Krauts and Japs."

"Don't call them that. We won that war."

"Well, we're losing the economic one, baby," he said.

Through the kitchen window we watched her park. The boys screamed with delight as the cloth roof of the convertible folded back, as though Beth was unwrapping a gift that contained herself.

"Ta-DA!" she yelled, hopping over the door.

Sam rushed her middle and Jake kept hold of the sleeve of her peasant shirt, looking into her face like she was the first Christmas tree he'd ever seen. Beth slapped open the front door carrying only a small leather overnight bag.

"Hey, jackass," she said, opening up an arm to Beau.

"Nice mouth on you," he said, lightly hugging her.

"Fuck you," Beth whispered, sweetly kissing him on the cheek.

"Been there, done you."

That was their shtick to lighten the tension of their history as high school sweethearts. It wasn't a big love, a long love, or a deeply profound love, but they were each other's first, and that mattered for something.

Beth first met Beau in shop class, and right away she complained that he liked her too much, sent her too many carnations on Valentine's Day, and hovered too near her in the smoking area, which he'd frequent even though he wasn't a smoker. They'd wrestle around in the dark of the living room until they heard Lou's Jeep pull up. Then Beau'd scamper off Beth's wilted body, deeply molded into Nell's old La-Z-Boy. Beau'd plop himself onto Lou's own La-Z-Boy, tossing a pillow over his swollen middle. Without touching Beth, he'd leave, as though an intimate pat would give him away, as though Lou didn't have a clue what the hell they were up to. He wasn't ignorant of the fact that Beth had had a reputation in high school. We once watched her get out of the back of some guy's Thunderbird, half of her dress absently stuffed into the back of her black nylons. We said nothing when she ran into the house and up the stairs, leaving her denim jacket in a pile on the foyer floor, the smell of stale smoke wafting off of it. What's to ask? Best he could do was cover the bases by making sure she covered her cervix with latex condoms that he boldly stored under the bathroom sink next to our tampons and the dusty hot roller kit.

About me, he worried less. I had experienced adolescence largely through Beth, much the way I like to think she'd later experience adulthood through me.

As a kid, I'd often interrupt Beau and Beth going at it, the first time on the living room carpet, Beth straddling him like a lazy cowgirl, poor Beau doing all the bronco work beneath her.

Beau yelled, "Get the fuck out, Peach. Don't you knock?"

"I don't knock on my own front door, asshole. Do this shit in Beth's room. I just vacuumed."

I stepped over their bodies and turned on the TV. Though they'd been dating for several months, I believe that constituted the first conversation I had had with my future husband.

I wish I could admit to mooning after Beau during those sweaty months when he was Beth's. Wish I could say I wistfully spied on them from the top of the staircase as they grinded on the living room shag, Beau peering over Beth's shoulder, shooting truer love from his pupils into mine. Fact is, I thought of Beau as the sputtering idiot with the perfectly feathered hair, who was always sweaty, who always wore too-tight T-shirts and had car grease under his stubby fingernails. To me their courtship simply represented the first and last time I had had my dad all to myself. During those months, Lou taught me to golf and canoe. We grew an herb garden, buying Mexican seeds from a specialty catalogue and reading up on natural pesticides. We canned a bunch of beets that fall. In fact, I had secretly hoped Beth would run away with Beau, so that I could finish growing up and out from under her dense shadow.

They had sex constantly, once in the dugout, and once in the back of Beau's mother's car, Beau's fingers working Beth quietly while Mrs. Laliberté drove them home from a school dance. After one of those rides I watched through the living room curtains as Beau's mom tipped the front seat forward to expel the spent cargo. Beth exited looking as though she'd had a good cry. She ran up the porch stairs and silently passed our La-Z-Boy gauntlet, sniffling.

"You okay, sweetheart?" Lou asked, half-distracted by the TV. "D'jall have a fight?"

"Kind of," she said.

Lou signaled for me to go after her, to see if she wanted to talk. It was his way of trying to raise us to be close, by helping me see the signs of her distress and training me to respond to them. "Beth's quiet today, Peach, go ask her if she wants to join us." "Beth seems a little moody today, Peach, go upstairs and see what's up." Thus began my career as Beth's interpreter, a hobby I honed into a science.

I found her in her room rummaging under the bed for a pack of cigarettes. She lit one, threw the match out the window, and nestled in the pane.

"Peachy. Everything's fucked," she whispered. Her face was flushed with what I thought might have been fresh sex. I was not completely wrong. She was pregnant. Beau wanted to keep the baby and was thrilled. Beth said she'd rather die than do that, let alone marry Beau. Indeed, after he proposed, Beth told me she threw up in the kitchen sink. She was seventeen and had the rest of her life to live, which didn't include—had never included—Beau. She was determined to get an abortion, with or without Beau's support, and I would have to help her.

"You have to drive me home from the clinic. They won't let me leave without someone accompanying me."

"I'm fifteen," I yelled. "I only ever drove the lawn mower!"

"Doesn't matter," she said. "They're not going to check your driver's license. I'll take over the wheel once we get far enough away from the hospital."

"No fricken way," I said. "Get one of your friends."

She raised an eyebrow at that. Beth didn't have many friends. Other girls had always been afraid of Beth, and because she gave the impression of someone just passing through, people weren't anxious to connect or commit to her.

"Why can't you tell Dad? He'll understand. He's prochoice."

That was true, but, as Beth pointed out, Lou wasn't pro-whore-for-a-daughter. He'd have been so disappointed in himself and his failed parenting skills he would have taken it out on Beth's considerable privileges, arguably ones that had put her in this position to begin with, but ones she'd grown thoroughly accustomed to nonetheless.

"Besides," she said, "I'm old enough to make my own decisions and to have my own secrets."

During the days leading up to the appointment, she stopped doing anything domestic. She stopped cleaning her room, doing chores, feeding the dog, or helping me with dinner. It was like she didn't want to play house. Sad House. Super Sad House. Smack the Unwanted Kid's Face House. Fat Ass Having House. Mommy Hates Daddy House. Beth never saw herself wearing cookie-crumb-studded shirts, smacking mouthy kids, hanging her clothes on a line made from a skipping rope as cracked as stale licorice. She wasn't built to stand in some welfare line in order to get what was coming to her—baby bonuses, retraining, government assistance. So she took out her frustration on the house, as though if she had kept up her chores, got sickeningly good at them, she would end up living on the farm for the rest of her life, becoming a horrible chain-smoking, farmhouse-living, cellulite-having, beer-out-of-the-bottle-drinking, teen-mom cautionary tale.

Newly terrified of his potent sperm, Beth dumped Beau by phone. Afterward, you couldn't find a boy more bereft in our county, and if I hadn't looked sideways at Beau before, I started to feel compassion for his shattered attempts to do the right thing. One afternoon he even brought flowers and his bank statement to prove that he had what it took to give the baby a good life. Beth dragged me by the arm into that conversation, afraid to be sucked into his vortex of sadness.

"Fifteen hundred dollars. Wow, Beau, that changes everything. Let's get married and have another one right away," she said, crumpling up the paper and dropping it on the carport floor. Beau didn't grasp sarcasm back then, so it was pitiful to see his face light up with her reply, only to dim seconds later when he realized she was joking.

She booked the abortion on a Saturday morning, ignoring Beau's last-minute phone calls. I only answered the third time to stop Lou from picking up. Beau cried openly and loudly that Beth wasn't just killing an innocent baby; she was also killing him.

I listened, hung up, and relayed the message.

"So now it's double homicide. Nice," she said, blowing smoke out the laundry room window. We had often discussed the dilemma over the running washer and dryer. "Believe me, he and his future wife will thank me someday. You and Lou, too, because you guys would be the ones taking care of this baby. Not me."

Beth told Lou we were going to the mall for the entire day, and he was so overjoyed at our seeming closeness he insisted on taking Polaroids. He peered through the viewfinder, set the timer, and ran to stand between us. Beth threw her arm around him and smiled big.

"Might want to put something on under that, Beth Ann," Lou said, clearing his throat at the way her braless boobs spilled out over the top of her scoop-neck T-shirt.

"I'm cool, Lou," she said, cupping one boob and adjusting it. For the six or so weeks she'd been pregnant, she couldn't keep her hands off them. She made me check out her boobs in every outfit she had tried on that morning. "I will definitely miss these," she said, bending over in the mirror and giggling.

The camera flashed and spat out a picture.

"Okay. Keep an eye on Peach," said Lou, shaking the photo dry.

"I won't let her out of my sight."

The clinic was housed in an ancient hospital where crackpots and rummies went to calm down and dry out. In the parking lot Beth put a bit of makeup on me, in case they mistook me for the fifteen-year-old that I was. She tended to my face with concentrated artfulness, standing so close to me I could smell her Juicy Fruit and Final Net. In the gift shop she bought me a bunch of glossy magazines and candy. And then we waited. I seemed to be sitting on every last one of my nerve endings, a little terrified of Beth's fearlessness. When they called her name, she sprang up like she'd been picked for something excellent.

"Okay, Peachy, just sit tight, okay? Back in a jiffy."

In those two hours I must have drunk about six cups of coffee from the automatic dispenser. I kept picturing how I'd drive out of the parking lot the way athletes meditate on winning their races. I saw myself backing out of the space with beautiful efficiency, gracefully negotiating the crowded lot before pulling over a few blocks away, sweaty but victorious. Beth would hop out and trade places with me and we'd be home in a half an hour, shrugging off our lack of shopping bags with words I had a hard time believing myself: if asked about the absence of purchases, we'd say we didn't see anything at the mall that we liked.

But Beth emerged a different person than the one who bounced through the swinging doors. She walked like the elderly, tippy and fragile, damp hair clinging to her face. Her features looked smushed, as though pressed in by a giant thumb. The nurse asked if I was taking her home, and I nodded. Good, she said, handing me an envelope of pills. Give her two tonight and two tomorrow. Make sure she drinks a lot of water and gets a lot of rest in the next couple of days, she said. If the bleeding doesn't stop in seven to ten days, bring her back. What bleeding? I wondered, half-expecting them to have sewn Beth up entirely.

We both mumbled thanks and I ushered Beth out to the Wagoneer. The sun was harsh and hot. I buckled her into the passenger side and took my seat at the wheel. I began a prayer in my head, but stopped when I realized that God had more urgent needs to attend to than guiding the ride of two teenaged girls leaving an abortion clinic.

"You're going to have to drive all the way home, Peach. I'll show you how," Beth said in a small voice.

"I can't. You said you would after the parking lot!" I was terror-stricken and angry.

"You can."

"I can't. If I kill us or anyone, it'll be your fault."

"Fine. Just put it with the rest of the carnage," she said. "I'm on a roll today."

I inched out of the parking lot in agonizing fits and starts, jarring Beth's limp body against the rigid seat belt. Beth leaned her head on the window, one hand covering her mouth.

"I have to get out of here," she said, her voice cracking with ire. "I have to get the fuck out of here."

"I'm *trying*," I said, speeding up slightly.

"That's not what I meant."

We hit all four red lights in the stretch to the blessed highway, Beth trying to muffle the winces my cautious braking caused. At one point she finally let the strap across her belly go slack. It was the last time I remember her ever using a seat belt.

At the farm, Lou was in the side yard with Scoots, watering the hydrangeas. I ran into the house, yelling a big phony hello through the kitchen window. Beth carefully crept up the stairs where I followed her with a glass of water.

"I need those pills now," she said, her forearm thrown across her eyes. It was like her body was a big empty puppet with old sprightly Beth still desperately operating the limbs.

"They're for tonight," I said, bossily. "You have to wait."

"Now, Peach. All of them."

I ran down to the kitchen and fished through my purse for the yellow envelope. I noticed Lou had secured the morning Polaroids on the fridge with several fruit magnets, our eyes betraying no hint of our true destination.

Lou never found out about the abortion. But after Beth broke up with Beau, older boys began to call the farm with alarming frequency. Lou often talked about that final year with Beth as one might describe a short trip to a dangerous country like Lebanon, or Liberia, a journey plagued by roadside skirmishes, shady men, rock throwing, late-night phone calls, police, and mysterious rashes. High school counselors called about Beth so often Lou eventually put them on speed dial. After a shoplifting stunt on a field trip to Cedar Point, during which she necked with a brown-toothed carnie on a dare and let the air out of the bus tires while it stopped to gas up, Beth was assigned to see a psychologist twice a week. Now with a captive, paid audience, Beth made up a story about how, after his wife had died, Lou was left with a sick sexual hunger. When he was done with us, she told her psychiatrist, he'd hand the both of us over to the bachelor brothers next door, in exchange for marijuana cigarettes and pornography. After the cops came, Beth had to admit it was an awful joke, that Lou wasn't even much of a tickler.

Still, the good doctor diagnosed Beth with borderline personality disorder, the root cause of all her emotional eruptions and burgeoning addictions, though the only side effects seemed to be Lou's chronic ulcers and my budding insomnia.

Lou dismissed her X-rated stunt as the product of leftover grief from our mother's death, the kind of thing, he said, that can make a person feel like they're a gas-soaked rag, begging bystanders for matches. But why hadn't these defects dented my own character? I was there that day too? And wasn't she my mother as well? Where was my buried grief, dramatically manifested? How come there were no expensive doctors listening to my sadness?

Around that time, Lou went to great expense to restore two minutes of Super 8 footage featuring Nell and Beth on the front lawn of the farm chasing after me. I couldn't have been more than two in the film, the smallest blur soundlessly running away from a medium-sized blur and a tall blur, presumably Nell.

"That's it?" Beth asked, rolling off the love seat. "We can't even see anything."

"That's it," Lou said. "The film's mostly damaged. Want me to replay it?"

Beth shrugged.

"Yes," I said. "Again."

Lou had hoped the film would jangle whatever was left of the grief stored inside her, but Beth lost interest after the third play. Eventually, Lou said no to the pills and the therapy, figuring plain old love and simple understanding would straighten Beth out long enough to reawaken her ambition to leave us.

In Beth's final year of high school, she managed to score not only entry-level marks, but her risky style sense secured her a place at Parsons School of Design in New York. Despite her rancid outbursts, Lou began to miss her long before her goodbye. Once, over breakfast, I watched as he became momentarily lost in Beth's puffy lips. She was absently stuffing pancakes into her mouth, her other hand negotiating an unruly sketchpad, the stainless-steel fan pivoting back and forth, mutely following what wasn't being said between them. I remember wondering if he was thinking, like I was, that Beth's lips were just like our mother's, before Nell's began to wrinkle around the edges like the dozens of clay ashtrays we brought home from art class. Every birthday and Mother's Day we'd bring her some kind of handmade round thingy which eventually took the form and function of an ashtray. Pick her some flowers, Lou would beg. Buy her candy, something she can't stub a goddamn cigarette out on. Lou was not being lascivious that morning, but something odd had made itself at home across his stubbled face, something I would call now nostalgic ardor. Finally, Beth looked up at him and grinned, her tiny teeth studded with pancake bits.

"Loo-ooou?" She slammed down the sketchbook. "You were, like, totally staring at me all weird there for a second."

Her syrupy finger hovered six inches away from Lou's face.

"Sorry, Beth Ann. I was staring and that is rude."

I tried to change the subject.

"Hey Beth, where's my book I lent you?"

Beth ignored me, waving the fork in Lou's face like a court lawyer.

"Why are you looking at me funny? Do you think I'm very beeeeooootiful?"

Lou threw down his napkin.

"Actually, yes, I do, Beth Ann," he said, crossing his arms and leaning back from the table as though he'd been challenged. "You looked just like your mother there for a second, and I was thinking, I miss Nell very much and I wish she could see how beautiful her daughter has become. And what a great success she'll be in New York. You do have your ma's mouth. Is there something wrong with that?"

"Yeah, old man. It's creepy," she said, seductively closing her mouth around a forkful of pancakes.

As Lou stood up to leave the kitchen, Beth rose too, and smashed into him. It looked like an accident. "Ow. Lou. My boobs!"

Beth covered her breasts and glared at him as he stomped toward the foyer. While he scrambled to put on his shoes, she dramatically collapsed back into the vinyl chair and laughed like a diva.

"Jeez, Peach. That was funny."

Lou headed outside, slamming the door behind him. Beth ran to the kitchen window, still giggling, as I wordlessly joined her, unsure of whether I could handle the image of Lou crying into his hands in the carport. But instead he seemed to be looking for something to smash to bits against a wall. His hand found the novel Beth had been reading, the one I had asked about, sitting dog-eared on the corner of his workbench. It was *Flowers in the Attic*, Nana Beecher's old book. He glanced at the back cover where it described a "tale of passion" between "innocent and beautiful siblings" who were "locked away from the world by their selfish mother." The opening chapter was titled "Goodbye, Daddy."

He must have skimmed through the book for ten minutes, seeming to stop on the first of several sex scenes between the young brother and sister.

"Beth reads this shit and passes it on to Peachy?" Beth said, mimicking Lou with a deep-voiced, Southern accent. "No wonder she's overly sexed-up and makin' funny 'bout incest!"

Lou wiped his eyes and carefully shut the book. In a house full of estrogen, he was the only one easily brought to tears by teasing. That was Beth's cue. She left my side, slapped open the door, and stood like a superhero, fists on waist, in the carport.

"*There* it is," she said, startling him. "You shouldn't read that book, Lou. It's not your kind of book. Or *is* it?"

"I'm sorry. I just found it over there. Here you go."

She snatched the book out of his hands.

"Don't tell Peachy you found it, okay? I'm not done with it yet."

"Sure, Beth. But it's not real smart reading, is it?"

She fanned out the pages of the paperback with her thumb, the slight breeze blowing back her bangs.

"Lou? Know what I wish for sometimes?" she asked, rocking on her hips. He seemed a little heartened. This was the kind of conversation he had always craved, had so wanted to have with her. He once told me he missed those times when we'd absently finger our wet hair while he dried our legs after a bath, the both of us nattering at him about girly things like ponies, the Fonz, unicorns.

"No, what? Tell me, Beth." Lou pulled up a stool.

"Well . . . I wish—I wish I had a *gorgeous* older brother," she squealed, holding the sickening book aloft and running back into the kitchen. "I'm kidding, Lou. It's just a joke!"

"I wish you had an older brother, too," Lou yelled.

He stomped after her into the kitchen, unfurling a finger inches from her shocked face.

"This must stop. What have I done to deserve this, Beth Ann? How have I made this environment conducive to such frank talk? Jesus Christ, I work long hours. I just want some peace in this house. And I want to see you learn to be kind, for godsakes. Why are you like this?"

"Lou, calm down," Beth said, plucking a cigarette from an open pack in the freezer. "We both already read that book."

"Smoke that goddamn thing outside. I don't want me and Peachy to die before our time just 'cause you're so damn stupid!"

"Fine. Let's go, Peachy. Lou's clearly got his period."

She sauntered out of the house, and I looked to Lou for that almost imperceptible nod that said *Go after her.* When she was like this, I did often join her. Not because I took her side. But rather because I was afraid that she'd feel abandoned or unloved, even when her banishment was self-inflicted.

We walked silently into town, over the tracks, past the high school, past the tavern and into the Starlite Variety. We strode down the toys and notions aisle to get to the cold drinks.

"Oh my God this place is depressing," Beth whispered, holding up a toy soldier whose stern little face was pressed up against a loud plastic bag. "Imagine buying this for your kid? Mom *was* insane." She tossed the doll onto the bottom shelf, then shoved a bag of Nibs down the front of her jeans. We paid for our pops and left, the glass door tinkling shut behind us. We ate and drank on the swing set until we sensed Lou's storm was over, the same trip I'd make a year later—a stop at the Starlite before a vigil in the park—when a different drama played out on the Archer Compound.

chapter four

Sam and Jake loved their aunt the way children do when they can sense someone's not terribly big on them. After Beth dropped her bag on the floor, and exactly twelve hours before she fucked my husband in our pantry, the boys had begun their aggressive preening. I loved how they'd trot out toys and tricks and books, hoping maybe one of those lucky props would do the job of puncturing Beth's mysterious ambivalence toward them. It was heartbreakingly great of them. And though it troubled Beau, I couldn't get enough of those parades. Made me root for them.

"Come here, boys, and let your gorgeous auntie grabble her hairy little monkeys!" Sam and Jake scrambled into her stomach, accidentally banging head-on into the fake boobs.

"Ow, boys, mind the machinery!"

Beth had recently replaced the old set of tits Lou accidentally bought her when she graduated. She had told him the money would go toward a Vespa to boot around Manhattan. But instead she parlayed the scooter into a stellar set of tits, which had sent Lou into a depressive funk for months.

"Where'd you pick up this idea that boobs are going to make you happy? How'd you come to think butchering your body's the thing to do after all these years in this household? You were perfect like you were. For godsakes, Beth Ann, didn't I teach y'all to be feminists? Nell would roll in her grave."

"Yeah, so sorry I'm not following in her stellar footsteps, Lou. And I *am* a feminist. But I also want to be feminine. I think of myself as a feminine-icist."

Eventually, she admitted that had she known some implants had to be replaced, she would never have gotten them done in the first place. But now that she owned no less than five thousand dollars' worth of imported lingerie, there was no going back to the old A's.

"Oh. That's a fine rationale," Lou had said. "Wanna know Victoria's Secret? She doesn't have one. 'Cause there's nothing mysterious about her."

"That's why I don't buy their cheap thongs."

Beth hadn't blown herself up to porn star proportions. She bought a firm pair of high C's, the same I sported twice with the pregnancies, before they reverted back to their default consistency of loose tapioca spooned into Baggies. But I loved her too in that moment. Beth was an unhappy woman, completely and utterly by choice, I thought.

"Hi, Peach," Beth said, straightening herself up and looking right at me. In her tone I could tell we had a long talk ahead of us.

"Hello, Miss Archer. Looking well," I said, smiling and hugging her.

"Thank you, Mrs. Laliberté. As are you."

"Tell me, Miss Archer, what brings you here on a Thursday may I ask?"

"Interesting question, Mrs. Laliberté. First of

all, we're not in production for six weeks, and since I own the show, I can do what I want, pretty much when I want. It's called the perks."

"How marvelous for you."

"Yes, it is marvelous. Also," she added, knowing her cover was blown, "on the morrow's morn we are departing this little hellhole called home, because Jeb and Nadia are hosting a dinner party in your honor tomorrow night in Brooklyn, and *we* have fancy reservations on Saturday night. More on that later. And on Sunday, breakfast at Tartine before I take you to the airport."

"Hmm . . . interesting. Are those places nearby? Because, you see, I have two young sons who need minding," I said, smiling over to the boys to cue their surprise reactions.

"Why no, they are not nearby. They are located in the city of New York, on the island of Manhattan. Come on down, Peachy Laliberté, you're the next contestant on *You're Coming to New York With Your Sister Tomorrow!*"

On cue, the boys knocked out their strangely aggressive little jazz numbers.

"So? Whaddya think, Peach? I know you've never flown and you don't want to leave the boys, but—"

"Beth. Really. I can't wait," I said, pointing to my already-packed carry-all behind the front door.

"Beau, you have a big mouth," Beth said, tiptoeing into the kitchen where he was digging out beers from the bottom of the fridge. She slapped his ass hard with an open palm. Then she began to dig down the back of his jeans to tug up his underwear, which made the boys giggle with delight. Beau squirmed away from her in discomfort.

"Ow. *Hey,* I didn't say anything. Peachy's the snoop."

He knew I could get touchy about any intimacy between them. So did Beth, which is why she would launch these little attacks in the first place. It was her way of reasserting that his body was territory she had originally conquered, then discarded. She got there first, not me. And though I couldn't imagine Beth wanting Beau again, he was, indeed, an average male starved for affection and attention, more so now since worrying about Sam's illness had long supplanted sex as the number one thing I liked to do with my husband in bed.

As though to cut the tension caused by Beth's teasing, the boys began their customary show-and-tell. Sam displayed several cool rocks he found by the river, one by one, on Nana Beecher's oak table. And Jake talked through a hand puppet into Beth's muscled shoulder, saying, "I'm Bernie. I can fly." Beau poured Beth a beer into a glass, no doubt fighting off the image of having sex with the both of us at the same time. What would it be called? The Archer Deluxe?

Lou came up from the salon stripping off his hair-dye gloves like Gypsy Rose Lee. He'd recently booked a clutch of teenaged boys from town who all wanted bleached crew cuts.

"Hello, my love. How was the flight?"

"Fast. Nice. Nothing," Beth said, standing up for one of Lou's hugs.

"You are thin, Beth Ann. I feel like I'm clutching a bouquet of lollipops."

"Good. That is the goal, Lou."

We sat around the table for a few minutes focusing intently on the boys, while Beau wiped down the granite counter top, took out the cutting board, and tenderly laid out chicken breasts he'd marinated in mustard and honey.

"Peachy, after the barbecue, let's go to the tavern for nightcaps. Beau can babysit," Beth said, tunneling through Sam's carefully placed stones to grab my hand. "I've got some more news about Marcus."

I felt my heart leap at the sound of his name.

"I thought that was all over, Beth," I whispered.

"Who's Marcus?" Beau asked. I couldn't tell if he sounded blandly curious or mildly jealous or both.

"Some guy who ripped out my heart."

"Wow, was there a reward for finding it?"

"Score one for Beau," Beth said.

Beau turned around holding a sauce brush. It was the first time I noticed he'd been wearing an apron.

"Hey, why is it, Beth, when a dad watches his kids, it's called babysitting? And when Peachy does it, it's called parenting?"

"Because, Beau, watching TV with your kids is not parenting. It's sitting."

"Oh, like you would know what parenting is? When's the last time you volunteered to help out around here? You treat this place like it's a hotel."

Beth's eyes widened and she looked at me as though to say, *Do something about your husband*. I too was a little shocked at the tension between them.

"Beau, just cook, okay?" I said.

Sam came over to Beth's side to straighten up his stones. She put a hand on his head and messed his hair a little, mouthing to me, "How is he?"

I searched for neutral words. "We don't know yet."

"What don't you know?" Jake asked, helping his brother with the stones.

"Anything. We don't know anything," I said, looking at Beth, trying to read the weather on her face.

"Well, *I* know something," she said, a hint of accusation in her voice.

"What do you know?" Sam asked, thinking we were talking in code about him or his condition, something he hated.

"Nothing. It's about your mother, Sam."

"What about Peachy?" Beau asked, keeping his back to us. I kicked Beth under the table.

"Nothing, I'm just teasing, Beau," Beth said. "As if Peachy's got secrets."

"Yeah, as if *I* would have secrets," I said, trying to deflate suspicion by acting exaggeratedly suspicious. She kept her eyes on me. The only person in the room who could tell we had been up to something was Lou.

"Okay, let's change the subject. Peachy, let's get drunk tonight, shall we?" Beth said, draining her beer and slamming the glass on the table.

"No driving then," Lou said. "I'll happily drop you off and pick you up at Earl's. Okay, ladies?"

Lou gave me his look that said, *I am not judging Beth's drinking, but I have been noting its subtle, though unmistakable, escalation, as are you, Peachy. So enjoy yourself tonight, but not that much.*

"Thanks, Dad, but I'm taking it easy tonight," I said, pointing to my beer.

The gravel driveway announced more arrivals.

"Uh-oh, Lucy and Leo are here. Be nice, they're having 'the troubles,'" Beau said, holding the plattered breasts. Beau's older sister Lucy fought with her husband so often that they indeed made the institution of marriage sound like Ireland, a once lush paradise ruined by messy children, too much drinking, and religion.

"I'm heading the hell out back," Beau said. "Tell Leo to bring the kids there. Boys, let's go. You can fire up the Water Willy, Sam."

"What about me?" Lou said.

"You ref."

"Not on your life," Lou said, scrambling after Beau.

"I'll ref," Sam said, making his way over to the laptop on the desk. "I want to play some Scrabble."

I felt a twinge of anxiety. I had been waiting for an email all day. But I didn't have the heart to force Sam outside. Jenny was four, Micha six, perfect ages for Jake, but Sam was trying to out-grow his cousins. Plus, he was afraid of having a spell and peeing his pants in front of the younger children. The doorbell rang.

"Why, I'll get it," Beth said, acting Southern and dopey.

"Be nice," I repeated.

"I am always nice. Lucy is the cunt."

Lucy's sturdy animosity toward Beth took root in high school and had flourished ever since Beth had broken Beau's heart. It was a weird resentment but so consistent I no longer chal-lenged its longevity. When Beth opened the door, Lucy's expression was of someone who had accidentally stumbled onto a teeming wall of maggoty garbage.

"Well, hello to you too, Luce," Beth said.

"Beth Ann. Hi, Peachy. Where's Beau and the boys?" She was holding a present for Lou.

"They're all out back," I said.

"I was hoping we could crash here tonight if we drink too much, but it looks like you won't have the room," Lucy said.

"You can share my bed, Luce," Beth said, knocking a cigarette out of her pack and heading toward the back porch. We kept her room almost exactly as she'd left it, though she often opted to sleep on the converted couch in Lou's air-conditioned Silverstream, especially in the summertime.

"Thanks, Beth, but no. I think I'd like to remain about the only person in town you haven't slept with."

"Sorry to break it to you, Luce, but you're not my type anyway."

"Please, people, please," I said, holding up my hands. "We are almost middle-aged women now, and no one's drunk enough for this. You guys can put the camper up if you want, Luce."

"We'll play it by ear," she said.

Beth slammed the back door and Sam turned around.

"Auntie Lucy wanna play Scrabble on the computer? It's very cool. I'll show you how."

My boy, my boy, my beautiful boy. I was trying hard to ignore him that night, or rather, to not monitor his every move and sound. Lucy sat down next to him at the piano bench. The corn boiled on the stove, and for an instant I felt a sense of fortune settle around my shoulders. I was thinking, This is a good life. Don't do anything to threaten this life. Why would you even want to?

Through the window I could see Beau out back standing over the barbecue like a conductor. Leo suddenly startled me by tapping on the glass with his awful opal pinkie ring. I gave him a weak smile. Years earlier, before Jenny and Micha were born, Leo had a fling with his Korean manicurist. I was shocked, not by the crime, but by the fact that he went to a manicurist.

"What kind of guy goes to a manicurist?" I had asked Beau. I had just had Sam, and my body had dropped so much weight from the breast-feeding, I could fit into Beth's sexy red hand-me-down sundress.

"The dickhead kind," Beau said.

After the whole thing blew up, Lucy spent six weeks with us crying as often as my new baby. One morning I held a firm finger, microphone-like, in Beau's face.

"No infidelity, no adultery, no divorce, no irreconcilable differences. Got me?" I said.

"None of those words in this house. There is no room for them."

Date, flirt, cheat, those were "Beth Words," single-people words, each a tiny, stupid Ikea-type name for replaceable things like lamps, cups, ashtrays. Beth could cheat on her guys, tests, and taxes, and the consequences were negligible. But we had a *mahogany hutch,* a *chesterfield, antimacassars, hydrangea bushes,* a burgeoning *oak,* from which we had plans to cut another table. Our kitchen was carved out of *granite* and *stainless steel,* these were all married words, and our house was full of them. Even the word *husband* had always invoked in me the permanency of mortgages, God, and cattle.

At the kitchen window Beau had put his mouth around my finger and gently sucked it.

"What about like other words?" he asked.

I was amazed to think we might have once had the ability to read each other's thoughts, but our minds were so uncomplicated back then there couldn't have been that many thoughts to choose from.

"What words did you have in mind?"

"Like 'fuck.' Like 'suck.' Like 'cock.' Like 'pussy,'" he whispered, stepping back to seriously assess the architectural challenges of that sundress, which would always give him a bit of trouble. I turned to press my back into him and saw Lou through the window playing with the baby in the grass. Beau placed his erection between the canyon of my ass and started to fiddle with the knot behind my neck. (Was it ridiculous to be angry at Beth for ruining this sexual position for me as well? Now not only couldn't I imagine facing my husband during sex, I couldn't imagine not facing him either.) Giving up, Beau lifted the skirt part, ripping it slightly at the hem.

"Oops. Sorry. Hoping to avoid that," he murmured into my unburdened shoulders.

"Liar, you hate this dress."

"No I don't. I love it on you. I just hate taking the fucking thing off."

What had I worried about eight years ago? Saggy boobs and an unpaved driveway? The creepy notion of my dad catching me going at it with my husband? My hip bones getting bruised against the granite counter? Being twenty-one with a new baby? Finishing school? I don't remember worrying about any of those things. For those few minutes, while my husband moved behind me with uncharacteristic grace and my father washed our stinking dog in the baby pool, our life was still only a series of regular vignettes—the wedding, then the baby, and then there should have been a graduation, and then a job, and then perhaps another baby, in that order, a long story with a happy ending. And though it had felt wrong having stand-up sex not twenty feet from my dad and sleeping son, I remember it had felt necessary, because this, I thought, was how husbands and wives inoculated themselves from disaster. This was how you kept the demons of marital disaster at bay.

The corn sputtered and hissed on the kitchen island. I glanced at the back of Sam's head; there had been no fit, no spell, so far that day. I made a mental note for Dr. Best.

"That's not a word, Auntie Lucy. It's a swear," Sam said, sounding manly, a bit too scolding and professional. I walked over to where they were sitting and looked over their shoulders. Lucy had organized her computer tiles to read "bitch."

"It's a word. It's a female dog. Scoots is a bitch, isn't she?"

"Actually," Sam said, correcting her, "Scoots is a guy dog."

"Then that would make Scoots an asshole," Lucy said, hand cupped under Sam's chin. "And don't you ever become one. I'm going to check on Leo and the kids."

It was going to be that kind of night, I thought, as Lucy grabbed another beer from the fridge and headed out back. Most likely she wanted to keep an eye on Beth, a wise move on her part.

"I'm coming too, Auntie Lucy," Sam said, scrambling after her, leaving me alone for a few blessed minutes to check my email.

At that point in our awful, rueful prank, no outright physical infidelity had occurred. But my thoughts and actions had all of the hallmarks of betrayal; obsessiveness, secrecy, sneaking around to check email, lying to myself that I'd stop, that it didn't mean anything, plus that rush of blood to the groin when I'd be driving and thinking about sleeping with a man other than my husband, in particular Beth's most recent ex, Marcus Edward Street. The problem was he felt the same way. About me. Well, not me, another me, a different me, a woman Beth and I have both come to think of as our "almost me."

Maybe I got easily snared in this mess because I was both bored and scared, and infidelity was spreading like a flu through many of the homes in our town, and what business did I have of thinking us immune? Still, nothing about our drama started out innocently. It was all venal— and ballsy and galling—and though Beth had been the plan's unapologetic architect, in the weeks prior to my first trip to New York, I had been the avid builder.

chapter five

During the summer between my first and second years of school, I had signed up for a stint (for credit) with physically and mentally challenged kids. They were sweet kids with gummy voices, sticker-strewn wheelchairs, hovering moms, and thick necks. In fact, I had wondered if perhaps special ed would suit me more than social work. Then I was handed the unwanted task of supervising special ed arts and crafts, myself in turn supervised by a couple of stern doctoral candidates, sent to evaluate my skills and report back to the university. I thought it would be a cinch. I had always stood up for the slower kids, those lumped with regular ones, kids forever screaming *Wait for me, I have asthma*. But I was not prepared for these ones. Regular kids are messy enough, but these kids moved like demented dervishes. None of our exercises were completed on time, if at all; nothing we produced was remotely close to the curriculum. The trees we drew were lightning bolts or freckles or flowers. The Popsicle-stick houses looked like what a tornado would see in its rearview mirror. The macaroni pictures reminded me of the table-scrap shrapnel on the floor around Scoots's bowl. I knew the point wasn't to produce perfection. I knew these kids were only to be coached on the attempt, and that art was merely meant to enhance expression and release. No one expected them to become accidental Picassos.

But I took their results personally. Somehow I thought it was my fault that I couldn't bust through the plasma that prevented them from creating little linear masterpieces. And my frustration rubbed off on them. I was too young to understand that teaching people to attempt the impossible, then to be unafraid to try again after failure, was about the best lesson you could grasp in life. Instead, I panicked. And then I insinuated myself in their tasks. I'd sit behind Chelsea, my hand firmly wrapped around her hand, and I'd make her draw what was assigned. I'd sit next to little Monty and efficiently shape the macaroni elbows into a radiating sun, even though he had no idea what I was building in his name. I'd pivot to catch and wash Joey's brushes. Then I'd helpfully guide his palsied hand toward the correct colors for oranges, bananas, or trees in summer. The kids were overjoyed at the results, the parents a bit less so after they discovered me to be the kids' arts-and-crafts Svengali.

Despite showing what I thought was real verve

and command, my evaluators did not agree. They wrote that I was "uncomfortably impatient, and overly protective."

Georgia Archer clearly demonstrates a deep fondness for the children in her care, but she has trouble allowing them to explore the limits of their own fallibility. She says her motives are to minimize the pain and frustration some of the children feel over completing the tasks at hand. But we feel she may be focused more on keeping the room clean than letting the children explore the outer reaches of the materials and the projects. In one instance Georgia brought in garbage bags (expense hers) to place over their artist's smocks to prevent too much paint from getting on them. In another instance, she completed an acrylic picture of a student's pet, after hours, and allowed the student to take full credit, even though the results obviously exceeded the child's natural capabilities. Though her intentions are admirable, and we do feel that Ms. Archer might make an outstanding teacher, we do not think she's a fit for special ed, let alone for the demands of social work, which requires particular detachment skills as yet unseen in this candidate.

I wasn't supposed to see that note, but a TA had accidentally slid the assessment in my mail slot at school. It was an odd feeling to read about myself, to picture myself doing those things, however wrong. But as with the artistic pursuits of my special ed charges, my intentions for Beth and her love life had always been good ones. My advice was always meant to help Beth; it was how I attempted to wrap my hand around hers so she could begin to spell out happier endings. But what she and her friends had hatched went way beyond casual interference or heavy-handed advice. It was near-criminal in its brilliance, and for the first time ever, I had been included.

Weeks before Beth's last disastrous trip home, I had returned from grocery shopping to find Beau splayed out on the couch, the top of his pants undone. His furtive masturbation had woken me twice that month. I didn't get angry because I wasn't doing anything to offset the need. He was welcome to play with himself all he wanted; I just didn't want the boys to catch him.

"Why not?" teased Beau.

"It would traumatize them. That's why."

"How?"

"They're just boys. And they don't need to know they've surpassed their father in every way. It would mess up their ability to admire you."

"There's a message from Beth. She's in fricken Thailand somewhere. I saved it," Beau mumbled, tugging himself out of the tail end of his nap. "She's crying again. I swear, you spend more time with her than me."

Beth's crew was on a two-week buying trip to find cheap batik and men's Hawaii shirts for a special episode on leisure wear. It was that aspect of her job that I had always found bafflingly enviable. She did these things, went to these places, and worse, she had a way of making the trips seem as important as G-8 summits.

I dumped the grocery bags on the kitchen counter.

"What time is it where she is?"

"I don't know, but she and her friends are pretty drunk. It kills me. She calls, you drop everything. I want something from you, you tell me later. *Wait. Not now. No. Quiet. Leave me alone.*"

"Don't be like this, Beau."

"It's true, man. I did the math. Fucking seven hours on the phone last month. That's more than you spend talking to me. Or anyone else."

"Where are the boys?"

I yanked a can of beer off its collar and threw it at Beau the way you'd pacify a caged lion with a lamb shank. I wanted to say that if I didn't have Beth, I'd have let the hair on my toes grow black and long like they want to. I'd be fat(ter).

I'd have cut my hair into that spiky middle-aged, manageable lady mullet, one you and the boys would be sporting a variation of, too. Worse, all proudly. Without the computer Beth gave us, we wouldn't have found that not-too-bad-looking, unobtrusive helmet that Sam can wear when we're not around, or when he knows he'll be negotiating hard surfaces. And forget about that red halter dress, the French perfume, the playful lingerie, the tasteful porn. Forget about those recipes you love so much you once said that you wanted to spread my eggplant parmesan all over your chest in front of the guys at the shop, like a monster, *It's that good.* Without my biweekly Beth dose, we never would have heard of *The Usual Suspects*, Lucinda Williams, or braised rapini, all your favorites now.

You have no fucking idea, Beau, I wanted to say.

"So. Where are the boys?"

"I butchered Jake and stuck his body in the freezer. Sam's out back choking on his vomit," he said, punctuated by a loud burp.

"Ass. Hole." I slapped him not lightly on the back of the head. "Don't joke about that."

"Relax, they're with Lou. He took them to the fair in Wheatley. He's gonna feed them lunch there."

"Lou take extra pants?"

"I don't know. Probably."

"Jesus. I told you, that's part of watching Sam, for chrisakes. Did you give him your cell?"

"No. I forgot."

"Man . . ." I took my anger out on the answering machine button, smashing down PLAY.

"Paging Dr. Peachy," Beau screeched through a *TV Guide* bullhorn. "Waa, it's Beth. Nobody loves me. Call me. *Waaa!*"

Peach, it's Beth. Check your email please, please, please. Then call me back. My cell. The hotel's a backwater. I'll call you right back. I did something kind of funny. Well, Jeb, Kate, and I did something funny. Anyway, can't wait to tell you. Miss you. Need some HDP.

Heavy Duty Peachy.

I used to ignore that laptop when Beth first gave it to us. Then I started researching Sam's illness, a terrifically addictive and terrifying habit that I was trying hard to break. Her email was titled "I Want to Die." The body of the email contained two Web links, the first one taking me to a New York newspaper's daily gossip section.

July 7—Media lawyer Marcus Edward Street probably isn't laughing about his girlfriend's latest antics last Saturday.

Potent party girl and TV fashion diva Beth Archer roughed up one of the bouncers at Marquee after she and her friends refused to vacate a reserved table. The incident escalated to the point where the bouncer, who has since been fired, allegedly put Archer in a headlock after she punched him squarely in the face, breaking his nose. Aggressive Archer had police called to the Chelsea hot spot after she was escorted out, but declined to press charges. Now that's, um, class!

The second link in the email took me to a dating Web site, specifically to an ad featuring a "Newly Single Lawyer," presumably Marcus. My heart actually leapt at seeing his handsome, happy face again, chin resting in his hand, making him seem professorial and wise. He looked exactly like a well-balanced, evolved, curious, committed, kind human man—no one like Beth had ever dated, including Beau. Plus, he ticked off an income category which exceeded that of everyone I knew or was related to, combined.

I finished reading, checked the time in Thailand, and phoned Beth's cell.

"Congratulations!" I said when she picked up.

"Fuck, Peach. You gotta be kidding."

"Whoa. Didn't you say you always wanted to make the gossip pages?"

"Not as Tara Fucking Reid!" she yelled over a loud crowd behind her. I could hear a man's voice say, "She was great in *The Big Lebowski*!"

"Fuck off, Jeb," Beth yelled, trying to muffle the receiver.

She told me they were in the hotel bar after a long shoot involving cauldrons of dye on the beach. It was almost midnight there, just after lunch for us. I looked at the back of Beau's skull, the alert part of his head facing NASCAR on that stupid flat screen we bought with the satellite dish after 9/11.

"Beau, turn that thing down, okay?" He raised the remote over the top of the couch and ratcheted down the sound.

"Peachy, did you see his fucking *ad?* We *just* broke up, and he had the balls to send the link to Kate, in case she had any friends who were single. I mean, he doesn't even like Kate. No offense, Kate," Beth said, presumably to Kate. I could hear people laughing in the background, but I could also tell Beth was on the cusp of some real pain for the first time in a long time. I whipped out my old voice, my soothing social worker voice, the one I had hoped to take out of its imaginary, velvet-lined box upon graduation.

"Okay, calm down, Beth. What happened? Walk me through it slowly. Start from the start. What sticks out? And go somewhere quiet, would you? I'll head out back too."

I grabbed a Coke in the fridge before letting the back door slam behind me. On my way out Beau muttered, "No, no, I'm good, Peach, I'll just stay right here, playing with myself."

"So tell me what happened, Beth."

"You wanna know what happened? You wanna know what he said? He said: 'Well, Beth, I wasn't sure I could fall in love with you before. But after that Page Six stupidity, it's doubtful I ever will.' He's looking to join a private firm. Make partner, or whatever law people do. Seems I'm not law-partner-wife material. But dammit, Peachy, that bouncer was a fucking tool."

Marcus told her he thought that they should take a long break, as though Beth was an arduous hike and lucky him coming upon a bench. I understood that urge, but sometimes that's all it took. A brief break, feet up, phone off for a spell, and then I'd muster up the business of missing Beth again.

"I want to know what's wrong with me, Peachy. Why I can't get a guy to love me?"

"I wish I knew too, lovey," I said. "Maybe your picker's broken and you should retract it for repairs. You know?"

Beau was right, I did spend more time on the phone trying to fix Beth's life than I did making sense of ours. I know now we had just begun the mysterious process of growing apart, something that used to baffle me about other couples. I used to wonder how, after seven, eight years together do you possibly "grow apart"? And please can you show me how to do it? I used to worry Beau and I had grown way too close, not in the cute way of finishing each other's sentences, but in the bad way, like a pot holding too many plants, the roots eventually strangling each other. After almost a decade of marriage, my body, my life, was becoming indiscernible from my husband's, a man who ate off my plate, used my toothbrush, and talked to me while sitting on the toilet, scouring his molars—worse, I understood every word he mumbled through the suds, standing there at the vanity wearing his tossed-off T-shirt and rubbing his medicinal hand cream into my heels. Even if I hadn't had sex with him, hugged or touched him, by the end of the day, I would smell like Beau. Once, after my hernia operation, I was about to scold him for clipping his toenails in the living room. But when he was finished with his toenails, he started on mine as though my feet were simply an extension of his own, a backup set, perhaps, and I loved him so much in that moment.

"Beth. Listen to me. Have you spoken to him?"

"Marcus won't talk to me. Won't answer my emails. Won't tell me why he can't love me. Then he goes and posts that ad and he *makes sure* I know about it. It's so cruel. I hate him, but I love him so much. Oh, Peachy, I'm going crazy. And now the Internet's down at this fucking hellhole hotel, and I'm fucking here for another week of fucking stupid models and fat Germans trolling the beach for kids. I hate it here."

I let her cry while craning my neck to watch Beau stretch off the couch, channel-surf, then fall back down after finding something else to watch. Like bobby pins under a high beehive hairdo, or the spider web of arthritic knots tied behind a delicate piece of embroidery, men have no idea how relationships are held together, the girdles and duct tape, the emotional scaffolding that hold two people together.

"Forget him, Beth," I said. "You have to just forget him. And no more emails, okay? He'll think you're desperate."

"It's just that I don't want this to keep happening to me. You studied social work. What's wrong with my social life?"

"Well, I flunked out so I'm just an antisocial nonworker. Maybe you pushed things too soon, too far?"

Beth had a knack for sending what I called "emotional canaries" into the hearts of the men she liked or loved. They took the form of anxious questions: Where do you see this going? When are you back in town? What should we do about dinner? How do you feel about meeting my people? My meeting yours? Where do you see yourself in five years, ten, twenty? When she wasn't using these questions to peck at her boyfriends, the questions would turn on her, stalk her, turn an otherwise successful TV personality into an urban Tippi Hedren, running in a panic to escape them. Because of this, I've never envied my prettier, smarter, funnier, skinnier, richer sister. Her uncertainty drained even me.

"Did you read his personal ad, Peachy? Doesn't he sound like a dream come true? Wouldn't you just want to meet him and love him?"

"Yeah, maybe someone's dream come true, but not yours. That's kind of dicky what he did, sending it to Kate."

"Well, he's trying to make a point. That it's over. Which I get."

"If it's any consolation, Beth, it actually looks like Marcus is looking for someone kind of like you," I said.

"Yeah, almost me, only *not* me."

"That's a good way to put it."

"Yeah. And so I feel like putting up a fake profile. A really hot one. Like the perfect woman." There was a pause, a rather long one, then she quietly added, "How hilarious would that be? Wouldn't that be funny?"

"Actually, 'funny' isn't really the word I'd use. 'Insane' comes to mind."

"Peachy?"

"What?"

"That funny thing I did?"

"Yeah."

"That *we* did."

"Yeah. What? What did you do?"

"It's funny more than anything. Jeb and Kate think it's funny too."

"Jesus Christ, tell me. This call is costing a fortune."

"Well, a couple of nights ago we were fucking around on my laptop and we were a little drunk, and . . . what if I told you that Marcus might be in love again. With someone we both know!"

"What are you talking about? Who do *we* know?"

"You."

"Me?"

"Yeah, he's in loooove with you."

"What the fuck are you talking about?"

She told me it was Kate's idea. Partly Jeb's. But mostly it wasn't her idea. Not mostly. Partly. Okay, all three of them thought it up. See, what they did was, well, they got to talking about how shitty it was for Marcus to send Kate the profile, so they thought it would be funny to contact Marcus with a fake profile of the perfect woman, someone who didn't exist, but they needed a picture so they filled out a form and topped it off with a real photo of me, my face at least, looking farm-fresh and windblown, culled from a recent crop of pictures Beth had taken during our unseasonably warm Christmas, which she had stored on her laptop, and wasn't that hilarious? Totally hilarious, right?

After a long moment, I said, "Wow. You are a piece of work. Even thousands of miles away you're dangerous to me and mine."

"I know, but listen I gotta run so remember this information. The password for the profile is Scoots. Don't ask. It just came to mind. And the user name is Almost Me. I haven't finished filling out the questions yet—Internet troubles here. But Peachy, please, please can you? Pleeeeease? It'll be fun!"

"Fun? For who? It's fucked. And no."

"Okay, fine. I'll do it when I get back."

"Jesus, Beth. What if he finds out it's you?"

"He won't. And look, I know it's a weird thing to do, but we're just fucking around. I just want to find out about his 'last relationship.' That's all. Then our girl, you, will disappear, a mystery to all who knew her. Hey, check out the email correspondence, Peachy. You might be a little interested in what my ex-boyfriend thinks of your picture. A young Julie Christie, indeed."

I looked over my shoulder into the house, past the dark kitchen into the dim living room. I could see Scoots's butt on the floor next to the couch, his elderly tail moving back and forth like a drugged limb.

"Peachy!" Beau yelled. "Get off the phone! I want a hand job!"

"Beth, I gotta go," I said, hanging up. I walked back into the living room, scratched the back of Beau's head, then sat back down at the computer to get another look at Marcus's face.

"Well? Can I have a hand job?" Beau muttered.

"No. Later. Maybe."

I had never been on a dating Web site before. The link off Marcus's ad led to even more faces. I scrolled what seemed hundreds of faces all looking like lost street kids on milk cartons, tanned attractive street kids. I felt so grateful for Beau, so grateful we had hooked up the old-fashioned way, using outmoded methods such as eye contact and beer. I punched in the user name and password. Seeing my own face on the site was thrilling, odd. It was a picture I'd never seen, taken on the porch of the house, face in hands, elbows on knees, the rest of my body out of frame. Jake's red parka was barely visible along my right side. I looked hearty, healthy, like a hair-commercial model, or like the third-prettiest woman on a soap opera. I clicked on MAIL and read Marcus's initial reply to Almost Me's wink. *Nice face. A young Julie Christie. Why no information about self? Write back. Would like to know more about u.*

"What are you doing?" Beau asked, still rapt by the fast cars.

"Looking for a new husband," I said.

"Well, keep an eye out for a new wife for me, if you don't mind. Better yet, I'd rather just have a girlfriend. Or just some chick to look at me a couple times a day. That would be nice. Touch me once in a while. She could even be ugly."

"What about someone who looked like a young Julie Christie?"

"A who?"

I closed the site and shut the laptop and walked to the pantry. I took down two boxes of Hamburger Helper and a can of sweet corn from the high shelves. I suddenly became so dizzy I had to brace myself on the butcher block, not realizing I was standing in the same position Beth would find herself in—or I would find her in—two sorry weeks later.

The next morning, after the boys went to school and Beau to work, I refilled my coffee cup and turned on the laptop, feeling as anxious as a mad scientist. The dating application was long and imposing. Number one was *Favorite Books,* in the plural. The plural. No one tells you that you must kiss books goodbye when you have babies. Unless you counted *Goodnight Moon*, I couldn't remember the last book I had read from cover to cover, let alone remembered. Where did that dreamy, distracted girl go, the one who wandered the farm with *Forever Amber* or *To Kill a Mockingbird* tucked under an armpit? *Most Humbling Moment? Best Advice Not Taken? Favorite Color? Favorite President? Moment? Ice Cream? Music that puts you in the mood?* Does the sound of my boys sleeping count? When the house is quiet enough to hear the grandfather clock? *Pet Peeves?* When the kids get up before seven. *Celebrity You Most Resemble?* Beth, maybe. A little around the eyes.

Introspection was exhausting, the idea that people do this every day, and then they update the information with more new things they'd digested, more books, new bands, exciting trips, fresh pictures they liked or disliked. When had I ever subjected myself to this kind of scrutiny, this kind of personal assessment? Maybe those old *Cosmo* quizzes I used to take, writing in a different ink over Beth's, trying hard to seem as unlike her as possible. I had been trained to assess others, to take inventory of other people's shortcomings, failures, and foibles, not my own. I became keenly aware of all the things I hadn't done, what I wasn't, what I'd never be, and what I didn't know about myself and might never find out.

In my twenty-eight years on this planet, I had done many lovely things, but I had never really done anything off-putting or different. I had never offended. I'd never been in a band, been to Europe, used heroin or cocaine, been alone on a boat, in a theater, or down a dark alley, written a novel, directed a play, or made a short film, had a near-death experience, seen a UFO, tried on a wedding dress (I had married in a muumuu on account of being seven months pregnant), gone bleach blond, submitted to a full Brazilian (they do the bum), touched a seal, worn anything made of vinyl, pleather, or ermine, been inside a synagogue, or a mosque, or truly understood how planes fly, or how war, famine, and childhood obesity could have gotten so entirely out of hand.

So I returned to hobbies and picked something that had nothing to do with predicting seizures. Beth had always liked horses, and so I gave Almost Me a pony and Italian, a language she might have picked up from time spent perhaps in a Swiss finishing school. Then I gave Almost Me a yellow racing bike to go with that life. And I chose photography, as it was something I wanted Beth to keep up, the least reason being she was the only person who took pictures of my family. Under *Likes?* I put: *hydrangeas, driving, reading, and anything that makes me laugh.* All true, for Beth and me both. Then back to books, I listed everything I had never got around to reading; Dickinson, Morrison, and even Austen, and so many others that weren't on my curriculum. But how could I? After one and a half years of school, I had a baby, three years later, another one. Under *Why should I get to know you?* I was thinking of Beth when I wrote: *Because in getting to know myself I am coming to believe it's a journey better done accompanied. Because life has a shoddy way of throwing me off my high-wire act and I'm sick of landing without a net.* I was thinking of Lou when I wrote: *Because being alone is really only good for a little while, then it becomes an unbreakable habit, one I'm getting too good at.* I was thinking of Beau when I wrote: *Because making love to myself is redundant, plus it's causing unsightly calluses.* And under *What are you looking for?* I was thinking about myself when I wrote: *Resuscitation.*

Then I wrote a casual howdy, said *Nice profile,* and that I was a *native New Yorker.* I wrote that since I had spent a *few years abroad,* was quite new to this online dating *thing,* and that I was *just out of a long-term relationship. So, be patient with me,* I wrote, *if I need a little time, back and forth on email, asking questions, before I take the plunge to meet someone new.*

And that I was very much looking forward to hearing from him.

And that he had a great face too.

Then I took out hamburger meat to thaw.

Then I picked up the stray toys off the front lawn, throwing a few worn ones the boys would never miss in the garbage can in the garage.

Then I cleaned out Scoots's food bowl and dumped in last night's Hamburger Helper as a treat. I kept a hand on his old back while he ate.

Then I called Beau at the shop to ask him to pick up lettuce.

Then I called him back and asked him to pick up some tampons, even though he hated to buy them, and I didn't really need them. Why was I being mean? Was it really boredom, or was I turning rotten? Was this a contempt for the truly familiar? I didn't really feel contempt for Beau, but I had begun to buzz inside like I was filled with hornets and he was handed a heavy stick.

Later that night, Beau drove into town to pick up some milk and I checked the account. There was an email—my first ever—from a man:

Dear Georgia:

First of all, Georgia was the name of my favorite babysitter. Fascinating profile. I've never been to Switzerland, let alone finished high school there. Must be where you began your linguistic endeavors. I'm flattered that you liked my profile. I, too, have recently ended a relationship. Not a terribly long one, but a rather complicated one, with a rather complicated woman. I don't normally e-date, as they say. But my friends urged me, and some have been successful. I also felt it was important to get back out there right away, (LOVED your line about high-wire acts, and also how you can get used to being alone, so true in this city!!!)

So besides being lovely to look at, where do you live in Brooklyn? What do you do for a living? (I don't understand what "mother of all multitaskers" means.) Me, I do entertainment law for a small company, but am making a move to a firm. It's mostly boring contract work for now, but hoping to liven things up a bit with the next career change. What about you? What does "Professional Juggler" mean? Or are you a professional juggler? Where do your folks live? Is that your cottage you're sitting in front of? When can we meet up? I live on UES, you? Can't wait to chat/meet/whatever. Oh and P.S., I can see why your profile's hidden. You'd probably get inundated with responses.

My first thought was, *cottage* porch. We live in a five-bedroom farmhouse, jackass! But I also felt a velvety flood overcome me while reading the email. It started at my feet and curled under my chin. *He liked my line about the high wire.* He thinks I'm *cute. Naturally* cute. Beau had never made me feel like less than a babe, but I'd always tossed him a spoonful of scorn whenever he'd show too much enthusiasm for the extra effort I'd put into an outfit for a wedding or a banquet.

"Oh my God, Peach, you're gonna give me a heart attack," he'd say, slobbering while I'd galomp down the stairs in a set of tippy spikes, my cleavage like an ass high up front, authentic ass in back harnessed in a Lycra girdle, lips lined and shimmering, hair and eyelashes curled, cubic zirconias like teeny cameras flashing at my ears and wrists. "Do we really have to go to this thing?"

Did I thank him for those hot words? Kiss him coyly on the cheek? Bat one frigging eyelash at my husband's unabashed joy at the sight of his poshed-up, curvy wife, her natural tits gushing over the top of a new, pricey bra?

No, I went with hitting him in the upper arm with my clutch. "What, I look like shit every other day? Is that what you're saying? Like I have time to make myself look like this every day. Lucy has the time to look like this every day and look where that got her."

I wrote him back thanking him for his note:

Dear Marcus:

Thank you for the note . . . you seem like a great catch, as they say, so you definitely have me curious about your last relationship . . . What went wrong? What was miss-

ing? When did you realize it was over? Don't mean to pry and am NOT audition-ing potential husbands. Believe me, I'm far too busy to pay much attention to a proverbial husband, let alone a real one, as I'm often told by people who know me well. Oh, and you asked, so I'll tell you, I work with special kids, one in particular who has my heart in his clutches. Anyway, much to do, gotta run . . .

How odd for people to meet and mate like this, I thought, scanning the faces, eyes full of marketing and menace. Still there were others on the site who appeared comfortable, built even for this kind of forum, their lives, likes and dis-likes, their minds and needs boiled down to their microscopic specifics and what was required for optimum compatibility. I want this and I want that and you need to have this and I hope you have that. I like this music, that book, those kinds of movies but not that kind of food. I'd rather eat Indian. Not big on red hair, but will tolerate if you turn a blind eye to smoking, split ends, debt. I hate cats. Love dogs, horses, antiques. I weigh this much, you must not weigh too much. Please make lots of money, live here, be from there, go to this school, work on this street and give it to me exactly like that, right there, that's right, no, don't stop, okay, move your finger, put the other hand here, bite me, kiss this, slap that, go home, call me, hurt me, marry me, hate me, leave me, love me, shoot me. I mean, Jesus, it took me a year and a half of marriage to find out that Beau hated ketchup. He assumed I liked ketchup. I assumed he did. So the bottle made its cameo on the supper table every night until one of those lulls in conversation found me scanning the food labels. The date on the bottle screamed *two years old.* I uncapped it and we were both hit with a menstrual vinaigrette smell.

Beau shrugged and said, "I don't eat that shit. Thought you did."

It took several sessions before I had realized Beau's foreskin was still intact. How was that possible that I didn't know that? Beth had never mentioned it in high school, and during the heady days of our counter screwing and boozy courtship, I never saw the damn thing unless it was already as hard and uncoiled as a full fire hose. And was it a sin that it was two years into our marriage before I found out Beau was afraid of elevators? Three years before I asked him about his favorite color? And it was only two years ago, after almost a decade of sharing a bed, food, clothing, smells, fluids, Lou, sons, and money, that Beau had told me in the dark of our bedroom that when he was nineteen, the day before he took the apartment over the tackle shop, his asshole of a stepfather broke into the bathroom, jackknifed him in half with a kick to the liver, and held his head underwater in the toilet for several seconds.

"He waited until I had finished peeing in it," Beau said.

He couldn't remember the infraction, perhaps an unauthorized bonfire, perhaps a lifted beer or three, but he did remember standing up, piss and water streaming in his eyes, thinking, I am taller than you now, asshole. But instead of beating him back, Beau went looking for Lou.

"Lou said, and I'll never forget this, and he's got his back to me the whole time, right, because he's making me this cold steak sandwich in the kitchen, and he goes, 'It's a sad thing to be an angry man, Beau. But it's a sin to make a boy feel your anger for you. You wanna get back at him, you just pick not to feel his anger, only your own.' And man I never cried like . . . I was like a fricken baby in this house."

"Why didn't you ever tell me this?" I asked, freshly spooning his back, cupping under him with a little extra thigh.

"I hadn't thought of it again. Much. I don't know. Next day Lou helped me get my own place. It was so cool of him because Beth and I had broke up so I didn't come around much, and it was way before us. Then, I don't know, I stuck around here and it just . . . the anger faded,

106

I guess. Then we got married and I made this family my family and I've been happy ever since."

Beau stretched off and away from my tight clutch, pulling his whole body taut with a shudder to the ceiling, a knife to my spoon.

"It wasn't a big deal, you know, him hitting me all the time. Slapping the back of my head like he did. Flicking at my ears and shit. But that night, that felt like he wanted me dead."

I watched my husband's profile, tears glistening in the valley of his eyes. Little sniffles echoed back and forth in the canyon between our bodies. He put a heavy hand on my stacked knees and we fell into an untroubled sleep. In the morning, Jake lay between us like something perfect we had made in the night. For a few seconds we both watched him dream in the nest of us. I remember feeling that if this is all that marriage is, then this is more than enough for me. Where did that feeling go?

That little email exchange had given me the oddest kind of buzz, making it somehow easier to relax with the kids while waiting for Beth's call. She would be arriving home early that morning, and I had hoped she'd sleep off the jet lag and airplane scotch before digging into her laptop. Imagining her scanning the completed profile, and my back and forth with Marcus, gave me a touch of nauseous jealousy.

"Mom!" Jake screamed, running to the other end of the slippy slide. I reaimed the hose in a high urinal arch. He tugged up his heavy bathing suit, his hair spidering across his forehead.

"What?"

"I just can't believe how much fun I'm having!"

"Me too, bud," I said, beginning to understand how affairs can sometimes spruce up a lusterless marriage. A little funnel of joy began turning in my center, all because a handsome man I had never met thought I looked like Julie Christie.

The slippy slide kept ripping Jake's trunks off before he could come to a stop in the wet grass. It was like he was being spat out of a boy factory over and over again, the same model, while Sam stood on the end to catch him.

I heard the phone ring inside and let Beau answer it.

"Here. It's your *waaaa*," Beau whispered, easing open the screen door and handing me the receiver. "She says her life's *gaaaa*."

"Keep them well watered," I said, trading the hose for the phone. The screen door wheezed shut behind me. I crossed the kitchen and the living room and moved out to the front porch, feeling Beau's eyes following me.

"What was that screaming?" Beth asked.

"The boys," I said. "I have two."

"Peachy. I just read your email exchanges."

"First off. Welcome back."

"Thanks. I feel sick. It's like Marcus is totally in *love* with you. And what's with you being a hundred thirty-five pounds? Jesus, I shaved off twenty."

"That would make me emaciated."

"No. That would make you a New Yorker."

"And you don't mean *me,* you mean Georgia," I said. My chest swelled with something—pride, fear.

"I know, I know. But are you in front of your computer? Did you read his latest?"

"No. Read it to me."

"Listen. *'Dear Georgia, thank you so much for your sweet, odd reply. I was looking at your picture while reading it and thinking, Yup she does look like this kind of person—playful, intelligent, and warm.'* Peachy! I'm jealous. Is that weird?"

"Yes. 'Cause it's Georgia, remember. Make-believe Georgia. Go on." My face was now shot with red. I was angry, actually angry that she read our exchange, that she had accessed his response before I was able to.

"So. Okay. He goes: *'And I hear you on the strangeness of Internet dating. I'm thirty-four. We'd barely heard of computers until I was about thirteen. But I'm not sure how I feel*

109

about purging all my past relationship secrets though. Why exchange sad stories before we even meet? Okay, I'll tell you this much. My last girlfriend, we'll call her B. We met at work, like millions of other people, and we dated for about six months, until about three weeks ago. You may think I'm putting myself out there too quickly, but I had one foot out the door for the past three months. I just didn't have the heart to tell her.'"

Beth's voice cracked at these words.

"Oh, sweetie," I said. "This is insane." And it was. I felt like a cheater already. "Why don't you just erase this message and kill the file? And I can't see anything good coming from this."

"Oh. So you don't want me to finish reading what Marcus wrote to you?"

Yes.

"No."

Yes, I thought, more please.

"No? Well here goes anyway: *'That said, B was a remarkable woman. Fun, funny, and accomplished. But her problems are legion. And her ego large. You seem different, like you're not looking for anything. Like if anything happens it's a bonus in an already full life. Or maybe that's just wishful thinking on my part. But that's what I'm looking for in a friend or companion.'"*

Beth went quiet. Save for the sniffling, I would

have thought she'd hung up on me.

"There you go. Your answer. We can close the file on this case now, right?"

"No way," she said. "I want specifics. I want to know what I did wrong. I want to know what moment, three months ago, did he know I was not the girl for him. And I want to know why he strung me along."

"Then talk to him, Beth. Call him in person."

But she wasn't listening to me. She was crying the same way she did when stuff was yanked from her hands as a kid. We are a family of criers. We cry to stave off death. We despair because we don't want to store, shelve, hoard that kind of stuff inside of us.

"*Call him?* Oh, that's funny. Yeah. I'll call Marcus and let him know just how pathetic I really am. Here's what I'll say. I'll call and I'll say, *Hey Marcus, a little bird told me you wanted me out on my ass three months ago, but you felt sorry for me so you stuck around a little longer . . .* aaaaaaaaaah! Peachy!"

"No. I'm done."

"*Please? Peachy!*—just write him just one more note. Gently pry him one more time. I want to find out why he stuck around for three more months. And then maybe prod him about his commitment phobia."

"But I don't think he has commitment phobia, Beth. I think he could commit, wants to commit

—but just to someone he's probably a little more compatible with."

"I can't believe you're defending him, Peachy. You don't even know him. And you don't know how close we were. We practically lived together."

"Jesus Christ, he took care of your fish."

"What are you saying?"

"Nothing. I'm sorry. I know you're heartbroken, Beth. And you must be tired from the flight."

We were both quiet for a few seconds, like a couple of boxers tired of circling each other, though not quite ready to land a punch.

"I am tired."

"Then sleep on it a little, okay? But I think we should stop this altogether, really. We're too old for this kind of stupidity."

I could hear the boys yelping out back, calling me to them.

"Fine. If you don't write him back, Peach, I will. And I'll tell him right off. How dare he tell a perfect stranger that I'm full of problems."

"Beth, you're insane. He was telling *me*."

"He doesn't know it's you."

"True. But he's gonna know it's you if you write him and tell him off. And then he'll think you're totally crazy. You can't tell him, Beth."

"I can."

"Then do it," I said.

Truthfully, I didn't want her to kill Almost Me, not yet. And I felt terrifically, embarrassingly territorial about my burgeoning correspondence with Marcus. I wanted Almost Me to live a little longer, maybe because I liked the feeling of someone preferring me to Beth. I knew Beau loved me, but I had never lost that sense of being his consolation prize.

"I will. I will shut this down, Peachy. But after one more letter to him. I want to know."

Beth threw down gauntlets so often it was a wonder she didn't have carpal tunnel syndrome. Fine, I'd always reply, go ahead. That's how she put her car in a ditch, driving it home drunk instead of leaving it at Kaponi's party where I waited for Lou to pick me up. That's how I got the scar under my chin, after Beth dared me to jump off the roof of the farmhouse into the above-ground pool we once had. I said, "No way." Beth said, "Step aside, chicken." And that's when I said, "Fine, I'll jump." And it was in the spirit of those ridiculous dares that I, instead of Beth, had been the one to find our mother that day.

"I don't want to play this game anymore."

"I've never asked you to help me before, Peachy."

"Bullshit. You're forgetting one or two very key moments from our childhood. But just this once, Beth, can you leave something alone? Just once can you not take something that's already a bad idea and shove it over a fucking cliff?"

"No. I want to know."

I exhaled.

"Okay. But let me write it. That way it won't seem like two different insane people writing him. This is so fucked up. Are we really this fucked up?"

"What can I say? We had a rough childhood," she said.

"You're *still* having it," I said, hanging up the phone. I listened to the gleeful shrieks coming from the back of the house. In the side yard, hearty reeds shot out of the willow stump and I thought about Nell, as I did every time I stared at that goddamn willow stump, its roots we kept meaning to yank up for good.

chapter six

Beth once told me she knew our mother was going to kill herself. She said it was a fact to her long before it happened, something she was merely waiting to see with her own eyes. We all knew Nell was depressed, but her depression wasn't just a part of her, inside of her. It hovered like a fifth family member, greedily taking up space, stealing oxygen from the rooms, occupying furniture, hoarding food.

The day she killed herself, I had been feeling sick, but I preferred to stay on the office cot until the lunch bell. Later, I learned that kids with mothers like ours, kids whose survival mechanisms were still intact, instinctively knew how to seek care elsewhere. I liked how the nurse touched my forehead with her cool, concerned hand. How she smelled mothery, like bread and coffee. At lunch Miss Brant told Beth to fetch me at the nurse's station, where I sat wilted over like a top-heavy flower, and take me home so I didn't spread my virus. They had tried to call Nell, but there was no answer. Beth convinced them that she was probably just outside, so she half-carried me back to the farm, taking the shortcut along the tracks. We stopped at the Starlite Variety, but the idea of anything sweet made me reel. I waited for Beth outside while she took her good old time picking out penny candy.

"If I get sick on the way home, it's your fault," I said when she finally sauntered out. She just shrugged, then dug deeper into her little paper bag, dramatically popping candy into her mouth.

At the house I couldn't wait to get away from her. I took the steps in twos, while Beth shuffled off her shoes in silence, enjoying the last of her marshmallow bananas. Nell's car was in the driveway, but we didn't hear her in the house. That was not surprising. We often found her napping instead of cooking or cleaning or buzzing around the house the way that other mothers did. But this time the rooms felt cryptic, tomby. Beth stood in the bathroom archway, unsure about Nell's whereabouts, while I sat on the toilet, completing a bit more relief. It seemed neither one of us wanted to be alone. Then we spotted the envelope on the console in the hall with "Lou" neatly written on the front. Beth opened it and read it aloud.

Dear Lou,

I am sorry for everything. I know you will be home before the girls. You can tell them I had a heart attack, which wouldn't be a total lie. You will find me in the tree house. The girls don't play up there now that the willow's rotted. You should have it removed right away. It's a terrible hazard. I figured it would be okay there, as I didn't want to spook up the house. I would like to be cremated in what I am wearing, please and the blanket. My mom can take the ashes back to Florida if she makes a stink. Some of them.

Lou, the girls are young, and they will come to understand in time, but I do believe they will be better off without me.

How can I describe how hard it is to stay really focused on living, all day, every day, every minute? It has taken everything out of me. Recently, it went from difficult to impossible. I can't live here. Like this. Not feeling anything. Dying is the only way I can think of keeping the kids alive.

Strangely, I am not sad while I write this. In fact, I am looking forward to the kind of life you will have without me. I will be happy when you find happiness. Tell the girls to be good. Tell them I love them. Tell Beth everything she needs to know, especially that it wasn't her fault. Remember she's just as much yours as Georgia. Maybe more so. And never let her feel unwanted.

Love for always, Nell.

My blood felt bubbly, like hot Pepsi had entered my veins. I soundlessly followed Beth to the side yard, where the willow loomed like a fat, strung-out ghoul, hair full of dreads and bugs.

"Don't go up there," I said, looking up the ladder.

"She could still be alive," Beth said.

I started to cry as a reply.

"Go see," she said.

"No. Dad says it's dangerous. We can't play up there. You go," I whimpered.

117

She looked up at the tree house. Her eyes were dry.

"I dare you," she said.

I took the dare because I wanted my mother, and part of me thought that, indeed, she could be still alive and this could all be written off as a big misunderstanding, a joke even.

I moved as slow as a bear. At the top I stuck my head inside the tree house, but my hands wouldn't let go of the rung. From the dark doorway I could only make out Nell's slippered feet, the rest of her body covered with her army blanket. I could see the dust floating in the slices of sun poking through the wooden slats of the tree house. I knew she was dead.

"Mum?" I whispered. I wanted to touch her foot; I wanted to reach out and pull her down with me. I stared at her foot, willing it to move. I had never been in so still a place. "Mum?"

"What can you see?" Beth yelled.

I don't remember the climb down, or walking past Beth and into the house. I don't remember pulling down a towel in the bathroom and draping it across my knees. And I don't remember how much time had passed before I heard Lou's truck pull up along the shoulder of the road. He'd been gone for two days on a run to Sault Ste. Marie, and was supposed to have picked us up after school and taken us to dinner, to give Nell a bit of a break. Instead he found me fitfully churning with a sweaty fever near the toilet.

"Teacher said she sent you home. Jesus. Are you alone, goddammit? Nell! Where's your sister, Peach? Where in the hell's your ma? Nell!"

I said nothing as he bobbed his head in and out of all the rooms, checking the closets, the carport, the old barn. I followed him into the side yard, where we came upon Beth crouched under the rotting willow. When Beth saw him, she didn't run to him as always. She just lifted up her face and then the letter she'd been clutching in her fist. Her features seemed shrunken inside a big skull.

"We went to the store. I made us late," she cried. She was eight years old. I was almost six.

I watched Lou bend down in front of her and take the note from her hands. He read it and looked up into the tree house and said, "You weren't late, Beth Ann. This is not your fault." And with that he lifted her into his arms and carried her into the house.

When the firemen took Nell's body down, they kept it draped in the army blanket she slept with, laid under, napped on, clutched hard, absently smelled, never washed. There was no blood. She had taken pills.

Years later Lou admitted that he too knew that Nell had killed herself when he walked into the house that day. Though he eventually forgave her for doing it, he never forgave the fact that I had found her first. We kept her suicide note and read and reread the thing as though its letters would somehow miraculously reassemble themselves into much better news. Then it took the consistency of inky feathers, then damp toilet paper, then around the time Beth moved to New York, it just kind of disappeared.

I was deemed too young to go to the funeral, a relief, frankly, but it was after Nell died that things got complicated for Beth. She said she'd always vaguely known that she wasn't Lou's biological kid, but she had no idea that she wasn't his legal kid either. Beth didn't even have a formal birth certificate, which was why Lou had never gotten around to fully adopting her when he married Nell. Beth had always had questions, but by the time she became old enough to ask them, Nell's depression obscured her desire to know. Then her death brought up the necessity to settle all of them.

During a long series of interviews conducted by well-meaning social workers, and at least one lawyer, all eager people who pulled up to our acreage to make better sense of a family whose precariousness was unknown to even us, Lou carefully meted out some of the details. Beth and I sat like two still owls, bookending Nana Beecher, who'd driven up from Florida with five suitcases, one filled with paperbacks, another with clips and bows to accessorize her stupendously long hair. Every morning she'd separate her hair into two pale rivers, braid each, then roll them into buns next to her ears. She reminded me of Princess Leia from *Star Wars*, only old, blond, and wrinkly.

She was my mother's mother, though having never seen them in the same room, it was a fact that never seemed quite true to me. But she knew the farm. She'd walk about the place like a bored mistress, demonstrating to Lou how toaster ovens and mixers work, what tampons and pimple cream were for, even though we were years from those dilemmas. She was efficient and severe, with the terrifying habit of filing her nails while driving, polishing them at red lights, and drying them on the dash. Still, I clutched at her with such embarrassing ferocity I accidentally turned myself into her favorite.

The story of Beth, the parts Lou didn't know, Nana Beecher filled out like they were subplots in a novel. It made Beth seem terribly famous to me, a real, live American orphan living in Canada, the product of romantic youth, geography, and war. As Nana Beecher recounted Beth's journey, she might as well have been talking about something that happened to someone else on the other side of the planet, which she was of course.

She told us Nell met Sam Drysdale in San

Francisco. Like a million other kids who staggered blinking from the darkness of the fifties and into the diamond skies of the sixties, my mother had long straight hair, a talent for socialism, hatred for Nixon, a guitar, and a crush on George Harrison. Against Nana Beecher's highly vocal wishes, after graduation, Nell had hitchhiked west to San Francisco to live in a city park with other damp hippies. That's where she met Sam, a gangly Oklahoman, whose nickname was Tooey, though no one knew how he'd earned it.

"He was one of the arresting officers during a raid on some park where she lived. One of the nicer ones, apparently," said Nana Beecher.

Just after learning she was pregnant with Beth, Nell tried to talk Tooey into coming to Canada instead of going to Vietnam, but he said he was a born soldier. Even after Beth was born he couldn't be talked out of his commitment. They said goodbye at a dock in San Diego. Three weeks into his first tour of duty, Tooey was shot in the back and killed, a victim of friendly fire.

For the next few months Nell went into a kind of critical shock. Friends were worried for the safety of the baby, whom Nell would often forget to feed or change. Nana Beecher convinced her to bundle up the baby and move to Florida for a while, even though Nell was worried she'd lose Beth to Nana Beecher.

Nell packed the Dart and planned on driving across the country alone. But then Lou stuck out a thumb north of Tyler, Texas, having just received his own draft papers. He was heading for call duty in Macon, Georgia. According to Nell, God was giving her another opportunity to save a man's life, something she wasn't able to do for Tooey. Lou too saw it as a sign from God, someone he'd gotten a lot closer to since he'd stopped drinking a year and a half earlier. It didn't take much for him to fall for his sad Canadian savior and her lively baby. Before they even crossed into Louisiana, they'd decided that Lou's reply to the draft board ("Fuck you") would sport a Canadian stamp.

When they reached Georgia, Nell called Nana Beecher and broke the news. Needless to say, no mother wants to hear that their daughter plans to marry a recently recovered alcoholic hitchhiker, but she wired the couple some money. Nell and Lou were married in Marietta, the town in which they'd later learn I was conceived, after which I was almost named, but Nell didn't like the sound of Mary.

They camped for two days, then took another two days to reach the Detroit border. When they showed the guards their marriage certificate, no one asked about the baby, whom Nell kept wrapped in Tooey's old army blanket. It wasn't uncommon for hippies to skip steps on their way to forming their ridiculous families, so as far as the border guards were concerned, Beth was simply no longer Lou and Nell's bastard child.

Since Nana Beecher had retired full-time to Florida, the house hadn't been properly lived in, so it needed a lot of work—a new septic tank, for starters, which couldn't be installed until the thaw. They used an outhouse Lou built from scratch, and though most of the land was still brush back then, the working land was fertile. He tried to grow soy, then corn, but farming wasn't in Lou's blood. So they leased a chunk of land to the bachelor brothers next door and lived off the proceeds. After I was born, Lou took up truck driving for a few years, so long as the routes kept him on the friendly side of the border.

Beth had relatives in Oklahoma. After they were notified of Nell's death, they sent their condolences, best wishes, and a half-dozen pictures of Tooey. They'd also promised to put money into trust for Beth, whatever the army had given him, whatever he might inherit, and what he had had in savings. It wouldn't be much, they said, but it might matter around college time if she decided to go. They sent Christmas cards for a few years, and Lou returned their queries with photos. Plans to visit were recycled but never fulfilled. As a draft dodger, Lou wasn't allowed into the United States, and he'd never put Beth on a plane alone. But even after the presidential pardon, he had long washed his hands of the American part of his life, especially after Ronald Reagan became the president.

Two weeks after Nell's suicide Lou called the bachelor brothers and coaxed a conversation out of them. Then he picked up an ax and walked across the street to the Rosarios to introduce himself. Nell never spoke to the neighbors, had avoided them since her return to Canada. We were told it was because of her depression, so when I was younger, I thought sadness was contagious, like colds. Lou told his new neighbors and eventual friends that in exchange for pulling down the willow tree they could help themselves to the firewood until it was gone. And that's when it began, when our farmhouse evolved from being a dark place to a light place. People drove up with gifts of day-old donuts, casseroles, carpool offers, and kittens. Behind our backs they referred to us as *the Archer Girls, those poor Archer Girls, did you hear what happened to the Archer Girls?* They talked to Lou while petting us, everyone hoping for an update, an explanation. *How are you faring? How's little Peachy? What's the situation with Beth? How's having June back from Florida? Is she still, you know, cuckoo?* Not long after, Lou started up his men's meetings on Sundays, much to Nana Beecher's consternation.

"It's fine now, Lou, but when the girls become teenagers, I don't want these drunks hanging around the house ogling them," she said.

"They're sober drunks, June. There's a big difference," he said.

"You confuse me, boy."

Beth did change rapidly after Nell's death. The first symptom of her motherlessness was that our sisterly scrapes turned biblical. Beth's sharp kicks and well-landed punches were accompanied with screams so high-pitched they'd deafen dogs. Her skills arrived almost overnight as though Beth had been replaced by a tiny ninja. You could see the transformation on Beth's face. I once compared her school picture from the year before with those taken the year after our mother died, and she had definitely become weary-looking and stiff, her very cuteness sucked from her cheeks, taking her dimples along with it.

For the few months she was with us, Nana Beecher did her best to dismantle Beth's bombs. She'd often stumble into one of our arguments brandishing a spatula, or a spoon, which she'd use to pry Beth off of me. She'd send Beth to her room and take me aside, her favorite granddaughter, and say: "If you feel like crying, don't. Tears are energy and they're a waste of time on someone like your sister. Turn them into something useful. But don't just sit there and bawl, Georgia Peach, it is of no use."

Lou took great umbrage with her no-crying rule.

"June, that's wrong. All's depression is is uncried tears. Don't listen to Nana Beecher."

Poor Lou. The man fell asleep with more self-help books than dates splayed across his white-haired chest; books with anthemic titles featuring low ordinals, hard steps, and easy promises, and always the A.A. *Big Book*, the consistent tent under which we'd find him snoring.

Just before Beth's adoption was finalized, she began to call our father Lou, and he didn't mind. "Call me anything that makes you feel natural," he said. "You're both still my girls."

Nana Beecher disagreed.

"Technically speaking, Lou, Beth's an orphan." She was sitting on the love seat wrapping an elastic around her long, damp braid. Once a week she washed her hair with Dove soap, then gave it an expensive hot-oil treatment. "You might as well stop pretending otherwise, because the damage of keeping the first secret is evident enough."

"What do you mean by that?" Beth asked.

"I just mean, Beth Ann, for a little girl who's almost nine, you have a lot of anger on account of people never telling you the truth. I am trying to change that, which I know sounds mean, but it is for your own good."

Beth had been using a heavy pair of pinking shears to cut out duplicate hearts and crosses for an Easter art project. "Nana Beecher, are you trying to kill me with depression?"

"No, Beth Ann, I am not. I am trying to cure you with the truth. Now come here and sit next to me and I'll help you cut your stuff," she said, patting the cushion on the love seat then splitting open one of her fresh romance novels. The cover featured a hunky slave ripping the dress off a deliriously busty woman.

Beth ignored Nana Beecher and walked over toward Lou, who was reading the paper on his La-Z-Boy. She put her heavy head on his chest and he patted her spine.

"June, don't ever say that again," Lou muttered over the top of his bifocals. "No one's an orphan here except me. And these girls are all the family I got. Why do you have scissors, lovey?"

"Because, I have to make hearts and I don't want to have depression," Beth whimpered.

"You won't have depression, Bethie. Who told you that?"

"Nana Beecher."

"June, stop saying stuff like that, she's just little. You're scaring the heck out of her."

"Lou Archer, I cannot tell what my daughter

saw in you. Now Beth, you come over here and give your Nana a kiss. I don't mean to make you depressed."

Beth collected herself and walked over to the coffee table, where I was bent over a coloring book. She regarded my work with phony awe, gently lifted and dropped one of my anemic braids. Then Lou and I watched as Beth moved closer to her intended target, lifted up then cut off Nana Beecher's long blond braid with one metal bite of the scissors. There was a split second where Lou could have stopped Beth had he really believed she was going to do it, which he did not.

"There!" Beth screamed, dropping the braid and the pinking shears on the table next to my book. I stared at the long tail of hair which must have represented at least twenty years of this old woman's life. I was only six, but even then I was quite aware that this thing was much, much older than me. And there it lay cruelly detached from its maker's head.

"What in the fuck!" Lou yelled, trying to propel himself off his saggy chair. He never swore at us like that.

Nana Beecher struggled to stand up too, but it was as though losing her hair had somehow affected her balance. She grabbed her braid with one hand, Beth's arm with the other, and yanked her out of the living room. Beth tried to sink to the floor, to make herself too heavy to drag, but Nana Beecher moved with the strength of a lioness carrying a limp jackrabbit in her jaw. Lou followed them out to the yard, and I followed Lou, nervously putting the ends of my braids in my mouth.

"Lay a hand on her, old woman, and I will lay a hand on you!" Lou yelled, keeping a slight distance from Nana Beecher, who still gripped one of Beth's arms. She raised her other hand at the ready for a slapping.

"Are you threatening me with bodily harm on my property, Lou Archer?"

"It is not your property. You gave it to Nell, who gave it to me. Now you let go of my daughter right now and leave this farm."

"This child is sick, Lou. Sick, damaged, and angry. If you don't beat it out of her now, she'll grow up rotten and spoiled and depressed like Nell. You mark my words, mister. Nell was just like this, and I shoulda been a lot harder on her when I had the chance. Running away like that. Making me look like I had done something wrong. Getting herself knocked up—not by one but by two feckless men. Wandering around with dirty hair, the neighbors said. Years like that and you didn't tell me. And then she goes and takes those pills and I swear, I don't know. I just don't know what I did wrong. I just don't know why this all happened to me," she said, the geyser of tears shocking her more than us.

Finally, she let go of Beth and daubed her wet face with her braid. Then she flung it into the high grass and stomped back into the house. Beth remained crouched in a ball, flinching slightly when Lou tried to approach. Maybe she thought he'd finish the throttling, but instead he scooped her up and carried her onto the porch, dropping her on the wicker swing.

"Stay outside, both of you," he said. "Keep an eye on Peachy." Then he disappeared into the house. We braced ourselves for more yelling, but it remained dead quiet inside. I was too afraid to talk to Beth, to find out what she had been thinking when she cut off Nana Beecher's hair. I left her on the porch swing, arms wrapped tight around her torso. From there she watched me comb through the grass looking for the lost braid.

Twenty minutes later, Nana Beecher burst out the front door holding two of her suitcases. Lou followed behind carrying the rest. Neither of them spoke as they packed up the car, putting some of the suitcases in the trunk, the others in the back seat. Her remaining hair had fanned out into an uneven bob, which looked quite lovely, actually, more age-appropriate than those ridiculous buns.

"Peachy, come here, dear, and say goodbye to me," she said, her voice hoarse with pride.

I became aware of the downside of being the favorite, how things could turn disastrous when the person who put you on the pedestal suddenly crumbled herself. I looked toward Lou, who stood leaning against the carport, placing his body between Nana Beecher and Beth. He nodded for me to meet her at the car, so I did.

"Peachy, how would you like to come live with me in Florida?" she asked, bending over to take my wrists in her hands. She spoke loud enough for Beth and Lou to hear. "Would you like that someday soon?"

I still can't imagine why she thought she'd get a different answer out of a six-year-old. Especially one who had only lost her mother a few months earlier. And though I did feel a certain tug toward Nana Beecher, I would have felt that way toward a cow or a bush or even a large piece of furniture if it had given me any solace.

"No, I wouldn't like that," I said. "I want to stay here."

"Well then," she said, straightening up and smoothing down her shirt. "You think about it some more, okay?"

I nodded, then ran to Lou and took his hand. She climbed into her car and without saying another word to Beth, she backed out of the driveway, honked once, and drove off.

I might have begun to hate Beth for scaring off the first of many people at least partially devoted to my happiness. But when Nana Beecher's car disappeared into the horizon, Beth's face went ashen, then completely slack, then her whole body rolled forward off the swing, fainting into a pile on the porch from the pain of clutching a broken ulna to her chest.

Every year for about ten, Nana Beecher would send a Christmas or birthday card, addressed to me, stuffed with a twenty-dollar bill and an invitation to visit Florida. ("I'll pay for the ticket. You can fly by yourself and I'll meet you at the airport, *Peachy.*") Whenever I asked about taking the trip, Lou would say, "Later, another time, when you're older." Then he'd file the cards away, urging me not to tell Beth, imploring me to buy something for Beth when I rode my bike into town to spend the money. Poor Beth, he'd say, adding that the wrath of that old woman was a rotten thing to visit upon such a troubled head. Then he'd tell me to pray for Nana Beecher, but mostly, he said, pray for Beth to not absorb any of Nana Beecher's awful words or deeds.

Soon after, memories of my mother started to fade by the day, by the hour. Suddenly, I'd forget her middle name, or that she was afraid of dogs, or what her favorite color was, and I'd have to look hard for something of Nell's to smell or touch to bring her back, hiding these attempts from Beth, my only female constant in the house.

At first Lou could only awkwardly mimic the way his wife had tried, and his mother-in-law had excelled at, running the house efficiently. He'd stiffly organize our arms and legs into flannel pajamas pulled straight out of a hot dryer. He'd carefully comb out the knots on our wet heads, cultivating a future affinity for playing with hair. The soundtrack of those early days was always an AM radio playing something soothing and country on the kitchen counter, Beth's crying and yelling turning to talking and humming, something awful in her temporarily lifting. For a few years we lived in a peace-filled, drowsy diorama, until Beth's legs began swinging off the crusty vinyl kitchen chairs with a newfound angsty rhythm.

Being raised by a man did not stunt our femininity; in fact, it brought out Lou's as he fell in love with fixing our hair, a skill that did not go unnoticed by other mothers and their daughters. I was never jealous of the few women who came around to get their hair done, who tried to hold Lou's gaze as he administered perms, or cut a straight set of bangs, all while marveling at our house with its acres of brush and big airy rooms, marveling at these motherless girls before them. *Oh, you poor things,* their eyes would say. Got no mom to clean this big old house, with two bathrooms, carport, mortgage fully paid for, no doubt, in this blue-collar town full of divorced drunks, deadbeat fathers, and unemployed jerks. And we knew if they reached for Beth's cheek or her hair with that look on their faces, their coats would mysteriously appear strung between two fingers. This was followed by a quick ride home to their rental over the florist's, or wherever they shared space with their own brats, or absentee husbands, or lazy roommates, Beth and I watching them from the passenger seat we'd scramble into, always making them take the back seat. I'd turn and wave weakly while Lou pulled fast away. Another one bites the dust, Beth would say, and it would be just us for a great long stretch.

After Lou decided his affinity for hair was a God-given skill, he went to school in Windsor for nine months of training. He found us a live-in sitter named Teresa Tran, a Vietnamese refugee who spoke very little English, so we never got the whole story, just bits about a farm she grew up on and the war that killed her dad and two brothers. Lou tried to explain to Teresa that he was a draft dodger, an almost Vietnam vet, pointing to his chest as though he expected her to pin something shiny to it. She just smiled and nodded. Despite her size, she also proved to be a formidable wood splitter, often joining the men helping Lou clear the brush where he would drop the trailer for his riverside hair salon.

I loved Teresa Tran, secretly hoping Lou would marry her and keep her on the farm, even though she wasn't more than nineteen, maybe twenty. I couldn't keep my hands out of Teresa's heavy horse-tail hair. I would touch her slanted eyes, too, and try to make mine go like Teresa's, pulling the outside corners of my eyes to my temples and fastening the skin with Scotch tape, leaving it like that overnight. Teresa would alchemically conjure her own dinners, the textures and smells Beth might have had the bravery to try, but not the generosity. She'd make Beth salty egg salad sandwiches, fish sticks, and corn on the cob. For herself and me, noodles and shrimp, soup that smelled like feet, and greasy rolls filled with wormy-looking salads. I loved her so much I used to sneak peeks at her sleeping in the little bedroom off the kitchen, which we later turned into a walk-in pantry. Teresa used bleach straight from the bottle when she washed down the counters; the house smelled hospital-clean and unfamiliar. She never ran out of things to dust, or fix, or sew. Two nights a week she took English at the high school and spent Sundays at the Catholic church, volunteering to help other refugees arriving in the county.

Teresa kept a jar on the counter labeled "The Swears of Beth and Peachy." She'd learned bad words to watch out for and any time we uttered "damn" or "goddammit" or "shit" or even "piss," she'd scribble the word on a piece of paper and drop it into the jar to tally later. She said God wouldn't allow us to fill up more than one jar in a lifetime. In her bratty need to see it stuffed, Beth unleashed a barrage into the kitchen air and watched Teresa Tran frantically rip a sheet of paper to shreds, trying to keep up: poo, dummy, fucker, kaka, asshole, bumbum, fart, mixed in with God, Jesus Christ, and Holy Mary Mother of God, filled the jar, pressing up against the glass like the guts of a dirty religious novel.

She stayed for nine glorious months, and there were times I thought that even Beth might warm to her. Once, she even asked Teresa about her own mother back in Vietnam, while she was cleaning the cubby under the sink. Teresa told us that she didn't get along well with her mother, but that she was fat and funny, and that people would bring her their wounded animals because she was the town's amateur veterinarian.

"A Vietnam vet!" Beth squealed, a joke that flew over Teresa's head.

"What about your mom? What do you remember about your mom?" she asked in her halting English.

After a long pause Beth said, "She always had gum."

Teresa looked at Beth with such concern I thought I'd cry.

Not long after that, Lou made the mistake of introducing Teresa to Lorenzo Mann, the man who took the truck off his hands for a fair price.

"You should marry that guy, Teresa," Beth said, after noticing the two of them hovering by the carport playing with one of the barn cats. At almost thirteen, Beth was easily a head taller than Teresa. And she must have felt filled with some kind of power when, a few weeks later, Teresa did just that, becoming Teresa Tran Mann before moving with Lorenzo to the Yukon.

I was devastated; Beth, nonplussed.

"Their kids will be cute," she said.

I wrote my first letter ever to Teresa Tran Mann. She soon replied that she was "bored in so many times up here," writing that it was "cold in the air, in the house, and in the heart of it too, though I press on as we all very must."

We stayed in touch for two months, then lost track. Then she, like Nana Beecher, like Nell, like every other woman I knew, left the farm too.

chapter seven

After the barbecue, Beth helped Lucy and me clean up in order to bust me free from the group sooner. When she visited home, we always stopped into the tavern for a drink, or in her case several, plus shooters. And now we had the ridiculous need for privacy in order to discuss our prank on Marcus, not to mention how she planned further debasement in New York. It was twelve hours before we were meant to leave for the airport, six before I walked in on her having sex with my husband, and my hands still smelled like the bubble bath Beau and I had given the boys before we kissed their wet heads and put them to bed.

There had been nothing off about Beau's demeanor during Beth's arrival, Lou's barbecue, the boys' bath, nothing to suggest that in a few hours he'd bang my sister up against the pickled beets in the pantry off the kitchen. Watching him wrestle the boys dry, I had even made a mental note to seduce him later. I wanted him. I did. I used to love Beau's brilliantly simple method of seduction, which, judging from what I had remembered, and what Beth had told me, hadn't changed all that much since high school. Once he had it in his mind, he was like a snowplow in his single-minded pursuit of sex. With stunning momentum, he would remove every excuse, shove aside any of my arguments, too tired, too late, too busy—too bad, he'd say. Then after a brisk chase, I'd find myself lying in a breathless pile at his feet, cupping a rug-burnt knee. I had wanted Beth to overhear a variation of this later that night. I'd been feeling guilty about my emails to Marcus and my subsequent filthy thoughts, so I wanted to assure Beth (and myself) that I was really in love with my husband. And I wanted her to know that, despite my complaints, I had made all the right decisions about my life, that I had not regretted staying on the farm and stumbling into marriage and motherhood at twenty.

It was still early, so the tavern was empty except for Mike Laroche and his girlfriend Shelly, and Mike Dannon, who taught high school gym and said hello to us by flicking his baseball cap.

"Fucking hell, here comes Dannon," said Beth, settling into her barstool. "Every time I get a goddamn beer here, I run into someone I fucked in high school. How can you stand living here?"

"Well, for starters, I didn't fuck Dannon."

"Well howdy-how to you, Beth Archer. Hey, Peach."

"Hey, Mike," I said, while Beth craned for Stu's attention.

"Mind if I join yous?"

"Yes," said Beth.

Mike began to pull up a barstool.

"No, I mind, Mike. I don't feel like making conversation and I don't much feel like sharing Peachy. Sorry. No offense."

"Oh. Sure. Okay. Tell Beau to call me when my carburetor comes in, Peach."

"Will do."

"Tell Stu the first one's on me," he said, making a circle with his finger around the empty bar in front of us.

"Thanks, Mike. Always the gentleman," Beth said with a salute. Mike clicked his heels like a soldier, turned, and left.

"That was mean," I said.

"So is a married teacher fucking a student in the back of his car during lunch break," she said, tapping out a cigarette from her soft pack of American Spirits. "It kills me that guys in New York wear those stupid baseball hats like they're some statement on being cool. It's just gay."

"Don't say gay."

"I mean it in the eighth-grade sense, Peachy. I love fags and you know it."

"Dannon got fat, eh?"

"Don't say eh, Peach."

"Beth Ann Archer," Stu said, dropping two drafts and two Southern Comfort shots in front of us. "What brings you home?"

"I'm here because of love. Loss of it. Shit like that," she said, making a pouty face. "Plus, I'm bringing this one back with me for a well-needed break in the big city."

I shrugged. The idea of a break had started to appeal to me, though I was unwilling to admit it to anyone.

"Well then, here's to love lost and found," Stu said, raising his shot. They both threw them back and Beth asked for another one. I was searching for an emotional on-ramp to open across my sister's face.

"I think he's in love with you," she said, staring straight ahead, wiping her nose on a cocktail napkin.

"Who?"

"Marcus, who do you think? You made him fall in love with you. I read your little correspondence with him. Pretty intense, Peach."

"I'm, umm, confused. You mean Georgia's correspondence with him." I was trying to keep the anger from tainting my voice. "And remember that this was all your idea. Not mine."

She pulled a piece of paper from her front pocket and unfolded it.

"Shall I share?" she asked, eyebrow arched. "Seems quote, 'you are someone I really want to get to know,' unquote. And that, quote, 'I want you to reconsider your reticence and meet me for just one drink, Georgia,' unquote. He says your note made him think you might be the, quote, 'last woman of conscience left in this city,' unquote. And that, quote, 'if there's no chemistry, perhaps there's friendship,' unquote. Oh and that, quote, 'there's no way I would get back with my ex,' unquote. Adding that this ex, quote, 'is troubled. I think she comes from a dysfunctional family, about which she was remarkably secretive,' unquote."

"Well, all the more reason to forget this guy, no?" I said, hiding the guilt. I had read that same email after Sam abandoned his Internet Scrabble game.

"Yes, I should forget him, I know. That would be the rational thing to do."

"And what were you secretive about? Mom? Your real dad? I don't know why you're so ashamed of shit? You need to get over that."

"I'm not ashamed. Just trying to keep a bit of mystery about me, you know. But I did something. Something kind of awful when you were bathing the boys."

"What?"

"I wrote him back."

"Wrote what?"

"I wrote him back and made a date with him. I made a date with him for Saturday night. That's when he's going to meet Georgia in the Village," she winced. "Well, not really. I mean, that's when she's going to stand him up."

She was hiding her face in the crook of her elbow, as though to protect her face from my punch.

"Um. No," I said. "I don't want to play anymore."

"Why not?"

"It's sick and cruel and mean. You think by standing him up on an imaginary date, you're going to get back at him?"

"Well. Yes. Kind of," she said. "He insulted me. He insulted my family to a complete stranger. So we are going to watch his humiliation from a bar across the street."

"Well, you're going there alone. I'm not a part of this. It's shitty all around," I said, putting my hands in the air in surrender. "I took it as far as I could stomach it. Besides, what if he sees me?"

"Oh, please, he's expecting someone who weighs twenty-five pounds less," she said. Seconds later she realized what she'd blurted out and slapped her hand over her mouth. Through her fingers she muttered, "Peach. I didn't mean to insult you. You're not fat. You have a beautiful body. I swear."

"Right. Thanks," I said.

"I mean it. I never meant to insult you."

"No. Course not."

The hand that had covered her mouth now clutched my upper arm.

"Please, Peach. I know the perfect place in Greenwich Village, a restaurant across from the bar where we can set him up. We'll disguise ourselves and get there a little early, and—"

"No. Put an end to this. Erase the account tonight."

"I can't. I guess I'm just made of harsher stuff than you. You can stay at the apartment and I'll go. I hate myself that I'm like this, but I can't tell you how good it will make me feel for Marcus to experience just a teeny bit of the rejection I feel. Just a teeny, tiny bit. Is that so bad?"

Her eyes were filling up with tears.

"Listen, revenge is not release," I said, running a hand down her spindly arm. "Humiliating someone to get back at them is only going to backfire on you. It turns into resentment, and resentment is cancer. Even if he doesn't find out, you've put bad karma into the universe and it carries your name on it. It does."

"That Lou's hippy shit or your Psych 101 crap?"

"Bit of both," I sighed, finishing my beer and signaling to Stu that I was through.

"I'll have another one, Stu. Do you have any Popsicles?"

"No, honey, the only food we sell hangs on clothespins."

Despite three more beers and three more shots of Southern Comfort, Beth was surprisingly lucid when we left the tavern. I had hoped by Saturday night I could convince Beth to drop the stunt and let the whole charade go, but I couldn't pull this idea out of her jaws that night.

Back at the farm Beau had long gone to bed, but Lou was still up. I pretended to be deathly tired, so Beth grabbed a bottle of beer and followed the lights leading to the Airstream. That's where I thought we'd find her in the morning, hung over and moaning about the early hour, me reminding her that the trip to New York was her idea.

I brushed, peed, and I threw on that yellow shortie nightie thingie Beau had bought me for Christmas. I had hated it at first sight, making fun of it with the boys that morning by dressing Sam in the top and Jake in the bottoms.

I climbed into bed and inched over to Beau's side, where he had fallen asleep with his clothes on.

"Hey, baby. Dja have fun?" he mumbled, a little drunk.

"Mmm," I said, moving my hand down to his belt buckle.

"Wait," he said, stumbling to the bathroom. In his absence, I arranged the blanket just so, leaving my ass exposed like Alps under moonlight and pretended to fall asleep. Since almost the day I had married him, I had been trying to get Beau to spank me. And though Beau had no qualms about positions, orifices, fluids and where to put them (or in whom, one would think), he would not submit to that. So I became fixated on requesting spankings only because Beau had refused.

While Beau carefully unbuckled in the dark, he let out a long cool whistle which totally cracked me up.

"I guess if Peachy's asleep," he whispered, "I could just stand here and jerk off. I wonder how that would go?"

"Suit yourself. Just don't get any on the carpet."

Beau gingerly climbed atop me, lightly straddling the back of my thighs.

"Do it."

My request was muffled by the pillow.

"No."

"Why not?"

"Because. I told you. I cherish you."

"Come on, Beau, it's right there for the smacking." I motioned toward my ass with a thumb like it was a suspicious stranger following me.

"But I don't want to *hit* you, Peachy."

"I don't want you to *hit* me either, Beau," I

sighed. He rolled off of me. I turned over. "I was only trying to be playful."

"I don't like violence, Peach. You know that. Any other fetish but that. I can't, can't, cannot do that to *that* ass."

"Jeez. You think because I asked you to take a whack at my butt I have a fetish? Beau, I do not have a fetish. I have a circumstantial request."

"But you only want me to do it 'cause I *won't* do it."

"So. Don't you think that's kind of sexy?"

"No. It's weird."

"You're weird."

"Okay. But, if I hit you . . . then . . . you'll probably have to hit me."

"Fine."

"*Fine?* You mean you'd hit me?"

"If you wanted me to."

"Well, it's not that I want you to. But it seems only fair."

"*Fine.*"

"So . . . hit me," he said. I could feel him brace up.

"It's not supposed to be a funny thing."

"C'mawwwn, give it to me, Peachy."

"Where?"

"In the arm. Do the arm."

It was dark in the room. By voice I gauged the general direction of his upper torso but my palm landed too hard by his left ear.

"Ow. Jesus."

"Sorrysorry."

"Boy," he sighed into the ceiling. "I cannot believe how horny that just made me. Remind me to let you smack me around more often, Peach."

I apologized and rolled over thinking how we used to "cherish" each other four times a week our first year, three the second, one the third, then after the boys were both toilet-trained, whenever the hell they weren't around, which was rare, or when both of us weren't tired at the same time, which was almost never.

He kissed my shoulder and told me he loved me. I said, "Me too." We touched bums, and as I listened for his snores to approach, I dug out another terrible, useful mind trick. When I'd begin to sound and seem like a whiny wife from afternoon talk shows, I would make myself think about how awful widowhood would be. It was a little sick, but it worked, made me feel physical love for the man who slept next to me, and, if everything was properly aligned, it sometimes made me quietly cry. Beth likened this trick to teenaged girls who cut themselves to feel anything. "Whatever," I said, "it felt good and it was less bloody." I would be so sad, I'd think. Then I'd imagine what I'd wear to the funeral; that sundress he loved, depending on the season, though he usually died in summer in my mind. Then I'd imagine his eulogy. *Beau might have been Beth's high school sweetheart, but he was the love of my life,* I'd say, choking up. *I only wish my mother could have met Beau; she would have loved him like the son she never had, and let's face it, had probably really wanted.*

I stopped sniffling long enough to hear one of the boys creaking gingerly down the hallway toward our bedroom. It sounded like the lighter, therefore younger, son. Jake padded like a spy across the bedroom carpet on up to the foot of the bed. There he paused kind of creepily, probably assessing the almost imperceptibly widening gap growing between his two sleeping parents.

"Jake. That you?"

His shadow froze.

"No more of this, didn't we say?"

I lifted the covers.

"I know," Jake whispered hoarsely, crawling toward my tunnel on all fours. "I heard yous come home and then I woke up and then I could hear Auntie Beth and Grandpa laughing and then music and I waited and no sleep came."

Jake inherited my and Lou's insomnia. We often gently bumped into each other in the hall in the middle of the night, something I had always found a little sad.

"You have to start sleeping in your own bed, guy. Or else," Beau said.

Jake and I fell into an automatic spooning situation, Jake's bony bum atop my softening thighs. I should start running again, I thought.

"Else what?" Jake whispered.

"Else your dad's going to have to start beating you up," I joked.

Jake snickered, nestled.

Beau groaned and said, "That's not funny. Hitting the boys."

"You go to sleep or I'll smother you with a pillow, Husband."

"Yeah, me too, *Father*," Jake said.

"Hey!" Beau said, his hand patting around for our bodies in the dark.

"Oh, now you want to spank me," I said over my shoulder when his hand made contact with my hip. "And in front of the kid and everything."

He waited a beat, huffed, got up, and grabbed a pillow.

"I'm gonna sleep downstairs. Wake me when you get up."

"Why?" I said, knowing the answer. He wasn't going to get laid in the morning now that one of the boys had captured the bed. He whispered goodnight and left.

"Mom," Jake whispered.

"What? Go to sleep, buddy."

"Mom. I just want to tell you something."

"Tell me, then sleep."

"I just want to tell you that you didn't even talk to me *all day*," he said, yawning, half-gone. "And all night either. And you're leaving in the morning."

The phony widow tears that had pooled now slid down my cheek into my ear. I squeezed Jake's rib cage tight to mine. He was thin like Beth, their rib cages like wicker baskets.

"Well, I'm talking to you right now, my sweetest boy, my little dude, my dolly man and darling sidekick. I am talking to you right now."

While Jake dropped off to sudden sleep, I lay thinking out an inventory. I am a good mother. Beau is a good man. I love my sister. I am glad Beth visits often. She inherited Mom's genes. I got Dad's. Lou is a good father. Beau is learning more from Lou than from me. My marriage is strong and true. This house is sturdy, and when the driveway's finally paved, we could make a mint. If we sell. Which we never will. This bed smells like us, like foods that don't normally mix; eggs and apples, milk and beer. We do okay with conflict. We have a clean well, and emergency candles. If there's a storm, we have a backup generator and good blankets—worst-case scenario, a barrel on the roof to catch the rain. Our post office is inconvenient but quaint. Our neighbors are angry but entertaining. Scoots is old and blind, but attractive and spry. Our sons are also attractive and spry. The youngest sleeps next to me, and though he is small for his age, he is in excellent health. The oldest sleeps alone, because he tosses too much and wakes with headaches, and because he sometimes pees in his sleep, we don't let him in bed with us anymore. Kills me now when I think about what I had put him through in the park a few hours later.

chapter eight

Hey, you're wearing your Bad Santa pajamas," Sam said, tugging a wad of my yellow nightie thingie from inside my housecoat. He was fully alert in the grass, and the park was beginning to fill up with morning dog walkers streaming out of the neighboring subdivision.

The boys loved when I named my clothes. I had my Scaredy pants, which I had been wearing when Sam got lost at the mall last year. I had my Bobby belt, which I used to capture a stray dog we later learned was named Bobby and belonged to one of those monster-home people who probably thought that moving out to Belle River meant animals could run wild.

"That's right, bud. Bad Santa."

"Maaw-*um!* Hear me!" Jake yelled. "We need

to go home!" I suddenly caught a glimpse of what a little asshole he might become at twenty or thirty, when he was grown up and hopefully some nice woman's problem.

"Maybe we could stay in the park permanently," I joked, stubbing out my cigarette and winking at Sam, who had his hands on his hips, twisting back and forth in his cute postseizure stretch. "It's fairly temperate. There's parking. We could set up house in the spiral slide. Wash dishes in the wading pool. Cook over burning garbage cans. We'd keep it clean. Order in a lot."

But Jake wasn't laughing, just bewildered.

"Okay. Let's go, boys," I said, tossing my cigarette and stifling my sniffles in case I sparked a nosebleed.

It was a short drive home. The boys were dew-covered and shivering in the back seat even though the sunrise had heated up the car's interior. As I drove Beth's convertible down the gravel driveway, the farmhouse suddenly looked completely different to me, like a different version of itself. I looked at the overgrown lawn, the dormers like ghoul eyes, the crabgrass strangling my heirloom tomatoes, defeated Scoots tied to the willow stump overnight until the smell of whatever he'd likely rolled in abated, the broken bike next to the house that Beau tugged from a garbage pile, promising to fix it into a chopper for Sam, the carp pails stacked in the carport, next to them the tarp-covered Dart, the back seat still probably strewn with the paperwork of my interrupted education, the detritus of Internet searches about epilepsy, spent Kleenex, empty coffee cups, broken doughnut boxes, and stray socks from lugging the laundry of boys and men to and from town, before the Dart, which I was more sentimental about than my mechanic husband, had finally died, and it occurred to me how right it was for Beth to leave this place when she had had the chance. From outside, it seemed like the rooms in our house had shrunk, but I pictured the furniture growing bigger, monstrous, vengeful, our grandfather clock shooting through the roof in slow motion like a launching rocket, Nana Beecher's oak table rolling sideways, smashing through the front window box, the antimacassars flitting through the air like bats, our mahogany night tables exploding out of the dormers, *baboom, baboom,* each landing feet first in the lush hydrangeas, which, that summer, had only finally bloomed the proper garish way the seed pouch said they would. And I saw Beau and Beth trying to escape, but as they reached the worn living room shag, it turned into a boiling blue ocean swallowing them both bloody under.

The boys were pups straining against me, now their least-favorite leash. Jake broke out of my grasp first when he heard the phone ringing in the house.

"I'll get it!" he yelled, running up the flagstones.

Sam looked at my face, then at his dad's Jeep parked crookedly next to Lou's yellow pickup.

"Are you guys gonna fight again?"

"I think so, sweetheart," I said, kissing the side of his sweaty head. "Go in the house and play with your brother in your room. Play Monopoly, okay?" Jake was too young to understand the game, but Sam was still at an age where winning was important.

"I hate it when you guys fight," he said, stomping a foot and walking off.

"Me too."

I watched our first born trip toward my childhood house, bumping directly into his dad, who was speaking to someone on the phone. He stopped Sam on the porch to hug him and to examine his bloody hand. Sam yanked it away and skulked past him.

I tried to look at anything but Beau's face, which was flattened with fear and shame. He leaned on the rail where the boys' bathing suits waved at us like sad flags. He said goodbye to whomever he was talking to and hung up with an angry digit. The cordless telephone was not invented for the enraged. Punctuating the tail end of a horrible exchange with a stern poke of a finger was wholly unsatisfying, which was probably why Beau hurled the expensive cordless into the house. I listened to it skip wounded along the wooden floor, causing even more unnecessary damage.

"Heyyy, DAA-aad," Jake scolded from inside.

"Where've you been?" Beau asked, his voice heavy with everything. His eyes were blood-shot from drinking and not sleeping. Or from crying, maybe. I wanted to believe there had been a lot of that.

The walk toward the house felt utterly uphill. I half-expected Beth to appear behind him wrapped in one of our wedding-present towels. I pictured her placing her chin on Beau's shoulder in casual ownership, as I had smugly done to chase off unwanted visitors. Maybe this was all a big misunderstanding, I thought. Maybe they were the ones who had gotten married all those years ago and I was the one *just stopping by.* Maybe those were their two boys and I was Beth, flying in for my monthly hair touch-up, my "slumming it with the family" weekend, and I would snap out of this electrified daydream.

"I was in town. At the park."

Beau had taken a shower, but he hadn't shaved. His freckles darkened in the summer. Though he still had all his hair, his sideburns were shot with dashes of white, the scalp along the part was pink and flaky with sunburnt skin. I'd known Beau since I was fourteen, when I was his and Beth's pouty gadfly. We'd married when I was twenty and he was twenty-three. Almost a decade later, I felt twice his age. I could smell Brut, a scent I found unsettlingly sexy, as it was Lou's smell too.

"You were at the park all this time?" Beau asked.

"Who was that on the phone?"

"Beth."

"Where is she?

"Lou's." She must have called on her cell phone.

"Peachy, come in the house," Beau said.

"Why is she still here?" I demanded, *and not strapped in a burning plane careening toward pavement?*

"Ah, well, you took the rental," Beau said, trying hard not to sound smart-assed.

"Right."

I noticed my red battered carry-on with the rusty metal buckles sitting slouched next to Beth's leather tote bag. The boys had helped me pack, my way of including them in our first goodbye.

"Peachy, come inside. Okay?"

The sun was peeking over the top of the Rosarios' barn across the highway, mocking us with its benevolent glow. I watched their leggy Doberman, Briar, run circles in the front yard like some big, demented toy.

"Are you two having an affair?"

I knew the answer, but it seemed like the question scorned women in soaps, in books, women elsewhere, asked in situations like this one. Annalisa Morrow must have asked Scott that question, and people would ask me if Beau and I split up over this, so I wanted an answer.

"No. Fuck. No. It was a stupid, stupid—we got drunk, Peachy. I am so sorry. You got blood on your face. Where'd he get you this time?"

"Nose. Where was Lou? While you were fucking his other daughter?"

"Jesus. The boys," Beau muttered, glancing over his shoulders and driving his fingers through his damp hair. "He was sleeping."

"You don't even like Beth."

"I don't. I don't. I don't."

"Then why would you fuck someone you don't even like?" I hissed. "Let alone my sister. A person who I love. Who I loved."

He just shook his head and showed me his palms. I walked past him, smacking him hard in the middle of his chest, partly to move him, partly to hurt him. I grabbed my purse off the roll-top desk and pulled my passport out from one of the upper slots. *Jesus,* I thought. *I am doing this. I am going to do this.*

"And you certainly can't say it was curiosity, Beau, because her goddamn pussy can't be new to you, let alone to the rest of the county."

I opened up the carry-on and it spilled across the floor. I kicked out a pair of jeans and a T-shirt. I wished for Beth to be in the house to take that in, but naturally only Sam had heard me say that. He was perched at the top of the stairs, chewing the bottom of his pajama top. Oh, the conversations Beth and I had had in front of Sam when he was a baby, it was a miracle his first word wasn't "fuck." Looking at his little face, I was suddenly aware of how easy it can be to earn the right to leave people, to shatter the very core of a family, and how difficult it would be to fix it. I had never insulted Beth. I had never thrown her past, her promiscuity, her selfishness, her arrogance, in her face, having never felt in a position to judge her. I wouldn't even tolerate lazy put-downs from Beau. Because if Beth was sad and angry, she had good reason to be, I said. And because she had always loved me, and mostly well, I even hated the very hate I felt for her.

"Where's your brother, Sam?" I tried to avoid looking into his loaded eyes while I manically dressed myself, tucking the yellow nightie top into my jeans.

"Asleep. He fell asleep on my Monopoly board and I want you to carry him to bed. Now, okay? And lay down with him."

I looked at the grandfather clock behind him. Poor Jake had run circles in that park for hours. His batteries must have just died.

"Let him lie there for a bit, bud. Okay? Daddy'll get him up later. Maybe you should get some more sleep, hey?"

"Are you guys going to fight?"

"No. Not anymore. But listen to me." He met me halfway on the steps. "I'm going to New York, like me and Auntie Beth planned. But she's going to stay here, okay? And I'm going to be back after you wake up and go to sleep two times. Before Disney Sunday night."

His mouth made the shape of the word "mom," but no sound came out.

"Look at me." I knelt in front of him and took his hands in mine. "You can be angry. That is okay. But I'm going to be gone for exactly two days. So listen to your father, and grandpa and Auntie Beth, okay? And how much do I love you?"

He was biting his lips and shaking his head, no.

"More than monkeys, mountains, or the moon?" he whimpered.

"That's right. Now give me a great big hug and a massive bye-bye and go back to bed and remember like I said, you only have to go to sleep and wake up twice and I will be home. Okay? And be nice to Jake."

"What if I have a seizure and you're not here?"

"We talked about this and it's okay, sweetheart. Everyone knows how to take care of you real good. So no worries."

"You're going by yourself?"

"Yes. I'm going to take a little break."

"From us?"

"No, baby, from me."

"What about Auntie Beth?"

"Well, lucky puck, she's now going to stay with you. So you'll have extra eyes on you."

"Aren't you scared to go by yourself, Mom? You're not supposed to."

"A little bit. But it's okay to be a little scared."

"You got blood," he said, pointing to the right corner of my cheek. I licked my hand and rubbed it. "You're coming back?"

I nodded. "Absolutely."

"Not like Grandma?"

I shook my head no. "Baby. No. Never like Grandma."

I regretted we ever told him how my mother had died. But Lou insisted we never lie after the legal and emotional debacles that sprung from her suicide. I wanted to tell Sam I would never abandon them like that, because the consequence of a mother killing herself is that she also kills her children's night- and daydreams, their imaginary friends, their favorite foods. She kills their private and public trusts. She takes with her their giggles and dimples and boo-boos. She breaks their hearts in half so that they grow up to

162

become doubly steeled to disaster. And they're meaner than they were ever meant to be. And they can't shake it off. It's a permanent slip of toilet paper stuck to the bottoms of their souls forever. So if not abandoning my sons meant they wouldn't grow up to be assholes like Auntie Beth, and, frankly, me, then I could live with the residual damage my hypervigilance might cause.

"I'm so coming back. Buddy, this is a quick little trip Momma needs to take. Now I want you to kiss me good night and go upstairs and take a shower and please do your neck and I will see you Sunday."

Sam grasped all of me with everything he had. Things were tight and terrible for several seconds and then he loosened and ran. After slamming the bathroom door, he screamed, "I hate everything!"

I'd never had daughters, and never once thought about my mother's suicide in relation to the shared sex of the kids she left behind. But in that moment I had a sharp vision and a darker bodily sense about how different my goodbye would have gone if Sam were a Samantha. I felt how much easier it was for me to briefly leave boys, but how much harder it would have been for me to leave the kind of girls I would have raised.

"Peachy? What the . . . what do you mean, 'you're going'? Please stay. Please talk to me," he begged, trying to block the living room archway with his body. "You can't leave. Who's going to watch Sam?"

"Don't use him. You, Beth, and Lou. There's plenty of people to take care of him here. Everyone who's been telling me he has to stop being afraid of being away from me."

The phone rang again. The lit-up window showed Beth's cell number, and despite Beau's plea for me to ignore it, for us to just talk, I answered.

"What do you want?"

"Hi, Peachy."

"Oh. Hi, Daddy. Where's Beth?"

"Here, in the trailer."

I pictured Beth shaped in the letter *C*, hands clasped to her knobby knees, head bowed, long shiny hair skimming over her beloved breasts, tickling the tops of her skinny thighs.

"Did she tell you what happened?"

"Kinda. Enough," Lou said, taking a deep breath. "Honey, breathe with me."

"I got a plane to catch, Pa. I got no time for hippy shit. Put her on."

"You sure?"

"Put her on."

"Stay calm, lovey."

"I am calm. Calmer than a fucking cow."

I walked to the kitchen and looked out the window toward the top of Lou's trailer through the reddening brush, picturing where Beth was sitting, trying to remember what she had on when I had backed out the driveway hours earlier.

"Peach?" Her voice sounded small but scarred from some serious drinking and crying. "I am so so sor—" She was suddenly overcome by sobs, which didn't sound fake. "Don't blame Beau. I got us all worked up. It's me. I'm a fuckup. I fucked up so, so bad. It was nothing I planned. I didn't mean for anything to happen. I swear to you, Peachy."

"Where's your keys?"

"It's just that we had a few too many drinks —then we smoked that joint and I . . . What do you mean, 'keys'?"

"House keys."

"To my apartment? Why?"

"Where are they?"

"Why?"

"Tell me!"

"In my purse. In the kitchen. They're in the outside pocket, I guess. Why?"

"Listen to me very carefully." I whispered harshly to Beau, "And you need to overhear this, dumbass. I am going on my planned vacation. I will be staying at your place, Beth. But without you, understand? You are staying here. Sam has an appointment with Dr. Best tomorrow morning at Detroit Children's. Beau has to work. And I want him to stay away from you while I am

gone. Write down everything the doctor says. If
—I mean when—Sam has a seizure, I've told
you what to do. But there are instructions on the
fridge and in the glove compartment. It is no big
deal. Keep him off the gravel. He knows to stay
on grass and carpet. When he starts to stare, or
mumble, or pull at his clothes, that means one's
coming. Stay calm. There are towels in the trunk
if it happens while you're driving, just pull
over, lie him down, and stuff a towel under his
bum in case he wets himself. There's extra
undies and pants in the white plastic bag in the
middle of the spare tire. Don't hold him down.
Very important. Do not stick anything in his
mouth. Take his seat belt off and try to put him
on his side. And don't worry about Jake. He's
very used to it. Ask him to sing something. If
you can time out the seizure, I'd appreciate it.
We're trying to keep track before the surgery."

"Peach. Stop. I can't. This is insane," Beth said.

"Have coloring books for Jake. Sometimes
they take a little while to pass. When Sam
comes to, just say 'Hello, welcome back, champ,'
something like that. Then carry on just as usual.
Before you leave for Detroit, make a lunch for
Beau. No meat. The fridge is broken at the
shop. His thermos is in the dishwasher. Washer's
still broken. There's four loads of laundry
already separated in the basement. Throw them
in the trunk. I find it's faster to do it all at once

when I have an excuse to go into town. The boys can play two games each on the pinball machine. I keep a bag of quarters in the coffee tin in the freezer. Grab a bunch. Don't let the boys see you. Jesus, it sounds like my life sucks. It does, doesn't it?"

"Peachy, I—"

"But don't use the dryers there. Sam's allergic to Bounce. Machines are polluted with it. Bring it back here to dry. Use the lines. Don't leave it out past dark. June bugs are still around. Be sure to fold the T-shirts just before they're completely dry, but not damp. Beau likes crisp lines. But make sure the jeans and towels are totally dry or they get moldy. You can use Lou's line too if there's too much."

"Jesus, Peachy," Beau said, running his hands through his hair.

"Get Sam to help you carry things, Beth. He's strong enough and he likes to. Your show's on tomorrow night, so make sure you tape it for Lou because he plays softball. He'll pick up the boys. They eat hot dogs for dinner there. Beau meets them after work. But since you're staying, make Beau's supper tonight. For tomorrow, it's Chinese, but pick up some iceberg lettuce at Silvano's next to the laundromat. But don't buy anything else there, it's too expensive. Lou likes to make the dressing. While Beau eats, draw a bath for Jake. Make sure you get behind his ears.

167

Sam takes showers. But if he's in there more than fifteen minutes, knock. It's rare for him to seize there, but you never know. Don't let him think you're checking. Just pretend you have to go. They can have dessert before bed. Nothing chocolate. And kudos to you if you can find the time to fuck my husband again in between all that."

"Peachy, I can't—"

"Yeah, I know. It's hard. Hence our no-sex dilemma, which, I guess is just my dilemma, seeing's he went and got himself some ass. So, I think that's about it. Let the boys wait up for me Sunday."

Beau was pacing like Jake had in the park.

"Peachy, I'm coming with you. We can talk in New York," she pleaded.

"No. All done talking."

"I'm at least coming up to the house."

"Don't. I'm late. Are you still drinking?"

"No. Jesus. Oh, Peach. I am so—"

"You should probably throw back some coffee. Days start early around here."

"What are you going to do in New York? By yourself?"

"What do you think I'm going to do? Rest, do a little shopping, and then I'll get ready for my date tomorrow night."

Beth went quiet. Beau stopped gently banging his head on the kitchen table, his eyes looking straight ahead into the middle distance. I looked down at his confused and stupid face and let the luxurious weight of my threat settle over them both.

"Peachy," she was calm and suddenly sober-sounding. "If . . . you . . . do . . . what I think you're going to do, I'll—"

I laughed hard and honestly at her. "Never forgive me? That is the funniest shit I ever heard you say, Beth Ann Archer. Well, it is up there anyway. Because you are a funny one. And don't even think about emailing Marcus to cancel plans. I've got your keys and your address book. I'll just call him, tell him I changed my mind again. I'll tell him I'm just a woman who doesn't know herself. I'll tell him it runs in my family. Wish me luck!"

I hung up on her, walked over to the kitchen sink, and turned on the tap. I stuck a plug in the drain and let it fill up a few inches. Then I took the laptop off the roll-top desk and dunked it under the water.

"I'm so confused," Beau said. His eyes were rimmed not just from the crying, but from pressing the heels of his hands deep into the sockets. "Who's Marcus? Why'd you do that to the computer?"

"Sam's on that damn thing way too much. Come to think of it, so am I."

"What are you talking about, a date?"

"Ask Beth. I'm in a hurry. And I'll have the cell, but only call if there's an emergency, like if one of the boys is dying, or you decide to do yourself in."

"Peachy, what's going on? What the fuck are you doing? I swear, it didn't mean anything."

"Why do people say that? It means everything," I said, walking out of the house and slamming the screen door behind me.

It wasn't fully light out when I started up Beth's convertible, checking for the rental papers in the glove compartment. I kept the top down to let my hair whip some feeling back into my numb face. I was running a little early, so I took Old Tecumseh to Riverside. At the bend the pink horizon where the lake dumped into the Detroit River looked toxic, man-made, the cumulous issue of American riverside factories. Then the Renaissance Center came into view, all shiny with the new sun. Ever since they put the finishing touches on the towers in Detroit, Beth had been chomping at the bit to be American, her right and birthright. She was born there after all, while I was spat out on the farm, my mother burying her placenta (or was it mine?) under the willow. Before she died, Lou and Nell used to bring us down to the waterfront to watch the giant metal cranes knit the five towers skyward.

After high school, Beth was done with Canada,

done with social welfare, boring TV, shitty exchange rates, and the feeling that she was on the outside looking in on a country that would appreciate someone like her coming home. She fixed New York on her horizon like a bobbing buoy, a place she'd have to swim toward or die. Lou was saddened. He had hoped his love affair with his adopted country would have worn off on his American-born daughter.

"No offense, Lou. You're not dull, but your country is," she said.

Driving toward the tunnel, the sky over Windsor did feel uncomfortably low. The early-summer heat gathered around my shoulders like an unnecessary shawl that I also wanted to throw off, thinking, So this is what it feels like to leave, to flee trouble, to ride a wild tornado out of town.

And then it happened. I finally started to cry like a child, the kind where your sobs make slow, choky connections to hiccups, nose and mouth all kind of linked with spitty suspension bridges that you have to unstring with wet fists and fingers because you never have a tissue handy. And I was grateful for the first time in my life for these hateful post-9/11 passport line-ups, and for WLLZ, Motor City Rocks, which I cranked up to drown my sobs.

After I calmed down a little, I checked out my face in the rearview mirror. I looked flushed and splotchy, like a pale pink balloon had broken open across my face. I could see why despair was tricky, what its free rein could do to the body. But the cry gave me the sense that I was capable of poignancy, and I let that softness propel me. I wasn't hoping for epiphanies or to ever hear the violins of heartfelt reunions; I hated my sister. My husband had punctured the force field around us with his ignorant dick. But for a moment there, I no longer felt as though my corner of the sky was a damp blue tarp, wackily pinning me beneath it.

"Purpose for your visit?"

I got one of the female border guards. They had a reputation for being meaner than the men.

"Going to the airport," I said, offering my passport, squinting up into her face.

"Are you okay?"

"Yes. No. I just caught my husband fucking my sister, but I'm okay."

It came out almost by accident, the upper quarters of my lungs bursting with the crime. I needed to let it out so I could breathe better. Also, I knew I was sending news out into a world that from now on would have to pick sides. Me or Beth. This was how I was going to gather an army against her, one by one.

The border lady winced without looking at me, as though this was the kind of information she gathered every day in her kiosk.

"Yeesh. That's rough. Where you going?"

"New York City."

"What for?"

I told her I was visiting a friend, which was true.

"Take it easy," she said, handing back my passport. "Don't cry and drive."

Both of us froze when my cell rang, flashing the number of the salon.

"Do me a favor," she said. "Answer that call, but pull over there and shut the engine off." She pointed to the parking lot where they direct smugglers and terrorists. "Answer it. If anyone bothers you, tell them I said it was alright. Pick up the phone."

I did. It was Lou giving me the same instructions.

"Pull the car over, Peachy. I'm not going to tell you to come home. I just need to tell you something important and I want you to listen carefully. It's my turn to speak." He sounded angry, which made me even angrier.

"Daddy, I can't talk right now."

"Then listen."

"She's toxic and I want her gone from my life. For good."

"That's not going to be possible, Peachy. She's my daughter too, and she needs a place to come home to, now more than ever. You may not understand this right now, but she's at a point in her life where she's ready to make some changes. You have to remember that she had a rough start, honey. She was born different than you. That's why her life's turned out different than yours."

"Yeah. Must be rough to be so rich and successful. Oh, and to be skinny and beautiful too? Rough, rough, rough. So I can see why she's so fucking miserable and has so few friends. My mother died too, Daddy. I was there that day too, and I was the one who found her, and did I turn into a fucking asshole? No. I didn't take my sadness out on the whole fucking planet. And I don't drink myself into oblivion over every little fucking thing that happens to me."

"That's right, Peachy. You don't. You're lucky. But because Beth does, we have to try to love her more."

"I'm *lucky!* How *dare* you. How dare you take her side in this when you know what she's done and what she's capable of doing. I have put up with her for years, her dramas, her crazy bullshit, her stupid, stupid stunts, but I am through. Now I got a busted marriage and a broken boy and another one who's not getting enough love. I have nothing left for Beth. You keep her for the weekend while I figure out what I'm going to do about Beau, and then you say goodbye to her, Daddy, because if I have anything to do with it, it's the last time she's ever going to see that fucking farm again."

The guard walked around to the side of the convertible and made a shushing motion with her finger.

"Either keep it down or put the top up."

"I can't have this conversation right now, Dad. I might get arrested."

"Just think back, Peachy. That's all I'm saying. Try to go back, and when you do, go back a little more, before you condemn Beth. Frankly, I'm thinking things are going to improve, if we let them."

"You are weird, old man."

"I'm trying."

"Listen. I know what you're talking about. But lots of kids survive what we survived. So don't blame me for Beth's shitty choices. She did this. Not me. Now, promise me you'll keep an eye on the boys, but make sure Beth takes Sam this morning to the doctor, okay? Not Beau. I want her to see a little of what real life's all about. I want her to take a good look at what she destroyed, okay?"

"That's the plan, Peach. No worries. And call me. Or I'll call you. And another thing. Beth's friend Kate's gonna meet you at the airport. She's told her everything, and Peachy, believe it or not, Beth's worried about you alone in the city. So you let Kate take care of you."

I told him I didn't need any taking care of, though I relished disabusing Beth's friends of any remaining notion that she might possess redeeming qualities.

"Well then, Peachy, try not to do anything stupid. You know how I feel about retaliation."

"I won't," I said, lying.

"Don't match hate with hatefulness."

"Okay."

"I love you a lot. But I love both my girls."

"I love you too, but I could do without the last part."

"Not me," he said. "Not ever."

We said goodbye and I started up the convertible. The border guard waved me out of the lot and gave me an aggressive thumbs-up, which felt corny and typical. I nodded. Until then, Americans had always killed me with those sentiments; their thumbs-up, their pats on the back, their way-to-gos, their you-can-do-its, their just-say-nos, a country of slogans to our footnotes.

chapter nine

Beyond the fantasies, beyond the daydreams and distractions, I'd thought of it, of leaving Beau and the boys, of never coming back. But where do you put those thoughts? Whom do you tell, I wondered, as the stewardess carefully pointed out all my new exits on the plane. Mothers meeting in parks don't talk about that while their precious kids play a few feet away on the monkey bars. I've never completely admitted to Beth how tyrannical *constant* togetherness sometimes felt to me, in part because I thought there was something wrong with me. Also, my marriage and kids were the only things that truly separated me from Beth, made me different, and at times, better than her, I thought. And I'd never heard any woman admit that maybe it was all a big mistake, that the marriage and kid thing was highly overrated and that the idea of never being alone again, pretty much as long as you live, was too horrific to allow yourself to contemplate, even when you actually were alone. Especially then. But because I was leaving the boys and men behind, and planned to do some terrible things, I thought I should be more afraid. Feel more ashamed.

It had been a morning of radical firsts: my first adultery, my first airplane ride, my first time away from the boys, let alone Lou, Beau, and the farm. But it was also the first time in almost ten years that I found myself completely alone, and I hated to admit this to anyone, let alone myself, after that morning, but sitting there, getting strapped in and sucked back in my seat upon ascent, I felt a bit wonderful. I never thought I was built for anything like abandon. But my constant vigilance was born less of altruism than of selfishness. I'd never left my boys before because I couldn't contemplate what would happen to them if *I* died. Sam's illness had bred a selfish morbidity in me; I pondered rueful, shocking thoughts. Who would take care of them? Naturally, Beau and Lou. But how would that go, all those men and all that testosterone under one roof? Jake and Sam were about the same age Beth and I were when Nell killed herself, so I've often fantasized about how much of me Jake would remember. Would it be as little as I remember of my mother? By virtue of being firstborn, Sam stored more of me in him as Beth had of our mother—something that had always made me envious. She and Nell had taken trips alone to the city. Nell taught Beth how to thread the sewing machine, how to roller-skate backward on the cement floor in the carport, and how to play "Merry Men" on the guitar. Beth got to have those memories even though I'd have appreciated them more. Yes, I was too young to learn these things, but I was left with so few memories of Nell mothering me, Nell loving me, that it was as though she had only ever existed in that brief watery home-movie reel that we had played and replayed.

As the plane hit its highest altitude and straightened up, I looked out the window at the checkerboard of farms stretching as far as I could see. Who knew there were still so many of us living so far apart from one another. Though we didn't really count as farmers. Maybe we should have made a better go at growing things instead of shaving off bits and pieces of the farm to afford to live on a farm that was no longer a farm. The last few acres on the other side of the river were the next to go, the offer from the builders too lucrative, and Sam's operation in Detroit too expensive, to turn down. Lou loathed the idea of having neighbors, but maybe they'd be good for us. Maybe being isolated and unaccountable was our problem. Maybe if there had been neighbors other than the Rosarios, I would have married someone else, one of the subdivision boys, and not Beau. Or had I stayed in school, maybe I wouldn't have married at all. I would have fallen in love with my career.

Instead, at twenty-eight, I had developed deep canyons between my eyebrows from worrying about people I couldn't love enough, especially Beau, a man I married, truly and honestly, because my sister didn't. And as ludicrous as it is, I kept the baby, went ahead with the whole shebang because an abortion would have made me appear to be copying Beth. My decision expressed nothing political, or maternal. I was merely avoiding embarrassment, the way a cat quickly, shyly, rights itself, as though it meant to roll off a high shelf while sleeping. Then I sealed the decision with Jake, because, I mean, who had two by accident? Asshole, I know. And even after Jake, I could have gone back to school and finished my degree. But aside from the work of raising kids, my career bubble burst after my internship in special ed. The day I snuck a peek at that assessment by the doctoral students, then drove home in tears, was the day I found Beau's legs poking out from under Lou's Jeep.

"You're not my father. What have you done with my father?" I said, holding Beau's ankles. Even though we often found him trailing Lou like a lanky shadow, I was genuinely happy to see Beau that day. A kind face after bad news.

"Peachy! Heyyy. Christ, we haven't seen you in a long time."

"What do you mean 'we.' You live here now?"

I embarrassed him. It was obvious to everyone that Beau stuck around because his stepdad was a merciless bully. Lou collected the indigent and upset like other people collected stamps. Some who came to the Sunday men's meeting stuck around to help repair a fence or patch a roof. Others, like Beau, pulled up to chat while Lou cut hair in the carport if it was a nice day and they were only looking for a trim.

"Nah. Just working on the timer. It's a beautiful machine, nice lines. Lou's thinking of painting it dark blue. Hey, Lou's gonna set me up with some work over at the co-op, fixing tractors and helping out at the oil field near Harrow. Can you believe it? Oil in Essex County. I told Lou we should stick a pipe by the willow and see what's under that stump. You never know."

"You never know. Where's Lou?"

Beau told me he took one of the bachelor brothers' trucks to Windsor to buy plastic piping for the new salon sink. Then he went on for a half an hour—while wiping his hands and putting away Lou's tools in drawers and jars I had never noticed before—talking about the price of gas, the fact that our high school music teacher had a daughter who was gay, some bla-de-blah about his stupid sister Lucy's stupid wedding and how it had cost twice as much as she said it would cost and how pissed his stepdad was and why should he pay for it if she wasn't his blood kid and why hadn't I been there (wasn't invited), and in the middle of all that he asked about Beth. I said she was great, seeing some stockbroker, flying to Europe, meeting the rich and famous. Beau's expression didn't drop or change when he said, "That's cool for Beth, I always figured her for a gold digger."

"You look really great, Beau," I blurted out.

"Oh. Thanks!" His grin did a slow spill across his face.

"I mean it," I said, plucking the middle of his shirt like a harp. Rejection had made me cocky.

181

Driving home that afternoon, I had come to the conclusion that I was going to quit social work and maybe go into teaching. By the time I had passed through Tecumseh, I had quit teaching and I was thinking about farming. By Puce, I had quit farming and upon approaching Belle River, I was learning how to cut hair, rewriting the sign to say CHEZ PEACHY, PLUS LOU. But when I saw Beau's wide-open face, I can't help but imagine that I had subconsciously landed on motherhood, because I now know I had been violently ovulating.

I dropped my knapsack on the garage floor.

Beau looked momentarily frightened.

"Do you want a beer?" he asked. "Lou doesn't mind if I keep cold ones for me in the little fridge out here. Plus, he likes to have drinks around for you and Beth."

"I'm aware of that, Beau. I live here. Often, I buy the beer myself."

"I know. I know. But we never see you anymore. I'm just saying," he said, still grinning from my compliment.

I followed him into the house. We sat across from each other on the vinyl chairs and drank our beers kind of quickly, both of us nodding at each other and grinning into uneasy silences. I mentioned the new countertop. Beau said it was a bitch to put in. Three guys to lift it. No idea how heavy granite was. I let out a burp. He laughed and cracked open two more beers, placing mine gently in front of me as if he dared me one more. Out of the corner of my eye something tiny and dark broke our game and bolted across the kitchen floor.

"What was that?" I screamed.

"That's that mouse, and by a mouse, I mean *a* mouse. There is *one* in this house. Lou's been trying to get rid of that fucker all day. Hand me that, Peach," he said, pointing to an empty juice bottle on the table.

"This?"

"Yup. Mouth's wide enough. Stand back." He got on his hands and knees, his top half disappearing under the sink. The stillness of his hips belied the bumpy activity going on behind the rusty pipes.

"I got it!" he hollered, his butt collapsing onto his heels, hands quickly capping the mouse inside. "Oh my God, I *got* it! Whooo!"

I peered over Beau's shoulder. The tiny mouse was trying to scurry up the glass but kept losing its grip in the leftover dreck.

I screamed again.

"Oh God, Beau. That was impressive. Let's take it down to the riv—"

"Are you kidding me? Lou tried that. No way. It'll just come back. I gotta kill it."

With that dismissal, Beau covered the top of the bottle with his wide palm. He began to shake it, slow at first, but then his arm became a blur, like a graffiti artist readying a spray can. He kept saying, "I'm sorry," over and over again, to whom or what, I didn't know, but it was a horrible minute and a half. I covered my eyes while the mouse made tiny thumping sounds. After Beau deemed it dead, he emptied the contents into the garbage under the sink and rinsed out the bottle.

"Whoo. Sorry, Peach, there was just no turning back. I put myself in a really difficult position there. Either it suffocated in the bottle, or I killed it quick. But that was fucking sick, you think?" He shuddered, shaking his wild deed out of his arm. I thought of the implications of having sex with a man who would do what he had just done, the brutality of which was hard to process, but was terrifically, disgustingly sexy.

"Sorry, Peachy, that was weird."

"Yup."

"Whew. All right, where were we?"

He grinned the grin of a guy who was completely comfortable in his own skin. He was different than the scholars and complainers I'd been surrounded by in university, with their brainy ideas about love. Beau walked over to where I sat, my head tilted up at him, my legs slightly splayed on a kitchen chair. This time I didn't, couldn't, stop him from doing what I knew he wanted to do. He got down on his knees in front of me. He clinically separated my thighs and wiggled his skinny torso between my legs, putting his face a few inches from mine. I smiled at him. He smiled at me and laughed. Then he tunneled his hands up the front of my T-shirt and placed them heavily upon both breasts. I put my hands on the top of his hair, which felt dry and wiry.

"I am totally freaked out right now, Peachy. Totally freaked out."

"Me too. That mouse killing was weird."

"No. I'm freaked out because I thought about doing this. A lot. And I was thinking exactly this when I saw you today."

"Thinking exactly what?" I teased, fiddling with his ears because I only had his head to play with.

"Thinking I'd like to fuck your brains out on Lou's new countertop."

"You think?" I laughed.

"Oh shit, though. I just remembered something. Fuck. I just started seeing someone, Peachy," he said, collapsing back down on his heels. He looked to the floor and then up at me like he was praying into my face.

"Who?" Not picked again, I thought. This after he'd placed his callused hands on my tiny tits.

"Janey Waterman."

"The dog washer from the vet's?"

"Yeah, but she's training to be a vet."

"Sounds exciting."

"She's gonna take it really hard," he said, thoughtfully rubbing a nonexistent beard.

"Take what hard?"

"That it's over."

"It is?"

"It is."

"I guess so."

"What do you mean, 'I guess so.' " He inched back up between my legs and began messing with the back of my bra under my T-shirt.

"Well, I mean, Beau, I wouldn't want you to break up with someone if you didn't want to." Pick me. Pick me, I thought. I helpfully pulled my loosened bra through the arms of my T-shirt and threw it over his head.

"But I want to break up with her."

"And then what."

"And then you can be my girlfriend."

The safety pin holding up the zipper of my jeans was giving him some trouble. Had I known this would happen, I would have worn my new black cords, with my tight, blue-and-white-striped boatneck top.

"Your girlfriend. Says who?"

"Says me, man."

"What about Beth?" I stood up so he could tug my jeans down, putting my hand on his shoulder to stay steady.

"Beth who? That was high school, Peachy, Jesus. I don't think about her. I don't even like her. She dates dickheads."

"Would you still fuck her?" I lost my balance and fell back onto the chair. I noticed that my bra had landed near the dog bowl.

"What a stupid question. No. I don't want to fuck her. Clearly, it's you I'm wanting to fuck."

"And then what." Me. Pick me.

"Well, then we'll . . . do some more fucking. And then maybe a bit more. Man, this is great. You have no idea."

He stood up and put his hands under my armpits and shuffled me carefully backward over to the counter, my ankles still shackled by my jeans.

"On the count of three," he said. "One—two—" and we hoisted my ass up onto the kitchen counter.

"Nice job this," I said, patting the granite with my fingertips. It felt so permanent. "Too bad about Janey though."

I pulled his shirt over his head too hard and it snagged on the earring he'd soon be parting with. I hated earrings on men. Even Lou finally acquiesced to my bitching about his gold hoop and tossed it. Both Beau's hands grabbed the bottom cuffs of my jeans and he unveiled my calves and feet like a sculpture he'd made. He tossed them over his shoulder onto the kitchen table. I put my fists on his belt buckle, one of those complicated metal affairs he had to help me with.

"Sure, I'm sad. For Janey. She's in love with me, I think."

"Maybe you should call her." I leaned back and fished for the wall phone, knocking the receiver off the cradle and handing it to Beau. Finish the job. Me. Pick me.

"Hmm. She'd be at work. I don't know the number by heart." He hooked his fingers into the sides of my underwear. "On the count of one." I lifted my butt off the counter like a gymnast and they landed at his work boots. I reached down and opened the drawer by the phone.

"Look at you," he said into my lap. "Peachy, Peachy, Peachy."

"Want me to look up the number?"

"I can do it."

While he slapped open the book across my naked thighs and dragged a finger down to the vet's number in Belle River, I reached under the book and split open the top of his jeans, snapping off the button, which hit the floor.

He dialed and covered the receiver. "Do you mind. I'm on the phone." His chest and arms were speckled with those dark freckles. He had a raised mole on his shoulder the size of a raisin and a hairy line down the front of his stomach. I could hear Janey Waterman answer the phone. She was always so nice to Scoots. She was the one who had told me that tomato juice was the best way to battle skunk stink.

"Yeah—hey, Janey. How are you?" he said, winking at me.

I could hear her say, "Hey, good, you. Where are you?" Her voice was so small I pictured her being pulled backward, slowly disappearing into the new horizon we were drawing for her.

"I'm good. I'm at Lou's. Yeah, uh, listen," Beau was looking into my smiling eyes. I had dunked my hands into the front of his pants, not too far, scratching gently at the hair poking up out of the top of his underwear. It had the same kinky texture as the hair on his head. I felt wicked and perfect, and Beau was so hard he had to wince and pull a little away from me.

"Yeah. The thing is . . . Okay. Janey, I can't see you anymore. And I feel cruddy calling you up to tell you this at work and everything, but I'm sorry. But something's come up, and I really gotta go. I'll drop off your stuff. I'm sorrygottago."

He was laughing so hard by the time he hung up he couldn't breathe. I took the receiver from him and slapped it back on its cradle.

"That was mean," I said.

But he was still rocking from his joke.

" 'Something's come up.' Classic."

"Are you sad? Wanna talk about it?" I said,

189

feigning a pout. The Beth part of me, the venal and selfish part that I'd always denied myself, was coming to the surface and I welcomed it. He grabbed the phone book off my lap, held it at arm's length to the right, and let it drop on the dog bowl, spilling the water on my black bra and on the floor, and I suddenly realized I had been wearing white underwear, but that this was just Beau, so what they didn't match?

"Yeah. Very sad. I'll probably need to cry all over your ass, Peachy."

He spider-crawled his fingers between my thighs and I let a couple of them inside with an unbearable sigh that tipped me forward into his smooth chest. With my heels I kicked down his underwear, and he pulled my legs forward until we were nicely lined up. I leaned back into the cupboards. His penis looked quite cute, kind of like a brave soldier peeking over an expensive granite trench.

"Is that for me?" I said.

He nodded.

"What should I do with it?"

"Whatever you want."

I started to shift my ass forward when the phone rang.

"Uh-oh," I said. "I think you've pissed off your girlfriend."

"Ex," he said, leaning toward the receiver. "Hell—o." Silence. "It's me. It's Beau. Oh, hey,

Beth. How are you?" Silence. "Good, fine. Yeah, yeah." Silence. "No, he's out. I was working on the Jeep. But, ah, Peachy's here if you want to talk to her."

Beau yelled my name out as though I was otherwise occupied in another room. I yanked the receiver and counted to three while Beau worked his fingers back inside me. I had to use his shoulder for support and for something to bite down on.

"Hey, Beth."

"Hey, Peach. What are you doing?"

"Nothing. Beau's working on the Jeep. Dad's out shopping," I said, suppressing a giggle. Beau was kissing a trail down the side of my torso, his other hand passed gently over my ass, which suddenly felt large and flattened. I was losing feeling in the lower part of my legs, so I lifted my heels into Beau's hip bones to relieve the pressure. He hooked his forearms under my knees and pulled me forward.

"Listen, I'm going out to Long Island next weekend after all, Peach," Beth said. "Joe's folks are there and he wants me to meet them. I'm sure they'll hate my guts, so should be good times."

"Who's Joe," I asked. By then Beau had pushed himself all the way inside me, his big hands firmly grabbing both ass cheeks, pulling the rest of me against him. We stayed very still for a few seconds.

"My new boyfriend and future rich fiancé. Oh, and Peachy?"

"Yeah?"

"I'm glad you're finally fucking Beau. It's something he's very good at. But for godsakes, use a condom."

"Okay."

"See you in a few weeks, you cheap, filthy whore."

"Okay."

"And bye, Beau!" she screamed.

I dropped the phone. We started making Sam on the new granite counter, and finished him off on the floor. Admittedly, it felt like incest, if incest was not only legal, but hot, and completely encouraged.

Sam had to have happened that afternoon because we didn't have sex again for a couple of weeks. Though for days afterward the air between us was dense with the deed. Beau would amuse himself by circling around me in the carport, or the kitchen, finding good excuses to come by the farm when Lou was there, and embarrassingly bad ones when he wasn't. I once watched from the upstairs window as he pulled out of the driveway, only to turn back around and inch toward the house. He idled his car in front for several painful minutes. That's when I knew.

Lead legs took me downstairs.

I opened the front door and yelled through the screen over the loud engine. "Did you forget something?"

"Yeah," he yelled back, scratching his head. "Can you check for my car keys? I think I left them on the kitchen counter."

"Sure," I said, turning around. I was patting around the newspapers littering the kitchen island when the screen door slammed behind me.

I knew then that he had picked me. But the decision to stay picked seemed to suddenly be mine and it was overwhelming. I was terrified of the responsibility the decision suddenly entailed. If I became a part of him, formed a pair, the rest of my life would happen to me. I began to look even harder for his keys.

"Peachy, just say yes," he said wearily, taking a step forward.

"Say yes to what?" I asked, standing still with my back to him.

"Pretty much everything?" he said.

"What if I don't want pretty much every-thing?" I said, struck with the idea that his keys could have fallen between the bread box and the coffee maker.

"Then say yes to something. Say yes to a little bit."

"What if I say no to it all," I yelled over my shoulder, looking and looking for the keys.

"Wow. For someone so pretty, you sure are stupid," he laughed.

"Fuck you, Beau," I screamed, launching what was handy, the loaf of bread, at him. "You do not have the right to tell me I'm stupid because I might not want what you want. Right fucking now!" My voice cracking with the authentic fear buried just below the phony anger. "I'm still in school."

"Whoa, whoa, whoa! I'm talking about my keys, Peachy. They're in my ignition, for chrisakes!"

"Well, what if I say no?"

He picked up the loaf of bread and massaged it back to shape through the plastic, and carefully placed the loaf in front of the breadbox.

"Then you force me to have to wear you down," he said in a somber voice I'd eventually grow to recognize as a five- or ten-second warning before he'd chase me around the house and fuck me where he caught me.

But the last thing he said to me that afternoon, exactly four days before I found out I was pregnant, was, "See ya, Peachy. Wouldn't wanna be ya."

Then slam.

A few days later, I peed on an expensive stick, and the first person I told after the stripe turned pink was Beth.

"Jesus. That man's sperm could reforest the

goddamn tundra," she said. "It could cure bald-ness. He should be caged and studied. What are you going to do?"

"I don't know," I said. I didn't.

"You haven't finished school yet. You have to finish, Peach. I didn't realize you guys were getting serious. I thought it would be a little fling or something. I mean, Beau? Really?"

"I know. I mean, I don't know. What's wrong with Beau?"

"Have you told him? Don't tell him."

"I haven't. I won't . . . unless."

"Think hard about it, Peach," she said softly. "You know I love you no matter what decision you make, but I want you to keep your options open. You want to be a social worker, remem-ber? But God, poor Beau. He's going to get a complex. Short of actually boning Lou, guy's been fucking his way into our family for years. Well, you could do worse than him. He's nice. He's a nice guy. He would have made a good husband. A good provider. He would have pro-vided me whatever husbands provide."

"Excellent endorsement. Nice to see Beau comes mildly recommended."

"You don't love him, do you?"

It was the first time I had ever heard the hint of envy in her voice, the first time something in Beth exposed a feeling of regret, completely against her will. And I was ashamed at how thrilling it was to hear, even though eliciting that sound was entirely unintentional.

"I do love him, Beth."

"Oh well, that changes everything. Congratulations, twenty-year-old mother and wife!"

"You say that like it's a tragedy."

"Peachy, it is."

"Fuck you."

"No, fuck you," she said. "Because if this is some weird way for you to fill my shoes, then knock yourself out, little sister. But we're talking about you bringing a kid into this world, as well as bringing Beau into ours. And I just don't believe you when you say you want all this. Sorry, Peach, I'm your sister, I know you. I have to be honest with you."

"Yes. Honesty. Your greatest trait. Thank you, Beth."

"And maybe I was hoping that my brother-in-law wouldn't be the first guy who ever went down on me. Just hoping. Dunno. Maybe that's too much to ask."

I hung up on her. It was extraordinary, not only Beth's talent for seeing any dilemma as hers, but for convincing me of it too. So I moved some of the leftover love I felt for Beth, the part she wasn't using anymore, over to Beau and the future baby.

When I told Lou I was pregnant, he cupped his hands over his mouth and closed his eyes.

"Oh, Peach, how great," he said, pulling me into a hug. "What did Beau say? What about school?"

"He doesn't know yet." He hadn't come back to the house after that day but had phoned to tell me to tell Lou he'd gone to an RV show in Ohio. These were the days before cell phones, when people were sometimes unreachable, and no one panicked and no one died and no one lost their minds because they couldn't speak to the person right now, right away, this instant.

"And I'll finish school. I have every intention of finishing school. I'll breast-feed in class if I have to."

My face flushed with hot blood, and my eyes felt suddenly itchy. Lou put his hands around my upper arms and shook me a little.

"You okay?"

"Fine. I feel weird, but fine."

"I wish your mother could be here for this. I'm sorry she's not, Peach. And I know Nell's sorry too. But we got Beth, so that's something. Let's ring her up!"

I put my hand on a kitchen stool. The floor felt like it was moving.

"Let's not. I'm very tired all of a sudden."

Lou walked me over to the couch. I had to laugh, because though it seemed dramatic and unnecessary to be escorted, I clutched him like an invalid. I couldn't have been more than a few weeks along, but the exhaustion was so sudden and acute, the surrender was less like falling asleep than fainting.

Typically, perfectly, Beau landed on bended knee and said, "Make me happy, Georgia Peach, and be my beloved wife." I went, "Yeah, okay." I wanted to wait until the baby was born, but four months later we got married at the Catholic church in town, the one to which we belonged, though had stopped attending after Nana Beecher left for good. Before agreeing to the ceremony, Beau and I had to sit through a series of courses on how couples under Christ should function. It was fun actually, and it made us both a little horny. After the ceremony everyone came back to the farm for a small reception in the back yard: Lucy and Leo, the Rosarios and the bachelor brothers, some of my friends from school, and Beth, who took me shopping for maternity wear the next day.

I had finals, so we took our disastrous camping honeymoon in Grand Bend two weeks later. It took Beau hours to set up the tent, while I sat and bitched, too tense to relax, worried my water would break in the night even though I was barely six months pregnant. We lasted two nights away, and I realized I wasn't much of a leaver. That was Beth's talent. Growing up, Beth culti-vated the fantasy of throwing a hat in the air in the middle of Broadway, while I priced cotton sheets in the Sears catalogue, mail-order, as even driving into Windsor seemed like too much of a trek to me. I ignored her florid descriptions of what her life was like living away from us, because when she talked like that it made me feel like I was built wrong, like I was a house with no front windows.

And in those years I hadn't traveled the world, hadn't done anything important or even interesting, but I had given birth to two sons, three years apart. And though there was nothing remotely immaculate about Sam's conception in the kitchen that day, he was my little savior, my godsend. He gave me purpose, that squalling blob of a boy who latched to my breast with such urgency I thought he'd turn the rest of my body inside out through my nipples.

As for Jake's conception, I had read how you could time and calibrate sex to make a girl. And I'll admit I wanted one. I read about vitamins you could take and positions you could initiate. While I was pregnant, the baby rode low on my front, and knowing women would press their palms to my belly at the A&P, swearing that he was a she. *Are you nauseous and moody,* they asked. I was. *So you already have a boy?* I did. *So you're likely stuffed with double the amount of estrogen,* they said. *A girl,* they said, *such good news.* I blithely installed a pink bed frill around Sam's old bassinet, because what if they were right?

When Jake was born, I was impressed. To keep that penis of his intact, he'd probably battled off a lot of magic, menace, and wishes in my womb. Later, while diapering him, when he'd cover his exposed penis with both of his hands, using strength that required both of mine to remove them, I got the feeling he knew I had tried to prenatally snatch it from him.

So I came to believe that the life you got, unlike the one you hoped for, could still be a decent consolation prize if you held it aloft like the winner's trophy. That's what I did, and had been doing ever since that day Beau and I had sex on Lou's granite counter. And though it was an exhausting skill, it came easily to me because I had never kept my eye on the bigger prizes to begin with.

chapter ten

For most of the flight I hadn't noticed that the seat between me and a chubby bleach-haired woman remained blessedly empty. At first, I thought it was luck that left it vacant before realizing it was supposed to have been Beth's seat.

"It's nice to have a little space, isn't it?" the woman said over the white noise.

"It was supposed to be my sister's seat," I yelled over the din, immediately regretting it. Small talk was always a big problem for me. That was Beth's particular talent, one I'd always left to her when we'd be out and about, meeting strangers.

"Oh, what happened to her?"

"I'm trying to figure that out myself," I said. I didn't mean to be mysterious or funny, but I was granted a sudden and captive audience in Lee, from Long Island, who worked as a regional manager for an expensive weight-loss franchise, the same company that had helped her slim down from about 300 to 160 pounds and counting. She carried a "before" picture around for proof.

"Wow, you're half a person!" I said, unsure if that was the right thing to say to a formerly obese person who was now just chubby.

Telling strangers terrible things had a way of making them feel less like they happened to me. So in the same way I unburdened myself to the border guard, I regaled this woman with the facts of my life; of Beth and Beau's crime, leaving out details of the sexual position I had found them in, sprinkling in a bit about our past and Sam's condition, and that this was the first flight I'd ever taken in my life, not counting the helicopter ride at Bob-Lo Island when I was eight. I didn't tell her about Marcus, as I didn't want to relent an ounce of my precious victimhood, the only thing that propelled me onto the plane to begin with. I still needed to feel badly wronged in order to continue on the destructive path I had begun to carve from my gravel driveway to Beth's marble lobby.

"Jeez, Louise," she said, with a long whistle. I felt stupid. It occurred to me that she might have been mocking my hickishness with that exclamation. Then to my great relief, she added, "My Perry cheated, like six, seven years ago. With some woman he met in a chat room, or what have you. You know, on the Internet."

"Did you leave him?"

"For a little while, yeah. I stayed with my brother in Vermont. Maybe a month. But we got on with things. Actually, I think it made the marriage stronger, the threat of not having it, you know?"

"Did he ever cheat again?" I felt such sudden kinship, love even, for this blowsy seatmate of mine. I imagined us having drinks on a beach together, on a girls' type vacation, something I'd always wanted to do with Beth. Lee and I would tell people how we met, arching our eyebrows at each other. We'd laugh about our wayward husbands, clinking fancy drinks to our uncommon strength and their common weaknesses.

We were banking near Manhattan when the pilot announced that we could see the black gap in the toothy skyline where the World Trade Center used to be.

"I don't know if he ever cheated again. I like to think not. He ended up dying in that mess down there," she said, pointing over my shoulder.

"You mean 9/11?" I said.

She nodded.

"I'm so sorry."

I kept my eyes on the island below, thinking, there I was, an imaginary widow attempting to comfort an authentic one. She was not looking at me at that point, but out and beyond the window, with a steely, almost practiced gaze. She could tell I was staring at her, which suddenly bothered me. It was like she had zipped on a snug suit of stoicism, one which she probably carried around for just such occasions. Still, I tried to fathom her sadness, to see past the strange celebrity that often comes from being party to such public tragedies.

"I can't believe three years have already passed," she said, sighing back into her seat. I felt very far away from her. I had no idea what to say, feeling as though my shoddy story of betrayal had been smothered under the ace of spades of her epic tragedy. I wished I could take back my words and the petty way I'd uttered them.

Beth had been in Belle River that September day, which she openly, deeply, selfishly lamented. She was down at Lou's having a touch-up on her highlights when the first plane hit.

"I should be there," she whelped into Lou's TV screen when the second plane made impact. We all scrambled down to the trailer, which had the only satellite dish at that time. "My city! I should be there!" I remember looking at the back of her head and willing its front part to shut the fuck up and be grateful. Despite air-conditioning, it was stifling hot, all of us crowding into Lou's watching endless CNN. And though I blamed 9/11 for a lot of rotten global fallout, long lines at the border, war and everything after, it was because of that godawful event that I relented and let Beau hook us up with one of those flat-screen TVs and a satellite dish too.

For the entire time the planes were grounded, Beth alternated between calling everyone she knew and crying in front of the set. Finally, she took a bus back from Detroit. I was worried, but relieved to see her go, sick of Beth's wrong-minded mourning. Still, having missed her shot at participating in history hadn't stopped Beth from knitting herself into the periphery of its ugly narrative.

"I had breakfast at Windows on the World not three months ago. That could have been me!"

On the phone to Kate: "Gosh, didn't we *just* fly into L.A. for that VH1 pitch? That could have been us."

To Jeb: "Man, my place is just a few blocks from there. What if the terrorists had miscalculated? And they slammed into my building? I mean, if I was there, then that could have been me."

I tried dismantling her reasoning.

"Beth, please, that would be like me saying if a different selection of Beau's sperm had hit my eggs, I wouldn't have had these exact kids."

"Yeah, but Peach, that *is* true. That *is* exactly what I'm saying."

Lee offered me her pretzels. "Trying to stay away from carbs. Sorry to be such a downer. The town I'm from lost a lot of people. We don't have much of a problem talking about it. Just blurting it out like that. I should remember that it shocks people."

"God. Don't apologize," I said, still looking at her profile. I thought of ways her husband might have escaped his fate: he could have been late for the train, or stalled in a lineup at a bridge or a Starbucks. Those were the stories I became fixated on, the people who missed their planes that morning because they got stuck in traffic, or they were delayed because it was their turn to drop the kids off at day care.

"But at least your marriage was a happy one

when he died," I said, adding lamely, "at least that's something."

"Oh, I wouldn't go that far. The marriage might have been stronger, but that doesn't mean it was happier."

I envied her her widowhood. I imagined that that would always overshadow Perry's ridiculous Internet romance. And Lee would be remembered for being a grand widow rather than a wronged wife. It made me sad that I couldn't tell Beth about Lee, that I'd met a famous widow, a true American mourner, though I imagined they were a dime a dozen in Manhattan. I wouldn't have put it past Beth to have made up a trader boyfriend, lost in the rubble, her one last shot at happiness now turned to dust.

Staring at Lee kept my eyes off the window, so the bounce and roll of the plane's landing took me by surprise. It forced a low laugh out of my diaphragm and a bit of pee escaped.

"Whoa," I said, "so that's what that feels like!"

Lee gave me a fleshy hug in Arrivals and told me to keep my chin up and that it shouldn't take too much work, as I was lucky to have only the one. And then she handed me a card with a 20 percent discount.

"Not saying you need to lose weight. My contacts are on the back in case you get into a jam. I live in Levittown. It's not far. But my advice, for what it's worth: don't do anything hasty, Peachy, okay?"

"Thanks. I'm sorry about your husband," I said.

"Life's life," she said. "Stay in touch."

We said goodbye, and as she walked away, I thought that there was still time to become a good woman. I could turn things around. I could stay kind through turmoil, like Lee. But after that weekend, I thought, Not now. Passing a bank of phones, I noticed the time. Beth should be with Sam at Dr. Best's by now. We were trying to monitor brain activity before, during, and after a seizure in order to perfectly time his surgery. I'd phone Lou later to find out how the appointment went. Meanwhile, fear and homesickness were duking it out in my stomach, my money on the latter. I felt young and dumb, and suddenly I wanted a mother, any mother, to wrap me in a shock blanket and take me home. I searched for the back of Lee's head. I suddenly wanted her to take me to her place in Levittown for the weekend. I could cry on a lawn chair, and she could bring me crackers and cheese and coffee. But before I gathered the guts to run after her, I banged into Beth's friend Kate standing in Arrivals and holding high a poster that read EVERYTHING'S GONNA BE JUST PEACHY.

"I think that's me," I said, pointing to her sign. "Peachy?"

"I really didn't expect anyone to meet me at the airport this morning."

"Sounds like you didn't expect a lot of things this morning," Kate said, rolling her eyes.

She already knew about Beau. Typical Beth, corralling friends and coworkers, I thought, while I'm seducing total strangers, one at a time. No wonder Beth always won. She goes for the players and I go for the bystanders.

"God, you look nothing like Beth!" she said, peering up into my face. Kate grabbed my hand with one of hers and pulled me into a brittle hug. Then she reached for my bag. "Not that that's a bad thing, lord knows Beth could put on a bit of weight."

She should talk, I thought. Kate had the size and carriage of a tiny, anxious fairy, with scarlet streaks striping her bobbed black hair.

"That did not come out right, Peachy. Sorry. I didn't mean . . . listen. Beth asked me to come meet you. She was afraid of you arriving here all alone. I hope that's okay."

I nodded.

"I did NOT mean to suggest you were fat. I mean, you're not *at all*."

"It's *okay*. And I didn't mean for anyone to go to any trouble. I would have been fine on my own. I have Beth's address and her keys."

"It's no trouble. Beth's paying. Remind me to keep the receipts. I'm at your service all weekend. And you know," she said, lowering her voice, "I'm really sorry about what Beth did with your husband. I know Beth can be a complete fucking idiot sometimes, but if it matters, she feels like a total ass right now." Her T-shirt said ASK ME ABOUT MY HONOR STUDENT, so I changed the subject and did.

"Oh!" Kate's face lit up as she turned around to show me the shirt's epilogue: THE BASTARD HASN'T CALLED US IN YEARS. "Thought it up myself. Trying to start up a kind of online business selling them. Beth said she might back it. She thinks we could make a mint."

We exited the terminal into a balmy wash of air that took me by surprise with its surprising tropicalness. I asked her where she parked her car.

"I've been asking myself that for ten years. No, sweetie, we're cabbing it. Nobody owns a car in New York. Not even Beth."

I knew that, but these are the things you forget to picture when you're picturing someone's life over the phone. You don't think about how they navigate from place to place, though I used to imagine Beth walking the streets alone, smoke rising out of the grates in the sidewalk, muggers and rapists lining the alleyways, waiting for her. There was always a dreary grey backdrop in my terrible nightmares of what it was like for my sister, alone in the city. I once dreamed she'd been shoved in front of an oncoming subway by a deranged stalker who turned out to be Lucy wearing a hobo outfit. Eventually, I got used to her living here, was less and less afraid for her, because in truth she was a taxi whore, a woman who lived in a SoHo condo that employed a full-time doorman, who frequented no establishment more than fifteen blocks from her doorstep, who had everything she bought delivered, including ice cream, hairspray, and dry-cleaning.

When Beth first moved to New York, we quickly had to develop a verbal glossary of terms for each other, our lives were becoming that different that quickly. Her new words for me were Ayurveda, Nolita, NPR, Missoni, Auster, E, and edamame. My words for her were episiotomy, CBC, soffit, raglan, Zyban, Enya, Ya-Ya, and Martha. But despite the differences, our conversations had always maintained the casual intimacy of two women in side-by-side change rooms, yelling over a high partition.

The ride into the city was languorous, except for Kate's constant narrative.

". . . one of the safest big cities on the planet. I swear in the like decade I've lived here, I've never been mugged, raped, shot, nothing—did Beth tell you I went to NYU, not Parsons? Beth is such a fuck-up. But we'll talk about that. I studied film. Not that I wanted to *make* films. That's the Chrysler Building. See the top? I never did really see myself as a director. Always liked the industry side. I'm interested in the producing. The financing side. I'm interested in the notion of the *perfect* pitch . . ."

The driver let me crank open a window to smoke, his Middle Eastern music adding a tinny soundtrack to our bumpy trip to Manhattan. I always knew I was in the States by the state of its roads. When Beau used to drive us to pick up Beth at the airport, I could close my eyes and feel us transition from Canadian-smooth streets, the cracks practically grouted with ground-up tax money, to the bombed-out downtown Detroit roads, its buckled concrete and neglected potholes rattling my teeth and bones.

". . . so I said, 'Beth, that's pretty unforgivable. No, completely unforgivable. But we'll talk about that.' I used to live over there. I mean, I know she's made mistakes in the past—beating up a bouncer comes to mind—ha-ha-ha—you know we always tease Beth that she's burned so many bridges in New York she should have a ferry named after her—that's the Lower East Side. Marcus lives here. He was a really nice guy. 'Beth,' I said, 'your sister's husband? I mean, that's just fucking mean. But we'll talk about that . . .' "

It was shortly after the abortion when Beth got the idea to move to New York. She went through a phase of watching *Bill Kennedy at the*

Movies with Lou. Beth loved Myrna Loy, but her favorite actress was Jennifer Jones, especially in *The Man in the Gray Flannel Suit*. After a sorry revelation about her husband's bastard son, Jennifer Jones frantically runs into their Connecticut yard. Gregory Peck wrestles her writhing body to the ground like an apologetic monster. Jennifer pretends to calm down, then she suddenly drives off in the family sedan, shooting down the gravel road, laying tracks like one long exclamation point.

To no one in particular, Beth announced, "I can't wait to live in New York, where I don't have to *drive* every time I want to leave."

". . . You will LOVE, love, love, the shopping on the Lower East Side, Peachy. I *am* getting that *fucking* kimono. Hope you have space in your bag for some new purses. They're knockoffs. It's all grey-market. No worries. But I have mentioned to Beth about her drinking. We all have. Marcus said the bouncer should have been a wake-up call. How cool would a kimono be? Saw it off a little? At the thigh maybe? With jeans? Yessss . . ."

Of course Beth lived here, I thought, scanning the skyline, almost dental in its craggy symmetry. I had memorized Beth's address from all the Christmas and birthday cards I'd sent, sometimes stuffed with a five or a ten, Canadian, just to bug her. And Easter cards, and Halloween

212

cards, and Thanksgiving (Canadian too) cards, and all the in-between cards filled with news of the boys, or just corny cards I'd send to woo her with their corniness.

When we crossed the bridge, I felt the vertigo of the city suddenly tipping forward, and I couldn't take everything in with just two eyes. I saw stores I'd never heard of and some I had; bloated Gaps next to tiny cafés, elderly brick houses slumped next to a stiff concrete slab, with a slash of a window cut in the center. Was it a salon? A museum? There'd be a tree, then many, then none for an entire block; dark, light, dark, light, the shadows carrying specific weight, the sun some real heat. We drove slowly, then quickly, the cab moving in nauseating fits and starts. The hordes of pedestrians, like cattle, seemed to have no interest in the yellow and red lights, or fear of the cars barely honoring them. Our driver parted people, Red Sea–like, around the hood of our nudging cab. Some buildings looked like they could be large homes or small colleges. It was like watching a noisy musical playing inches from my face. We barreled down canyon after canyon, some streets narrow and some harrowingly wide. My neck hurt from gawking and craning, up then down; it was Detroit times a thousand; Belle River, a thousand million. It wasn't a bad feeling, just overwhelming, the same feeling I'd get as an eight-year-old with five dollars in my pocket pulling up to the Starlite. I wanted to feel flush with choices and happy to make them. But instead I'd worry about buying the wrong thing, something I didn't want or wouldn't like, and a bit of that fear followed me to New York.

"Here we are," Kate said, clambering out of the cab.

Beth's condo was in an old building made newer by bright green awning, smoked windows, and two huge granite vases framing the doorway.

Kate pulled out an envelope of money and counted out the fare, handing me the rest.

"Beth wants me to give this to you. She was going to pay for the whole weekend anyway, so no arguments, okay?"

"But I have money. I just have to hit a bank—"

"We've seen your people's money. It's very pretty, but very useless here," she said. "Now, I'll call you later, okay? I have a million things to do, but I'm taking you to a dinner party tonight and tomorrow night I was thinking we could—"

"*No!* No. I mean, I'll be fine, Kate. You don't have to baby-sit me."

I wasn't sure how much she knew of my participation in their Marcus fraud, or of my threat to meet the hapless man tomorrow night, instead of standing him up as Beth had planned for "Georgia" to do. But I didn't want her to muck that up. Plus, the thought of spending another living minute with Kate made even my hair hurt.

"Well. Okay," she said, fiddling with the bottom of her shirt and glancing around. "But I have explicit instructions not to—"

"Look. I am sorry, but I'm here on a break. I have a lot to figure out and I didn't plan on having an escort. It was very generous of you to meet me at the airport. Very. But I am fine from here on, okay?"

Beth didn't have friends, she had minions, pets, errand runners, I thought, as Kate handed my bag to a man who looked like he belonged to a South American army.

"I can take my own bag," I said, snatching it from his hands.

"Okay then," the man said, surrendering his hands to the sky.

"It's Jonathan, Peachy," Kate said, yanking my bag out of my hand. "Jonathan works here. He's Beth's doorman."

"I'm *Beth's* doorman?"

Jonathan took a step back and scratched his chin. "*Really?* Now, I was always under the impression that I also worked for some of the other nice people who live here, too. But per-haps I've been wrong all this time. And where is Miss Archer, may I ask?"

"She got *delayed*," Kate said, looking at me. "This is her sister, Peachy. She'll be staying here

215

for the weekend. So you be good to her, okay, Jonathan? It's her first time in New York."

We were practically yelling at each other over the traffic sounds.

"Of course," he said, raising his hand. For a second I thought he was going to slap Kate across the face. Then a cab screeched to a halt in front of the building.

"Thanks, doll," Kate said in his general direction. She folded herself inside the cab. "It's going to be a great dinner party tonight. It's in your honor."

I silently followed Jonathan and my bag into the lobby, which was flooded with the sound of a loud golf game echoing out from behind the marble kiosk. Jonathan dropped my bag and dove over the counter.

"Let me turn that down. That's not your sister's favorite sound."

"That's funny," I said, looking around, "Beth loves TV. She makes TV."

I couldn't imagine entering this lobby after a long, stressful day and uttering "Home at last." It had all the charm and warmth of an empty underground pool.

"Well, your sister was one of the few 'no' votes on me getting the thing. I try to keep it low. I can't see the resemblance," he said, turning back around to look at me. "Between you and Beth."

"We're only half-sisters," I said, thinking he could probably tell which half's mine.

"You got a key and all that then?"

"Yes, thanks. I do. I'll take that."

He picked up my bag off the floor and handed it to me as though it was carved out of expensive leather and not formed of blue vinyl and covered in the boys' Pokemon stickers.

"Let me know if you need anything. Peachy. Is that from the South or something?"

"Kind of. No. It's Georgia. Peachy's just a nickname."

The elevator was taking a long time, and I seemed to need to flood the lobby with my words while I waited.

"Well, it's my middle name," I said. "But I was, you know, conceived in Georgia. Born in Canada. Where we lived, Beth and me. But *I* live in Canada, Beth doesn't live there anymore. She lives here. As you know."

"Oh. I thought Beth was from California. I know she has a *weekend* house near Grosse Pointe. But I thought—" He suddenly stopped himself as though remembering that he had to do something urgent behind the kiosk.

"A *weekend* house? Huh. In Grosse Pointe, Michigan. Yes. Well, Beth was *born* in California. But she lived most of her life on our farm. Since she was two. In Canada, in Belle River, which is across the *lake* from Grosse

Pointe, Michigan. I guess that might be where her *weekend* house is located. But I've never been there myself."

I put my bag down, took a step toward him, and crossed my arms. An elevator came and went while I continued.

"No, see, Beth's at the farm where she was raised, and where I live, weekends *and* week-days. With my sons and my husband and my dad. She's never mentioned that?"

"Nope," he said, shaking his head, still pretending to look for something. "So Beth's *Canadian?*"

"Not anymore. But she was. Yeah."

"Huh."

It was like we were both blindfolded and describing the same animal to each other.

"So this weekend house," he said. "Big stone place? Few hundred acres? You live there too, with your family?"

"Yes. We *all* live there. Only it's thirty acres now. The land got chopped up to pay for Beth's college. And we're likely going to chop it up some more. And the only thing stoned about the place is my husband, sometimes. Beth visits us every other month or so, and my dad does her hair for free. He's a hairdresser. She's never mentioned that?"

"No. She once mentioned something about him being a fighter pilot in Vietnam."

It wasn't until after I replied, "No, he's about as opposite to a fighter pilot that you can get," that it occurred to me Beth might have been talking about Tooey, her real father, who now sported phony pilot credentials.

"So Beth's delayed on the farm you live on with *your* family. Getting her hair done by her dad the hairdresser."

"That's right. She's also taking my son to his doctor's appointment, and after that she's supposed to drag four loads of my laundry into town because our washer is busted."

That image, of Beth doing laundry, seemed to amuse Jonathan. But after a brief silence our words, which had begun to bounce around the marble cavern, started banging violently into each other.

"I'm sorry. You know it's none of my business—" he said.

"That's okay. This is all—"

"It was unprofessional of me to—"

"No, no, no, it's okay—"

"Please don't mention to Beth that I—"

"Of course not—"

"I mean really, it's—"

"I won't—"

"I need this job," he said, pressing his finger lightly on the kiosk and stopping the conversation on that point.

There was restless history between them, that much was obvious. And though he was not bad-looking, I think even Beth would draw the line at her elderly black doorman.

"Do you live here?" I asked.

"Yes, I do."

"What floor?"

"I don't live *here* here," he laughed. "No, I live in Yonkers. My wife and I. Our son's in college. Syracuse."

By then his face had melted into complete bemusement, eyebrows fully relaxed alongside his eyes.

"You should know that Beth and I aren't much for conversation these days, I'm sure she's mentioned that."

"No, she hasn't," I said. "But then again, we're not much for conversation these days either."

I re-pressed the elevator button, feeling suddenly exhausted by Beth even though she was hundreds of miles away. It occurred to me that this man saw Beth morning, noon, and night. And before she dumped her dramas on me over the phone, she likely lugged them past this man who likely made minimum wage and maybe Christmas tips, and still was able to put a kid through college, a man who probably commuted from wherever Yonkers was, probably at least an hour away, every day, to and from SoHo, so he could stand guard for people like Beth, a woman who never, ever dropped her guard for anyone, except for maybe me.

"Okay then, I'm going up now," I said as the next car arrived.

"You do that, Peachy."

I held the door open for a second.

"You do realize, Jonathan, that my sister is completely and utterly full of shit."

"I have had my suspicions, Peachy," he said, spreading a sympathetic smile across his face.

I pressed the CLOSE button. "Twelfth floor, right?"

"That is right. Now you let me know if you need *any*thing."

"Oh, I will."

chapter eleven

By our farmhouse standards, the apartment was surprisingly small, but by Manhattan standards I knew Beth had scored with this place. It was nicely proportioned, boxy and clean. In the living room, which was a step down from the narrow hallway entrance, there were two intentionally mismatched dark wood end tables bracketing a white couch that I could only call obese. It seemed a piece of furniture so alien in color and texture to me that when I sat on it I had the nervous-visiting-mother-of-brats kind of dread, as though my kids could dirty up this kind of couch telepathically, through my own proxy fingers.

Funny how I'd gotten so used to the primary colors of the boys' sticky toys studding every living space in our house that their absence in Beth's seemed like a strange trick to my eye. I expected a red Tonka truck to careen out from under the couch if I nudged under the slipcover with a toe a little, or to hear the squeak of Scoots's gummy yellow chicken toy if I sat atop the pile of Beth's carefully placed pillows. The lack of dog and boys was instantly odd. Her place could never include them. What would they do in a place like this except sit still a lot, hands folded in their laps, fear on their faces? The white leather armchair was less a chair than a flabby letter *L,* its top and bottom strung between two gleaming metal poles. A pale green shawl had been thrown over it for effect; I could picture Beth set-designing the place, preparing it for our imminent arrival. Little Chinese boxes and souvenir masks from all her travels littered the shelves and dotted the walls. The low-slung, kidney-shaped, glass-topped coffee table was appropriately "Beth," very arty and very useless; no place to store magazines, no coasters, nothing on it, not even the remote or a vase of flowers. Her suspended wine rack reminded me of a full holster of bullets hanging sideways from the ceiling. She had the flat-screen TV I had wanted, half the size of our space portal, through which I'd joked we could all step through standing.

The two living room windows boasted a decent view of the Hudson River several blocks away, but sunlight didn't flood the place as you'd expect this high up because it had to negotiate around several similar buildings nearby. Her white laptop lay closed on a brushed metal desk. The parquet felt cool and clean under my bare feet. (I had removed my dirty sandals, of course.) The window in the kitchen, between the steel stove and steel fridge, looked onto a cluster of plants suffocating the fire escape. I opened the door and peeked below to a courtyard of brush-cut grass. I slid a finger in the pots hanging over the grating. All freshly watered. Perhaps that was one of Jonathan's jobs, though he had left me with the impression he'd just as soon pee on her plants as feed them.

Her surprisingly large bathroom smelled like her, like lemon grass and cigarettes and Final Net, the only beauty product besides Great Lash mascara that Beth had been loyal to since high school. The rest of her products, the ones I'd fingered on her visits, and now found in mother lodes lining the bathroom shelves, were capable of curing things I never thought I was afflicted with until I'd read the instructions. Some cream eliminated "fine lines" I'd never noticed. Another contained "light diffusers" for that younger-looking glow. There was a lime-salt rub that cut down on "orange-peel skin" and increased "subcutaneous circulation." Its companion cream sat on a tiny pedestal slung over the claw-foot tub's lip. It promised to "visibly lift" saggy areas, and I imagined filling the tub with every ounce of all of this stuff and dunking my whole ass in the mess. There, get rid of that, would you? Another tubside unction, which smelled like clean laundry and baby's feet, promised to "lock in moisture," but where? And still another toner contained "noncomedogenic" properties, a word that reminded me of the kind of humorlessness you'd have to possess to believe these products could work. The boys often dug through Beth's cosmetic bag with the enthusiasm of two tiny drag queens. She'd let them, winking over at me with that look on her face that said, *Goodie, maybe one of them will be gay!* Two summers ago, as I was doing my pickles over the sink, I watched out the back yard as Beth lovingly fashioned dark mud masks on Jake and Sam's upturned faces. She stretched out next to them on the lounge chair, and while her toenails dried in the sun, and the hot-oil treatment baked her hair under a towel, I timed the boys as they sat, side-by-side on the picnic table, waiting for their masks to dry.

"Imagine if aliens came down right now and landed in the back yard, Auntie Beth," Sam said, trying not to move his lips. He looked like a mini Al Jolson.

"They'd probably think they were home," she said, encasing her hands in paraffin wax.

Sam laughed and Beth put up her finger.

"Shh. No laughing," she said firmly, which made it harder for Sam.

"Feels like a volcano," Jake murmured, lightly tapping on his face, his feet swinging off the picnic table. He couldn't have been more than four at the time.

"Don't touch it, buddy!" Beth scolded. "You have to let the Dead Sea emollients *seep* into your pores. That's where the magic happens!"

A miraculous twenty minutes had crept by as the brown caked to beige. Every once in a while, one or the other of the boys would gingerly lift Beth's hand mirror up to take a look at the "magic" happening on their faces. They had never been so still in their lives.

I had not seen Beth take more than an aspirin in my presence, so I was shocked at the contents of her crowded medicine chest. Some of the prescriptions I recognized as sleep aids and nerve calmers. Others carried so many of the alphabet's least-used consonants—*Z, X,* a *Q* even—they seemed to be for someone older and sadder than Beth.

Her bedroom was wallpapered with a retro-old-ladyish pattern of light green scribbles and dark leaves. The bed made the room seem suffocatingly regal compared to the rest of the place. The hip-high queen-sized bed was layered with white sheets, over which was placed a doughy white duvet, the whole confection punctuated with still more pillows, white, red, and a couple of little pale gold ones. There was a high bookshelf featuring only hardcovers, austere biographies of writers I'd never heard of, a couple of popular feminist tomes, guy writers galore, some Indian too, and the bottom three held expensive-looking books on fashion, photography, textiles, and makeup, some on design and furniture, quite a few yoga books, and the biggest was a collection of photographs of famous American summer houses, in which I'd no doubt find a tasteful layout of her imaginary weekend place in Grosse Pointe, Michigan, directly across the lake from our farm.

In the cupboard of the bedside table, under a drawer that housed condoms, pens, tea candles, and a pink plastic rabbit thingy which I knew had a sexual purpose, she stored a paperback collection of self-help books, most of their spines shamefully facing the back. Seemed that Beth needed to help herself with a lot of things; how to find, get, and keep love; how to save, spend, and invest money; how to know if you drink, smoke, eat, or fuck too much, too little, or not enough; and what to do about it. I felt oddly criminal fishing through her things, looking for evidence, flaws, and clues, but it was impossible not to. This is the kind of snooping that wouldn't have been available to me if I had accompanied Beth back to New York. She would have had furious plans to fill our time. She would have ushered me quickly in, and out, of the building, avoiding any conversation with Jonathan in the lobby, lest he bring up the weekend place, or God knows whatever else she'd invented about her life. I could picture her rolling her eyes in the elevator by way of explaining any obvious tension between them. ("You don't even *want* to know, Peachy.") All weekend we wouldn't have eaten a meal, or turned on the TV in the apartment, and in fact the fridge was empty except for a bottle of champagne, a half bottle of Perrier, three bottles of white wine, a half-empty carton of American Spirits, a drawer of cheese, a stack of congealing takeout containers, and film.

The guest bedroom, a bit bigger than the bathroom, was painted a cozy pale yellow, with a quilt-covered double bed shoved up against the wall. I didn't notice the bowl of four ripe peaches, bums-up, in a bowl on the cedar dresser, until I finally sat on the bed. The entire apartment seemed to belong to a person Beth hoped to be when she grew up. Maybe it was the absence of toys and games, the lack of a meat product thawing on the counter, or dishes piled up in the sink, but her place felt like a hotel to me. And the strategically placed and elegantly covered boxes of Kleenex gave the impression that a lot of crying had been done here. I couldn't imagine containing my life in such small rooms, however nice everything was. And though Beth bragged that she was still paying less than three thousand dollars a month in mortgage payments and only nine hundred in condo fees (which combined was still more than Beau's total monthly income), it was to me an inconceivable amount to pay. Lou was always on Beth's back to move home or at least to Detroit, claiming for the amount of money she was paying to buy an 1,100-square-foot condo, she could have actually bought a house in Grosse Pointe, Michigan, if she'd only taken the job with *Channel 7 Action News* back when it was offered to her.

"Just think," he said, "you could have drinks with Bill Bonds." He was Lou's favorite local anchorman. "You could have invited him home for a barbecue. Just sayin'."

Still, it wasn't envy I was feeling, keeping my bare feet on the posh area rugs as I floated through the rooms. I never envied Beth's life, but I envied the craving she had for it. It was a very different life than what she was born into, where I had remained. Yet I couldn't imagine living in a city where olive oil could cost as much as a tank of gas, where a person couldn't afford a car, yet could spend thirty thousand dollars on clothes and shoes.

I turned on Beth's laptop, and while it warmed up, I stripped off my clothes, leaving them piled at my feet like a sculptor's shavings. After all, I too was going to be someone else here, someone different for a day or two. I threw on a bathrobe and walked around talking to myself in Beth's perfect news-anchor-American accent: *Hi, yes, welcome, make yourself at home. Do sit on the all-white couch if you want. Can I offer you anything to drink? Why, I don't think I have any Budweiser, but I do have some Grey Goose vodka in the freezer and a bottle of Veuve Clicquot in the fridge. Oh, and what's this? A wine rack? How novel. My sister Peachy told me she and her ex-husband couldn't imagine using a wine rack, as they always drank the wine too fast to fill one. Can you imagine? How white-trash is that? No, of course you can smoke in here, but all I can offer you is American Spirits. Do you like baba . . . ga . . . noush? Well, I don't know what it is either, but I'm going to smear a bit of it on a table water cracker, because fuck it, I'm hungry, and I'm on vacation. Hmm. Meanwhile, I'm going to pour a lot of this expensive French bubble-bath shit in the running water. I'm not much of a decorator, but I wonder what the white couch would look like with a single cigarette burn hole in the middle of the middle cushion—*

My fantasy of sullying Beth's perfect couch came to a halt in the kitchen. The black and white picture of our mother on the beach in Santa Cruz, the one where she's holding up three fingers, sat framed atop Beth's fridge. I missed Nell immensely in that moment, thinking about how things would have been different if she had been a happier person. I kissed my finger and pressed it to Nell's head, then over her heart, meanly skipping the belly part where Beth had been growing. Tooey must have taken that picture. Beth never talked about him, and hadn't displayed any of his pictures her Oklahoma relatives had sent after Nell died. In fact, the only other picture in the apartment was a framed one of me and Lou on the bumper cars at Bob-Lo Island. I wore the same goofy, apologetic smile that seemed to haunt all my photos. There were several pictures of the boys on the fridge, but they were so clumped together and randomly picked, it looked like Beth had just hung them there for the benefit of my visit.

I looked for some CDs or a stereo but could only find a white pedestal holding a small white square thing that was probably an iPod. It was docked on what looked to be a single white speaker, but I had no godly idea how to turn the thing on. Instead, I turned on her countertop radio, automatically tuned to a jazz station. The running bathwater drowned out the traffic sound. It had been ages since I had taken a bath.

But before I could slide in the water, an unfamiliar phone rang in the living room. Call display showed our number in Belle River. If I hadn't had two young sons, one sick, I would never have picked up.

"Peachy? Peachy? Don't hang up." It was Beth sounding tired. Welcome to my world, I wanted to say, when noon on Saturday feels a lot like a Monday's midnight. "Kate told me you got in okay. Are you okay?"

"Where are the kids?"

"Sam and I just got back from the doctor's. Jake stayed here with Lou. And I think Beau went to work, but I didn't see him this morning."

"Too bad. That's his favorite time for it."

"Peachy, don't. I hate myself as it is."

"Me too."

"I'm so sorry. I'm going to do whatever's necessary to repair this, Peachy."

"What happened at Dr. Best's?"

"Not much. He adjusted his meds, I think. I got a new prescription filled, and the doctor wrote down some things for you to do about his diet. I have it all here. He has to go back in six weeks. But he hasn't had one today. Lou's only got two appointments this afternoon, so we'll both be around in case."

"Can you put him on?"

She muffled the receiver, and I could hear her call out twice for Sam. My mind was picturing him flailing in the bathroom, or going down in the back yard, his head nicking the picnic table en route to the booby-trapped grass.

"Mom! Where are you?" He sounded breathless and happy, which knocked my heart across the room.

"I'm in New York, buddy," I said. *Being an asshole. A vengeful, angry asshole. A nonmom.* "How are you? What are you doing?"

"Do you like it there?"

"Yes. It's very nice. Very big and loud," I said. "I miss you so much though. I didn't expect to miss you so much. Where's Jake?"

"When are you coming home?"

Why do I bother trying to have a conversation with my children when I know they're only interested in knowing a few things? What are we eating? When are we eating? Where are we going? When are we getting there? And why can't we have more of whatever it is we want more of?

"Sunday, honey." I felt my voice cracking, and I desperately tried to caulk it with a bit of calm, in case Sam became afraid of my fear.

"'Kay, bye, I gotta go," he said, darting off before he answered my question about Jake, before I could remind him of how much I loved him, pushing the love through the little holes in the receiver, like sweet-smelling Play-Doh.

Beth came back on the phone.

"Is the laundry done yet?" I said, not expecting it to be, not wanting it to be.

"That's next on my list. Sam helped me load it in the trunk just now. That's where we were going. I wrote everything down," she said with a kind of pride in her voice I hadn't detected before. "Peachy, are you going to meet up with Marcus tomorrow night?"

"I don't think that's any of your business."

"Don't, Peachy," she said, her voice haunted from this morning's crying. "Please don't let this make you mean like me. And I don't care if you tell Marcus everything. At this point I really don't care who knows what a screw-up I turned out to be. I'm sure Marcus won't be surprised anyway. I just hope he doesn't tell everyone. Actually, I don't care if he does. You know what? I don't care about anything except for making things right with you. With us."

"Go do the laundry, Beth. Try to find parking on the street. They charge at the lot."

"Will do. And Peach?"

"Yeah."

"I love you more than—"

"Just don't."

She was quiet.

"Did you see Nell's picture in the kitchen?"

"I did."

"She wouldn't be too proud of me right now, would she?"

"Doubtful."

"There's a good walking map in the drawer by the sink. There's a subway one in the wicker basket by the door. But take cabs and I will reimburse you. God, it's so weird you're there without me."

Her voice sounded reedy, beaten.

"Okay. So. I'm gonna get off the phone now. Tell the boys I love them and I'll see them Sunday afternoon, by which time I hope you will be gone from there."

I hung up on her, threw off the robe in the living room, and caught a glimpse of myself, my whole body, in the full-length mirror hanging outside of Beth's bathroom door. What a template the mother's body is, I thought. A fleshy notebook upon which her children's stories are told. My stretch marks weren't too pronounced, my sides merely lined with the light claw marks of maybe a playful cougar that might have tried to mangle me from behind. Twice. My legs were thin at the base, but they bloomed up and out at the thighs like a vase with generous handles. I didn't mind my arms, my collarbones, my shoulder blades, and I liked most of the skin over me except for the parts that hadn't sprung back, that now remained the roomy evidence of my body's former inhabitants. But even after they had left it, the boys kept returning to my body, which was still theirs. They'd sit on my flabby lap and play with my greying hair. They'd rest their hot heads against my chest and ask questions about my freckles and my bruises and my scars, for the same primal reason, I supposed, that people would sometimes drive by the homes in which they used to live, to remember what it was like, and to note all the new changes.

Once, while Beth was visiting, I was sitting in my underwear and a loosely wrapped bathrobe, breast-feeding Jake. Sam would have been about four when he asked why I didn't have a penis.

"Because we don't need any more of them. We have four penises in this house already—five, if you count what Auntie Beth has stashed in the inside pocket of her suitc—"

"Peachy!" Beth screamed, looking up from peeling potatoes. Sam looked at her utterly confused.

"You have a penis, Auntie Beth?"

"No. I don't have a penis. But it's been said that I have a fine set of balls."

"Beth!" I yelled back.

"You started it," she said, pelting me with peel.

God, my boobs shrunk so unevenly after breast-feeding, my torso wore the expression of someone dinged in the head too often and rendered stupid. My nipples were wall-eyed and sad-looking, and the flap under my belly button (which was the nose of the face) looked like the mouth of someone strange and dopey, someone you'd run away from in a schoolyard.

"Hello, Peachy," I said, taking my fingers and making my tummy flab talk in a Muppety voice. The boys loved when I did this, though it caused Beau to cringe and leave the room. "You're in New York City by yourself because your husband fucked your skinny, skinny sister. What are you going to do about that? And by the way, what are you going to do about me? I keep getting bigger and bigger."

I cupped my breasts and made the nipples look me straight in the eye.

"We're going to get in shape. That's what we're going to do. But first we're going to take a bath and then we're going shopping to buy expensive clothes to cover us up. Make us look super nice and pretty and we're going to meet Marcus and maybe let him touch us. Would you like that? No? Just a little? Maybe? Well, we'll see."

After my body's puppet show, I shut off the water and sank under the suds, realizing that the last time I'd had a bubble bath—alone—was the night I tried to induce labor with Jake.

Almost six years ago? Jesus. I felt around down there with a kind of numb purposelessness, suddenly wanting Beau so badly I felt angry, as though I had rained more betrayal upon my body just thinking about him. If I was exhilarated during the plane ride, my freedom suddenly felt terrifying, like a balloon freed from a bouquet. At first it was a wild and unfamiliar ride, being away from them, but the farther I got the smaller, the more untethered, I felt. I saw myself floating up and above all the action, unable to will any weight into my legs, now two noodly strings, drunk on wind and fury. I had no real plan and I had always had a plan. I learned in school that before diving into the toxic soup of a situation, social workers had to have plans. You had to be able to anticipate dilemmas with textbook assessments and well-placed questions, open-ended and benevolent. But my training left little room for understanding Beth. Beyond the vagaries of our childhood, the things we shared and those we kept secret from each other, she remained a mystery to me. Her drunken mishap and Beau's lack of vigilance led to an event as rare as a centennial comet to us. But I lingered in the water, sad for myself, the cuckolded baby sister, sad for the boys and their rotten parents, sad for their aunt, born with a vile bent, and sad that Lou had tried his best and failed us both.

When I pulled the plug, the drain made the

sound my heart would have made if it could have made a sound when I found them. I deliberately dripped water all over Beth's shiny parquet floors while pouring myself a half a glass of wine, a daytime luxury as uncommon as the bubble bath had been. I sat my wet ass on her expensive office chair, a black, springy contraption, and logged into our email account, remembering our dead laptop at the bottom of the kitchen sink. Even if Beth had wanted to muck with the account or warn Marcus, she'd have difficulty finding the time to go into town.

Dear Marcus, I just want to confirm tomorrow night, 7 P.M. Hope we're still on. If something comes up, call this number. It's not a local cell. Belongs to a friend. Long story.

I threw the robe around me and stretched across the couch and closed my eyes for what I thought was a second, only to jerk awake to the sound of a faraway doorbell, and to a sun that had dimmed considerably. I had had a nap, my first in several years. During those few seconds between sleep and full alertness, I had the sudden understanding that my kids were far away, which explained the hollow thudding in my chest. The boys would be bracketing the supper table by now, I thought. Beau would probably linger in town after work, stopping in at Lucy and Leo's, perhaps, or at Earl's to eat and watch whatever was playing on the giant TV. Who would he talk to? Who would he tell about what he did? Lou knew, but Lou had a preternatural ability to forgive any transgressions.

Beau also wasn't the vengeful type, which is what I loved about him. I also loved his hands and arms, and how he'd wrap them tight around his torso and scratch himself awake in the kitchen, pajama bottoms sagging around his bony hips, one hand still scratching as he dopily pinballed from the coffeepot on the counter to the sugar pot on the table to the cream in the fridge, his yawns smelling exactly like the pond. I remembered knowing we were young in the beginning. But after the kids I don't remember when it was that we got old. And so fast too. Was it awful to be in love with the fact that, with Beau, I didn't feel the need to talk about every little thing? I had talked to neighbors, to Beth, and the boys. I talked to Lou, and Sam's doctors. I talked to Lucy, even to Leo. I picked Beau because I thought his body had already contained all my unsaid words. He knew me. He knew Lou, my sister, our past. And I thought he had extra room under his skin to store more unsaid words, the ones we'd gather over the years we'd be married. That's what made him mine. My prize. But Beau was Beau. He was just a man, who, given the opportunity to get away with having sex with someone other than his wife, would take it and run with it. Even if it was with his wife's sister. Where I thought he was solid and steady, he turned out to be tippy and hollow, like the rest of us.

The noise of the city twelve stories below sounded like an enormous outdoor party, the honking traffic an awful sort of jazz band providing the music. And I was invited. I stretched and realized I had all weekend and good maps. I had money and Beth's backup closet. I had a date with a handsome lawyer tomorrow night, and I seemed to have finished crying. The tiny ding-dong sound that had woke me from the nap was actually Marcus's email reply. He wrote, *"U bet. Can't w8."*

chapter twelve

And that's all it took to send me out the door. I covered my sad-faced body with my best pants, cream-colored corduroys, knowing nothing in Beth's closet could come close to covering up my hips and ass. Even her tops, dresses, and blouses had the cut and consistency of tattered flags, each seemingly festooned with some kind of string or wrap, requiring fussy little buttons and hooks. I managed to find a pretty orange tunic that fit, with tasteful embroidery framing the V-neck. I pulled it over my head and tucked it in, then untucked it, then tucked it in, then finally untucked it in the elevator down. I passed Jonathan wearing my first genuine smile of the day.

"Good color on you, Peachy," he said.

"Thanks, Jonathan, I think so too."

"You got a map?"

I slapped my purse and nodded.

"Where are you off to now, then?"

"I don't know. But not far, really. Just around the neighborhood. See some sights?"

He scribbled a number on a piece of paper and gave it to me.

"Call me if there's trouble," he said, and I thanked him, thinking, Lou would love you. I love you.

When I hit the city air, I suddenly felt starving from the hurry of the morning and dizzy from the mouthful of afternoon wine and the nap. But it made Manhattan seem all the more Technicolor and amazing. I found myself looking up at people's houses, the high stoops, the lack of privacy but utter mystery each building seemed to contain; the strange color paint jobs (Who paints a living room red?), the gorgeously ornate ceilings and cornices of the imposing brownstones, stacked as they were, side by side like orderly tombs. Sometimes, I could see the tops of paintings or high bookshelves. I didn't go so far as to climb the stoops, to peer right into the windows, right into the beautiful homes, right at the beautiful people inside, but I wanted to. What stopped me was Beth's imaginary scolding, her snobbery, which would have surely accompanied us on all our jaunts had she been with me.

"Jesus Christ, Peach, you're like the phantom of the fucking opera. Get down from there!" I could imagine Beth saying. "You're embarrassing me."

But Beth wasn't here. She was in Belle River sorting my laundry, fingering my stained bras, my worn T-shirts, Beau's sweat-stiffened work socks, and, hopefully, she'd be close to fainting by now over the fact that little boys and grown men seem to leave behind an astonishing amount of skid marks in their underpants.

But though I was in her city and wearing her clothes, I was nothing like Beth. Because unlike Beth, I ducked inside the first restaurant I found, careful to keep her building within my view, lest I become lost and permanently forgotten. Where I was terrified, Beth was fearless, throwing herself into this cauldron of a city at the age of eighteen, just to see what would stick. And it all stuck. I thought how brave she must have been, how scared and yet how brave. I couldn't imagine being tossed into a city this big, loud, and fast, and blithely rising to the top as Beth had. I would have curled into a ball at the first sound of sirens, remaining that way until Lou came to get me.

In the diner I ordered dinner: a hamburger, a Diet Coke, and a side salad. Later, I asked for fries, too, which I ate slowly, one by one, avoiding all eye contact with strangers and regretting that I hadn't brought anything to read. In my head I toasted to an imaginary Beth sitting across from me.

"Here's to my first big weekend away from everyone but you."

By the time my hamburger arrived, my hunger had been replaced by heavy sadness. While I sat alone, an unremarkable woman eating an unremarkable meal in an unremarkable diner, Beth was, at that moment, surrounded by my beloved boys, and at least one of the two troubled men I lived with. Lou would be keeping one eye on Beth's awkward caretaking, the other on filling in the gaps: finding the other sock, counting out pills for Sam, digging out Jake's favorite story book, which he kept tucked under his arm for at least an hour before bedtime. Beau wouldn't be there, of that I was certain. He'd stay away as much as possible that weekend without alarming the boys or overburdening Beth and Lou. He'd probably eat at the tavern or stay late at the shop, slouched over a work bench, slowly chewing take-out fries and staring into the middle distance. His head would be running a looped argument with himself, his internal voice by turns reproaching and defensive, giving him the demeanor of a man watching a boxing match on a tiny TV. A new and awful uncertainty had crept into our marriage, something I hadn't felt since Nell died and something Beau hadn't known since a childhood spent tiptoeing around a volatile stepdad. He was in anguish, and I didn't care. I wanted to yell, *You did this! You brought this on! You, you jackass! Not me.* But his own self-loathing would be nothing compared to Beth's hatred for him. If there was animosity between them before, now there was war. They might hiss at each other over the kitchen island, or curse in the carport over cigarettes, out of earshot of the boys and away from Lou, the standby referee. Beau would blame her for taking advantage of his dopey vulnerability. Beth would blame him for being too stupid to realize that she was too drunk to know any better.

I could see Sam sitting at the head of the table, poking at something unfamiliar that Beth likely made for supper. Despite my warnings that he wouldn't eat anything weird, Beth probably whipped up something like risotto or sushi, something involving weird mushrooms, booze, and fire. Then she'd wonder why a shy kid with a bad brain would balk at eating it.

"Don't want to try it, honey?" she'd ask, eyebrow arched, trying to hide her disappointment. This would be Lou's cue to wordlessly slap together a cheese sandwich for Sam, after which he'd plop himself down in front of the TV with a bowl of green grapes and the remote. Sam would know, too, that something was wrong with the way the weekend unfolded. He had picked up more than enough information during my dramatic departure to be wary of Beth and any of her awkward affections. So if he rejected her meal it would have more to do with loyalty than loss of appetite—a thought that triggered both pride and shame in me.

Jake, however, would try anything. Last year, Beth made osso bucco on a visit home, and he sucked the bone like a Viking, refusing to toss it to Scoots. If he was thrilled by her attention, he was thoroughly delighted by his ability to please Beth. He was a boy whose love of girls and women had never been subtle, even as a toddler. So I had no trouble picturing Jake with his legs swinging off the cracked vinyl chairs, hands under his thighs, grinning mouth covered in the stained remains of something exotic: curried goat, lamb stew, goddamn paella, Beth mussing his hair in deep appreciation. *Somebody loves me,* she'd be thinking. *Somebody from my sister's home doesn't want me gone for good.*

I paid my bill and left a too-large tip and headed to the small park across the street, still keeping the top of Beth's building within my sights. It felt enlivening to be jostling with other people probably heading home from work. But I admit I was a little disappointed that there were no weirdos, no punks with high hair, no crazy-looking hookers, no gay men dressed as circus performers. The crowds looked mostly normal, like people strolling a mall, or exiting a church, just more of them. I watched a young couple clutching hands on a park bench, their hair still damp from showers or sex. The man said something. The woman whipped her head to look at him. He looked away smirking as she stared moonfully into the side of his head, then down at his shoes as though contemplating her good fortune, or his good taste.

Even though it was just down the street from her apartment, Beth had probably never been in this park, let alone noticed it. I couldn't imagine her purposelessly sitting anywhere, for that matter. Or if she was, she'd be nose-deep in a newspaper, carefully avoiding wrinkles, a woman you'd never see sporting tennis shoes, then changing into heels at work. No, Beth always said if you can't afford the kind of heels that can survive the city sidewalks, stick to bloody Birkenstocks.

Still it was romantic (if not a little creepy)

watching this couple squeeze in a few intimate minutes in public, neither one of them distracted by the traffic or the children buzzing around them. I watched great gulps of people coming in and out of the subway entrance, up and down a staircase in the ground. If I lived here, I would love having a subway, I thought. I would never drive. I would always take the subway to work. I would carry a Metrocard and I would memorize the routes like a pro. I hoped to muster the courage to ride it at least once while I was here, despite the way the map made me gasp. How do the cars not crash into each other? How does someone descend down into that underground labyrinth and not get lost? And though I didn't miss my imaginary career, I would have loved the idea of going to work, of moving along with other commuters in the morning, of having some place to be. Even the drive to the city for an appointment with Sam's doctors was a welcome meditation. As I left the farm, I used to feel as though I was unraveling a spool of thin worry that would run out halfway to the hospital. At which point I would take up the strings of the efficient medical system, severing one set of concerns, then clutching another.

The cell-phone ring jangled me out of my trance, flashing a number I didn't recognize. It was Kate. She was in the lobby of Beth's apartment.

"Where are you?" she asked.

"I'm just across the street. Not far."

"We're going to Jeb and Nadia's for dinner, remember? It's in your honor. Come, come, come, come, come. Please?"

"But I ate."

In my honor. I pictured myself on a throne, wearing a funny hat at the foot of a long table, fielding questions about Beth's absence, knowing they all knew by now.

"You ate already? It's only seven-thirty. Anyway, you can eat again. Wait. That didn't come out right."

I was too exhausted to fight her, plus too curious about Jeb and Nadia's place (and marriage) to say no. I wanted inside some of these buildings, to see how people here lived, where they stored their tampons and toilet paper and what kinds of pets they kept. I told her to give me a minute and I ambled across the street. Then I skipped toward the silhouette of Beth's building like an anxious kid who'd strayed too far from her minder's sight.

Jeb and Nadia lived near a bridge in Brooklyn, in an old building that, from the dark street, looked terribly menacing. It was plain, square, and flat, with mismatched brick around the lower, newer, windows. I felt nervous to go in, not just because it was my first dinner party, in my honor no less, but the area looked poor and dangerous.

"Does everyone know why Beth's not with me?" I asked Kate, suddenly feeling ashamed. But what had I done wrong?

"No," she said, shaking her head. "You're just here on a little break and Beth got delayed. That's all."

When the freight elevator deposited us onto their floor, things didn't improve. The hallway was dim and cavernous. I had driven by projects in Detroit that had more charm. And good parking. Surely they both made money, I thought, feeling grateful that Beth lived in a place that was recognizable from magazines or TV shows. So when Kate said, "You're going to die when you see this place," I began to wonder if she was being serious.

Nadia hauled open the creaky barn door using what looked like her full weight and welcomed me with drama.

"PEE-chee! Everybody, Peachy's here!"

A mild "yay" emanated from behind her. Some weak clapping. I felt thoroughly sick. But the place was enormous and more beautiful than anything I could have expected from the street. In fact, it was the opposite of the street, despite its alley-type features; brick walls and the ceiling exposed to all the inner workings of the apartment's heat and hydro. It was rich-looking in the strangest kind of way, like Jeb and Nadia lived in a tastefully furnished factory, lit by fat candles and warm lamps.

"Wow," I said. "It's so beautiful."

Nadia clutched me to her bosom like Nana Beecher might have, had she had a bosom.

"You are much prettier dan your sister," she said. "Much."

Nadia was a big blond Polish *woman*. Not fat, not at all. Large, wide-shouldered, a woman who possessed the presence of an entire room of people. I followed her into the kitchen, where Jeb stood wearing an apron that said KISS THE COCK.

"Peachy. So good to meet you finally," he said, holding my face firmly and planting two kisses, one on each side. He whispered, "Sorry Beth couldn't make it."

A thin man with strange glasses sitting at the island coughed "whore" into his fist. The room exploded with laughter. Not uncomfortable laughter, the real kind born of a real joke.

Nadia shot him a dirty look. Kate told him to "fuck off" in a singsongy warning kind of way.

"Kidding! Kidding! Sorry," the thin man said, smiling, holding up his hands in surrender and offering me one. "I'm Anthony and I'm *kidding*. I love Beth. So nice to meet you."

I shook his hand, and Nadia guided me over to a group of people in the living room area who seemed to be in the middle of a conversation about Cuba.

"We should be there. We should be investing. We should be putting up infrastructure. We should be developing hotels. We should be passing out free Coke."

"Cocaine coke? Or Coca-Cola coke?"

"Both, fuck."

"Dis is Peachy. Beth's sister. On a little visit from Canada," Nadia said, her hands framing my shoulders. It was hard to take all of their faces in at once.

"Hi, Beth's sister," a couple of them intoned in my general direction. I flipped up a hand and slapped it back against my thigh.

"Anthony you met. You know Kate and Jeb. Me, of course," she continued. "And dis is Louis, Frieda, and Stacey."

The names were familiar from Beth's stories, but the only things that stood out were the seedy bits, the stories I'd laughed at, and lived off, frankly. For instance, Louis and Anthony used to date until Louis insisted on being bisexual in case he met a rich woman and could retire. In fact, he had recently found out that he had a kid with a woman from college, a one-night stand, and that he resented paying child support, not because he didn't make enough money on Wall Street, but because the kid was unattractive. Years earlier, I remembered that Frieda had flashed a bouncer to get the lot of them into a club. And that she shaved five years off her online dating profile. Stacey once sued a Ukrainian woman who burnt her vagina during a Brazilian wax job. She got $265,000, which she now considered her "entrance" fee, in that any man who made less than that had no chance of getting in. There were so many other places I wanted to be just then: a darkened bathroom suffocating under a horse blanket in the tub, lying down in the back of a pickup truck that was careening over a cliff, stuffed in a cannon about to be shot into a boiling lake. I almost prayed for Beth to pop in, to shelter me from having to make conversation with people to whom I had nothing to say. This was Beth's kind of room, these were her people, arch and fierce, funny at the expense of others. I stood there hands clasped in front of me looking like a kid about to give a boring speech about Ancient Egypt or the awful business of wearing braces. *Ladies, gentlemen, esteemed judges . . .* Beth would have swanned in, wiggled herself down between two of the meanest ones here, interrupted their conversation and demanded a cigarette. Even better, they would have loved her for it. After which, she would have joined their conversation about Cuba like a fast car merging into loose traffic. *Blah blah blah embargo, blah blah blah black market,* all just run-on

sentences until Beth would provide the punc-
tuation, the joke, the final word, and when the
subject was exhausted, she'd change it into
something better. These thoughts didn't make me
jealous. They made me miss her. I realized why it
had always been so wonderfully easy to go
places with Beth. She cleared the path, made the
entrance, laid the groundwork, did all the hard
work of elevating the evening. I just carried the
train.

"I must go cook," Nadia said, turning and
leaving me with these people. *Noooo. Don't
leave me,* I yelled in my head.

"That's my broad," said Jeb. "Broad" seemed
silly but very apt. Not just because Nadia looked
to be older than Jeb by a few years, but, like
Beth, she carried herself differently than everyone else. But where Beth's rails ran low to the
ground, Nadia's were higher than all of ours. I
could see why Nadia rankled Beth. "She thinks
she is sooo great," Beth would say. But it was
precisely that aspect, that pride of place, that
made her seem great.

The group in the living room resumed their
conversation under a dusting of cigarette smoke.
I looked past them at what I thought, for a split
second, was a poster of the Manhattan skyline.
But it wasn't a poster. It was the skyline in all its
gaudy brilliance. It was dusk by then, and the
buildings were washed in the kind of color you

could never find in a can. As I moved closer to the window, the moon suddenly joined the buildings and I couldn't help but laugh to myself. I couldn't believe how beautiful it looked, hovering over the skyline. I felt choked up, like even the moon knew it looked better over here.

Jeb came up behind me, slapped a vodka and soda in my hands, and lit a cigarette.

"So. Tell me. What happened?"

"This is amazing. Look at that moon," I said, smiling and sipping. I never thought the moon could put a person in a better mood, but it had. I pointed to his cigarette pack. He pumped one out for me and lit it. "What do you mean, 'what happened'?" For a second I really had no honest idea what he was talking about.

"You *know* what I mean. *Beth*. Kate mentioned something about her and *Beau*. What the *fuck?*"

I tried not to look around the room at all the faces suddenly trying hard not to face me. Kate seemed to be eyeing the bottom of what must have been her second martini, pretending to pay attention to something Anthony wasn't saying. Out of the corner of my eye, Nadia was moving slowly in the kitchen area in case the pots and pans she was messing with drowned out what Jeb and I might say to each other. They reminded me of bored hyenas, dying to gnaw on the entrails of my wounded family. Beth would have launched a witty barb into the tense crowd,

254

something sharp enough to counter their curiosity: *OK so yeah, my husband fucked my thinner sister and all I got was this lousy, extra-large T-shirt,* she would have said, to guffaws all around. The thought made me wish for my husband, a man whose job it had always been to shield me from this kind of menace. Whenever I'd been bored, out of my element, over my head or off my game, at the party, a barbecue, the tavern, or a banquet, I needed only glance sideways at Beau, and he'd appear by my side with my coat. If Beau were here, I thought, he'd have long since called us a cab. Before leaving he'd have smashed their faces together, Frieda and Stacey in particular, nose job to nose job—whack. Then he would have hoisted me into his arms like a rescuing prince, or an avenging angel (the kind who have sex with their wives' sisters and then feel really bad about it), and carried me across the darkening room. But there was no one coming to get me, no one to save me from these people whose only real sin was to give me a supportive audience for my indignation, to allow me the necessary luxury of ripping into Beth. But I couldn't do it. Even though I had never hated her more, I probably would have still thrown an arm across her chest if I slammed on the brakes at a stop sign.

"I don't want to be rude, Jeb," I whispered. "But I'd rather not discuss my personal problems in a room full of people who don't know me."

"Oh come *on,* Peachy," Anthony yelled from across the room. "We *know* Beth!"

Kate snorted. A bit of pimento landed on Anthony's arm. He carefully lifted it and returned it to the rim of her martini glass. "I believe this is yours, madam."

"Ank oo," Kate said, mouth full of olive.

There was more laughter from the faux comedy club audience, now off the subject of Cuba, and onto the subject of me.

"Well, I think it's totally fucked what she did," said Frieda, who was sitting in the middle of the sectional couch. "Totally wrong."

Stacey, wired and tight, added, "Well, if Peachy doesn't want me to be her friend anymore, I won't be Beth's friend."

She was kidding, but there was a smattering of nods and yeahs to that childish comment.

"You all know?" I asked, looking directly at Kate.

"We're all best friends with her," Louis said, shrugging. "She would have told us herself. Eventually."

"Peachy," Nadia yelled. "Come into da kitchen wit me."

I practically ran across the massive living space, past the chain-smoking gauntlet. Fury moved my legs, but embarrassment and anger were the fuel. Nadia glowered at Jeb from across the room.

"What are you looking at me for?" Jeb yelled. "I didn't do anything."

"Jeb, you should be fucking gay for all da stupid gossipy girl shit you get yourself involved in. No offense, Anthony. Louis. And be careful of trowing stones," Nadia said. "And Kate! You should shut your mout sometime."

She was being meanly playful, but her Polish accent made the scolding come out in a religious hiss.

"Peachy, stay away from doze people, dare awful," Nadia cooed, motioning for me to come to her in the kitchen. I felt coddled and protected, and since the vodka was kicking in too, I felt a bit bolder. Beth's betrayal seemed to lend me a necessary edge in the room, made me kind of feel a bit interesting. Plus, I didn't relish the thought of wandering the neighborhood below looking for a cab.

"And scat, you two! Go," she said to Kate and Anthony. "Go sit in da corner wit da udder bad people. We don't like you."

They skulked off, leaving us alone in the kitchen, which was bigger than any restaurant kitchen I'd ever been in. I gulped the rest of my drink, slammed it on the cutting board, and asked Nadia what I could do to help.

"Hand me dat rifle," she ordered, pointing to the top of the fridge.

I turned and scanned the wall above for a gun

rack, for a second thinking she might just finish them off in a hail of bullets. I could only see a big bowl of cream and fruit perched next to a standing photo of chubby girls in a line wearing bathing suits.

"What rifle?"

"No, *try*-full," she said, laughing. "Put it in da fridge, please. Sometimes, I wish I did have a gun, dough. I hate Americans."

I moved the bowl and then pulled down the picture of the bathing beauties. Their excellent posture, red lips, pin-curled hair, cocktail-weenie thighs jutting out of bathing suits, reminded me of a still from a 1940s water musical.

Nadia grinned fondly, pointing at the girl in the middle. "Look at me how beautiful. Tirty years ago, can you believe it? Only tirteen and look at my legs. Very strong. I believe I should have won because I feel I was standout, no?"

I laughed, thinking that around the age that Nadia was expertly posing, one meaty thigh in front of the other, Beth would have been tugging on satin shorts, obsessing about imaginary cellulite, hating her nonexistent breasts and her very real set of braces. No wonder Jeb, or any man, would rather marry her than Beth. I would have married her because she really was standout. In a place that seemed full of self-abusive, self-flagellating self-loathers like Beth, Nadia indeed stood out.

"You must terrify Beth," I said.

Nadia stopped braising what looked to be a dozen tiny heads of thin lettuce splayed on a strip of foil.

"Not on purpose," she said. "I need a sharp knife, Peachy, hand me."

I unveiled a long knife from the block, feeling like her assistant surgeon. "Smells good, what are we having?"

"Boudin and spaetzle with braised endive. Trifle for dessert. Jeb bought da sausages. I can't cook a pig's head."

The menu sounded like the starting lineup for a Finnish hockey team, but I didn't care, I'd try it all.

"Do you love him?" she whispered, glancing over my shoulder at the guests behind me, seemingly entertained by a story Anthony was telling them. She moved the little lettuces into the bottom of the stove.

"Beau?"

"Your husband. Do you love him?" She stood up, put both her fists on her hips, and fully faced me.

"I think so. I don't know. I'm angry. As you can imagine," I said, feeling suddenly so tired.

"More dan imagine, Peachy. I know. But if you love him, you can get trew dis."

"I guess I do. Yes. I mean, we have two kids. And one's sick. And I don't want to go it alone.

But that's not why I'd stay. I just—I don't want to hurt the boys. My dad loves him. But what he did. And with Beth. My sister. And *she*—"

My voice caught in my throat again, but I was not going to cry at Jeb and Nadia's. I didn't want to give them the performance they seemed to be keening for.

"Let me tell you someting, Peachy. I don't know if Beth told you dis, but before I was married, Jeb had a one last fling wit your sister."

"No. She didn't," I said, stunned. "And you're still friends with her?"

"Yes. It may seem strange, but day had been broken up for years. Can you hear me in the udder room dare? And Jeb, I don't know. Beth was a reliable person for him to fuck because she didn't want anyting from him. Didn't want to destroy our relationship. Didn't want him back. She just wanted to have some fun. A nutting ting, day said. Jeb too, and dat was supposed to be all. And day tought dat I would understand, even if I *did* find out, which I was not supposed to find out—right, Jeb? Dare not listening now, you see, because dis is an embarrassing ting for Jeb listen to. He feels shame. Even still."

I glanced behind me, and it was true, the party suddenly seemed deeply ensconced in a discussion about Sardinia, pros, cons, celebrity spottings, the yucky pebble beaches, anything to desperately not overhear what Nadia was unconcerned about saying in their company. I suddenly wanted to be Nadia's best friend, to make Nadia like—no—love me. I wanted to tell her that I would never hurt her, never betray her, that I was nothing like Beth. I would be a soldier-friend, loyal, honest, and kind. And probably, to these people, as boring as hell. It suddenly dawned on me that they loved Beth precisely because she was so spectacularly fucked up. She entertained them, which had made them as complicit in her crimes and dramas as I had been.

But they knew nothing about me, nothing about how my insides work or the depths to which I knew things. My love for the boys, for instance, was so limitless and impenetrable that there could be no real harm done to me there. I could see these people for who they were, sad, care-worn, and a little lost. I had never believed, like some parents, that you can't really know what love is unless you have children. But after I had the boys, I found it impossible to hate the same way again. And while I could hold some soft-ness in my heart for Beth's people, they likely found me as dull as a spoon. I was okay with that. I knew otherwise. So did Beth. Once on the radio I had heard a piece of classical music, just a snippet. It was slow and then it built, like a small dancer quickly tiptoeing up some stairs. It built up and up and up like that, hung for a second, then released into a cascade of instruments before abruptly ending. The silence just started me bawling. It wasn't the music so much as the end of it that cut me right in half in the kitchen. Twenty minutes I cried standing there. I have no idea what that music was, who composed it, whether it was a symphony, an opera, a concerto, whatever. But years later I told Beth about it, how that bit of music seemed to be inside of me at first. How it curled right around my spine and then pulled something awful and hidden out from behind my heart.

"It felt like a miracle or something," I said.

Instead of teasing me or snorting at the sentiment, Beth, eyes welling up, said, "Peachy, I was just going to say nothing has ever moved me like that in my life. But you just did."

I suspected that it was the kind of thing that I could tell Nadia, too, one day. If we ever really became friends.

"So anyway, I find out. Doesn't matter how, but I do. And I cry. I call da whole ting off. I cry for weeks and weeks and weeks. She never told you dis?"

I shook my head, marveling at Beth's appetite for ruination as Nadia sliced diagonally across the boudin sausages, sprinkling a little dark oil in their centers. Placing them back in the oven, she plunged both hands in a bowl of dough, lightly massaging it.

"I need you to turn on da water on da stove dare, Peachy, to boil. And I hated your sister with all my might. A person. Who I asked. To speak. At my wedding," she said, punctuating her sentences with her kneading. "Dat she would have sex with my fiancé. But den one day she comes here to my door. Face all swollen and fat like a crybaby's. She had deeze flowers and she begs me to come in, pleeze, she says, I will never ask anyting of you again. Hand me dat strainer."

Nadia described how Beth paced and smoked, and I saw my sister working the room, using the exposed-brick wall as the backdrop to her dramatic monologue. I could hear her voice, bruised with just the right amount of patented regret, saying all the right and soothing words, words that go beyond sorry and into the realm of celestial expiation. Her story would describe a heinous deed not committed by her, but someone not her, as though she'd been momentarily abducted by a bald-headed, shriveled demon who, once finished committing the crime, giggled over its shoulder as it gleefully exited her body. I had heard that regret in her voice before, sometimes in minor dollops, like when she'd canceled a trip home for Jake's graduation from preschool. It came in a bigger dose when she couldn't be there after we were told of the full scope of Sam's dilemma. Beth's potent apology was followed by three dozen roses with a note attached that read: "I am there for you, whatever you need. I will do it. If you need it, say so." And she meant it, she always meant it, which is why I had always forgiven her. Though she was only kidding when she said she'd be on the first flight home for Nana Beecher's memorial, held at the church in Belle River after Lou picked up her ashes at the Windsor airport. ("The last place you'll ever find me," Beth said, "is crying over that bitch's coffin.")

"So I forgive her. Not completely. Not right away. And you know why? At first because you should keep your friends close, Peachy, your enemies closer. But den, I knew Beth. I knew Jeb. I knew dey could make trouble like children do. But once day were caught, I never was loved better by eeder one of dem. And I love Jeb. I know he loves me. And I would miss Beth and her stories, and she's so funny and generous too. You know dis. Mostly it's because I feel sorry for her. Someting about Beth makes me want to take care of her, even dough she hurts people she loves. And you know, wit her childhood and everyting, and how awful it must have been to —anyway. It's best to forgive."

We all began to gravitate around the dining room table. The boudin was delicious, though I had to chase the image of the face of the pig from my own head in order to eat it. Frieda and Stacey asked me affectionate questions about my boys, which I happily answered. Lou was an object of real interest, a mythical draft dodger Americans really only hear about but rarely meet. But when I brought up the time Nell tried to convince Lou to cross the border before draft dodgers were pardoned, just to see what would happen, the table went nearly silent.

"Yeah, before she died, she was always on him about moving back to the States," I said, filling in the sudden blanks at the table. "You know, 'Let's go to the States, I want to move back to the States, I miss the States,' but he really didn't want to leave Canada. He's totally in love with the country, I swear. It's like a person to him. A woman even," I said, laughing into the silence, taking an uncomfortable sip from my wine.

"Sorry, Peachy," Nadia said, taking up some of the empty plates. "We didn't mean to bring up your mudder."

"Um. It's okay," I said, looking around, confused. "I mean, I brought it up. But I don't mind."

The table seemed to exhale.

"What is it?"

Then Louis piped up and said, "Oh well, Beth made us totally sign our death warrants *not* to bring up the subject of your mother's suicide in front of you."

Kate kicked someone under the table.

"Must have been awful for you two to lose her so young," Stacey said, lighting a cigarette, handing it to Frieda, then lighting her own. "The real tragedy is that Beth was so little when she found her. I mean, do you ever wonder if part of why Beth's the way she is is because she discovered the body?"

I covered my hand with my mouth, freshly stuffed with a forkful of spaetzle that I was suddenly finished chewing.

"Can we change the subject, Frieda?" Kate asked, one eyebrow twisting into a ferocious comma. I looked around for something to spit the spaetzle in, because I couldn't deposit the goop in Nadia's linen napkins. That's why I never used cloth. How could I with two kids who were both such finicky eaters? But there was no possible way for me to push spaetzle past the bile beginning to rise in my throat.

"Excuse me," I mumbled through my fingers, rocketing to the kitchen to grab my purse, where Nadia was dividing the trifle. She used a big spoon to point out the guest bathroom by the entrance. I nodded and punched it open, carefully shutting it behind me. I could hear the sound of Nadia quietly scolding the whole table, the sound of the whole table quietly defending itself.

I spat the food into the toilet and pulled out

the cell. The phone rang three times before Beth picked up.

"Peachy! Hi! Where are you?" I could hear a loud TV in the background.

"What did you tell your friends about Mom?"

Beth exhaled.

"I don't remember, really. I think, a long time ago, I think I might have told Jeb that I was the one who found her. I don't know why. Then it never came up again. And then, knowing I had said something to that effect, I guess I just felt I should leave it alone. That's why I told them not to bring it up. I couldn't remember what I'd said. Why? What happened?"

"Why would you lie about something like that?"

"I don't know," she mumbled. "I'm sorry. I always felt ashamed that I didn't go up first. You were so little."

"So were you."

"Yeah, but I was the oldest. I should have—"

"What are the boys doing?" I cut her off. I couldn't have a conversation like this sitting in Nadia and Jeb's guest washroom.

"The boys are here with me. We ate hot dogs. We're watching *Dukes of Hazzard*. The TV show, *not* the movie."

"They should be in bed by now."

"I know, I just—"

"Where's Beau and Lou?"

"I don't know. I saw them take off a couple of

hours ago. Peachy, what happened? Where are you?"

"Jeb and Nadia's. I'm in the bathroom. Hey, do you know the address here?"

She told me. I wrote it on my hand.

"Peachy, don't leave by yourself. Not that Williamsburg's dangerous," she said. "Unless you don't want someone to steal your style. Listen, get Kate or Jeb to call you a car—"

"Okay, I gotta go," I said. "I mean, I really gotta leave."

"Peachy, don't hang up. What's going on? Did Nell come up? What did you tell them? I'm so sorry—"

"Stop with the sorry. I didn't tell them any-thing, Beth. Okay? I said nothing. But I don't understand why—listen. Fuck. I gotta go."

I hung up. I felt cornered between exposing Beth's lie and the inability to betray her. If I went back to the table, they'd force me to choose, and since I was a terrible liar and hadn't been properly prompted on all of the finer details from the site of Nell's new deathbed, I had to leave. There also was a part of me that preferred Beth's version to linger a little longer in this milieu, because I didn't want to betray Nell, to use her awful tragedy as my dinner party lubrication. It was my story too, my mother, and I didn't want to abandon her sadness here, to be kicked around after I left, like it was a dead mouse being toyed with by dumb cats.

I dialed another number and Jonathan answered after one ring. I told him I was stuck at an awful party in a dangerous part of the city and that I needed a cab to come and get me. He said no worries, a friend of his had a car company not too far away, so sit tight, he said, one will be there in a minute.

"Also, in the future, you don't have to tell me you're Beth's sister first when you call. You just say it's Peachy from now on."

"Okay."

"See you soon."

"Thanks. Bye."

Three minutes later, the doorbell buzzed on the other side of the bathroom door. I could hear Nadia clomping toward me, then faint knocking.

"Peachy, darling, dere's a man here who says you ordered a car."

I opened the door and took Nadia by the arm, using her body to shield me from the dining area as we walked out.

"Thank you for the lovely evening, Nadia, but I really have to go now. Bye, everybody!" I yelled over her shoulder to mild protestations.

"Nobody meant to make you upset," she said, framing my face like I did with the boys using my two hands. I nearly started to cry from missing them.

"I know. But I have to go."

"What are you doing tomorrow? Let me take you to lunch or someting. I will call you, okay?"

"Okay," I said, accidentally kissing her good-bye on the mouth.

chapter thirteen

It was almost ten o'clock when I woke up. I wasn't hungover, but I felt drugged and disoriented from the unnatural amount of sleep I had enjoyed. Almost ten hours, I realized, patting around the quilty mountains for Jake's phantom limbs. I had slept so long and so deeply my entire right side had gone numb. For the first time in almost ten years, I had woken up alone. A person could get used to falling asleep alone, but waking up alone felt altogether odd to me. Odder still was not having to spring out of bed to rouse the others. I didn't have to set a table or stir up eggs. I didn't have to yell up for Beau, twice, sometimes three times. I didn't have to take Sam's temperature, or check his bed for pee, pulling the plastic liner off and flipping it if the mattress was damp. I didn't have to let Scoots out, then in, then out again. I didn't have to feel guilty about dumping his fresh food in last night's crusty bowl, always meaning to wash it later, which I sometimes did, but mostly didn't.

There was nothing in Beth's apartment for breakfast except booze and cheese, so I boiled some water for tea. I was eating my second peach when Nadia called. She reiterated an unnecessary apology about last night and told me to expect her at Beth's in an hour for some shopping and sightseeing. I was excited to be hanging out with Nadia rather than Kate, who I would have eventually shoved in front of a subway car if I had to pass any more time in her presence. I took my tea out onto the fire escape. The city streets below made me feel like I was hovering above the deck of a crowded cruise ship.

"Ahoy," I yelled like an idiot.

I thought about Beau's anger, which, judging from my dreams, had reached New York and stirred me in the night. I remembered nothing in particular. No dream scene stuck out. But I woke with the sense that I'd done a lot of running and screaming, that there'd been fights of some kind, and that I had ground my teeth on account of how tender my jaw felt that morning.

The sun beat heavy on my pale shoulders and I ducked back inside. As I made my way to the computer to check the email, I tripped over an area rug and spilled my tea across the white fat couch.

"Fucking fuck," I screamed. I had seen myself doing this, had envisioned it several times before it happened, my body likely doomed to fulfill that destiny. I scrambled to the fridge for something like soda water, snatched the Perrier, and poured it on the cushion. Then I pulled at the paper towels off the rack, yanking the spool across the living room floor. I sopped and prayed, prayed and sopped, and the brown turned to beige then to a blush only detectable if mentioned, which it would never be, I thought, flipping the cushion over, only to expose an even bigger stain, far less faint, on the other side. Expensive red wine, I thought. I also found a tiny packet of white powder folded in Saran Wrap and lodged in the couch fold. I knew what it was. I had never seen Beth do hard drugs before, but after nosing through her medicine cabinet this should hardly surprise me. Yet, I winced at the sight of the packet. I bit it open with my teeth, careful not to spill any into my mouth, and poured it down the sink under running water. This was something I'd need to discuss with her, I thought. Or better yet, I'd discuss with Lou, who could, in turn, discuss it with her, my ability to conjure any benevolence toward Beth still badly impaired.

The New York subway was cleaner and more navigable than I had imagined. Nadia impressed me with how she knew exactly where we were going, what hallways to go down and staircases to go up, minus any maps. The way she walked, her slightly imperious strut, made her look like the opposite of a lost and stupid target, and I tried to copy it. But my outfit betrayed me badly. I saw no one who looked like me, a tourist in discount black sandals with the worn, sloped heels of someone who chased after children full-time. My five-year-old jeans, belted high at the waist, bagged low under my bum. My purse, utilitarian beige, had about as much style as an old rotary phone and weighed the same too. Even magnanimous Nadia seemed to cringe when I reached for my denim jacket, saying, "It's too hot for dat. You won't need it," though it would have gone a long way to conceal what I once thought was my best blouse, which the kids named the Babysitter shirt, because when I wore this V-necked, long-sleeved red confection with its hint of Lycra shimmer, it signaled that Beau and I were going out. But here, in Midtown Manhattan, it signaled too much effort too early in the day. Even I knew it, glancing around the subway at the put-together women who wore artfully knotted scarves, patterned skirts, and brand-new high-heeled shoes.

When Nadia told me she was taking me to Macy's first, I felt the rush of childhood joy, though I only knew the place from Christmas movies and parades. But what does a person wear on a date? How could I have never been on a date? Beau didn't date me; he knocked me up and married me. No boy had ever pulled up our long gravel driveway to pin something gaudy to my chest.

"What you need is one nice outfit, Peachy," Nadia said. "And den we can accessorize around it. What plans do you have for tonight? Kate tells me you are meeting a friend you know from here."

She seemed to have no idea I planned on meeting Beth's ex. In fact, it occurred to me that Nadia wouldn't think much of Jeb, Kate, and Beth's ridiculous prank, so they probably never told her about it.

"That's right. An old friend. And I think dinner's just going to be casual. Not too fancy. But I want to look, I don't know, pretty."

"Dat won't be too hard."

I blushed, confused by a crush that was anything but sexual. Nadia was dressed in smart black culottes over which was draped an oversized blue caftan, cut off at the thighs. Her hair was tied back and low with a frayed ribbon. I rarely shopped with other grown-ups, and never without the boys. Shopping to me was having an exit time and a list, keeping one keen eye on both kids, the other on the clock. If I found something I wanted, which was usually something I needed, I'd stuff all three of us in a changing room. I'd tell them to pretend it was a fort they had to hold down if I ran to the rack for a bigger size. How many times had I brought home the wrong color, thinking the navy was the black, the ivory was the white, shopping at lightning speed to keep the kids on their schedule and Beau and me out of debt. But I loved shopping for them, picking out their cute outfits, their stripes and pants and matching socks, the smell of chemicals on new cloth bringing me back to those days before back-to-school, when Lou would do his damnedest to outfit Beth and me as best as possible. He would watch what the other mothers were buying for their girls and trail behind them like a seagull following a cruise ship, pecking at their castoffs. My fingers grazed a pair of jeans that were a size zero, a category I had heard of before, but rarely spotted in places I shopped for clothes.

"These could fit Sam," I said.

"Yeah. Or dey could be leg covers for your kitchen chairs," Nadia snorted.

Nadia yanked a half-dozen pairs of pants, two dresses, and lots of tops off the racks, smacking them up against my body while avoiding my eyes.

The hour passed with increasing frustration. It wasn't that nothing fit, but nothing looked like it was supposed to on my body. The waist would jut out if the pants fit my ass, or the shirt would tug too tight across my shoulder blades, or it would pucker across my tits too much.

"Do you know your size?" the salesgirl finally screamed over the change room door, behind which I stood, spent clothing piled around my ankles.

"I thought I did," I yelled back. "I thought maybe I was an eight or maybe a ten. But now I don't know."

I looked down at the sartorial carnage. I must have tried on a dozen pairs of pants and jeans and cords in those sizes, reluctant to ask for a twelve or fourteen, even if they made them in those sizes, which they did not. I felt like the fattest, poorest kid in class, fully expecting to be chased back to Beth's place by a taunting pack of elegantly dressed scarecrows. I sat my ass on the little shelf, pants shackling my ankles, and started to tear up. I had in mind a picture of me that perhaps didn't exist, someone pulled-together, confident, and happy.

"Hello in there? I could start removing some of those castoffs if you don't mind," said the saleslady. Gathering up the clothing, I angrily flung them over the top of the door and fell back on the shelf feeling like the cornered dunce.

"Open da door please, Peachy," Nadia demanded. She'd been gone for a while, during which time I had lost the battle with the long-legged jeans.

"Here." Her hand proffered a springy pile of heavy material. Its comforting pattern looked like the close-up of a painting of a lake, all curvy blues and greens and creams. "Dis is it. Dis is da ting."

"I can't afford that," I said directly into the dress's price tag.

"Dat's good news, because I can," she said.

"That's ridiculous," I said. "I don't want you to buy me anything."

"Just shut up and try it on."

The price was the equivalent of a fancy barbecue with a burner for corn, or a pair of cross-country skis, two things I recently wouldn't allow Beau to charge on the credit card, claiming it was only to be used for emergencies.

"What emergencies?" he whined.

"Fire burns down our house and we need to stay in a hotel."

"But we'd stay with Leo and Lucy," he said.

"The hell. What about Lou?"

"The fire wouldn't reach the trailer, dummy."

The dress folded heavily around my body, the cut and weight of the material containing me making me feel grown-up. I held out my arms as Nadia expertly threaded one strap through a hole and wrapped the other around the thinnest part of my waist. She lovingly tied a bow and let it gingerly drape a hip, and I watched my face instantly unbuckle out of its pretantrum angst and melt into the relaxed grin of a person falling a little in love with themselves. I traced my fingers up and down the valley between my breasts.

"Holy shit."

"If you won't let me buy dat for you, Peachy, den we're going to have to make a run for it," she said.

The salesgirl, arms full of castoffs, moved toward us as though in a trance herself.

"Diane?" she asked, taking in my body in that dress.

Nadia nodded and repeated the name. They both regarded me with pride, as though they had carved the silk itself.

"The woman's a genius."

"She is," said Nadia.

I had no idea who they were talking about, and I didn't care. Because I had found the woman I was looking for, and her name wasn't Diane, it was Georgia. All I had needed was this dress to point me to her.

So this is what it's like to be a girl, I thought, while taking out my charge card at the cashier's. A dueling plastic smackfest ensued and Nadia eventually won. In the end, I let her buy me the dress because, as she said, it was her idea and she wanted to take all the credit. She promised to let me pay for the shoes but only if she could pick them out. How could I argue? What did I know, after all, about being a girl, shopping with a girl, and letting her mother the hell out of me?

My mother died when I was five. Beth left when I was on the cusp of needing all of this so badly I didn't even know it until Nadia wrapped a perfect dress around my body and found a pair of sling-back sandals I swore I'd never take off. As we sampled perfume in Bloomingdale's, poked through the stacks of a bookstore bigger than our downtown library, and hit a bustling deli for turkey sandwiches and Diet Cokes, I was infused with a kind of ghostly nostalgia for days I had never experienced. Soon after Beth left, my life had become all male so fast that anything feminine about me seemed to have been washed away in the constant laundry of my life, the sweat socks and skid marks and pee of my boys and men. My natural scent had become the lemons of dish soap with a dash of wet dog thrown in. While wandering in the temple of women, among other women, I felt like Cinderella's secret sister, the one who wasn't even informed that there were Polish godmothers to be had or city princes to meet or sling-back shoes to try on and buy or dinner reservations to get to on time, let alone depart from before your ride home turned into a monstrous gourd.

I turned to Nadia in Saks and said, "I believe I am having what is known as a great day."

"I'm glad, Peachy. Let's hope you have a great night," she said, placing a wide-brimmed hat on top of my head and adjusting it.

chapter fourteen

The last person I expected an email from, the person I had the most difficulty imagining sitting in front of a computer, composing and sending one, was Lou. But there it was, waiting for me at Beth's after I'd kissed Nadia goodbye (both cheeks) and jostled past Jonathan with my oversized bags. I looked like a cartoon girl on the cover of those novels I'd never read because the shopping they celebrated seemed altogether malevolent. Lou's email, which had come from our family account, was titled "While You Were Gone."

Dear Peachy,
Just writing that now, and it's been so long since I wrote your name, I'm thinking maybe we should have just stayed calling you Georgia. I always thought it was a kind of regal name but too big for such a little girl. I am trying hard not to interfere, trying to leave all this in God's hands. You know my take on pain, that we are nothing without it. I believe that's

why God made the family to begin with. Training wheels for real life. But it is awful when family's where the biggest pain comes from.

Since you drowned the laptop, I write this from the copy shop in town. Beth wrote your email address, and this young woman here showed me how to work this thing. You should know last night I made my home on the couch to clear space for Beau to ruminate and sulk in the trailer.

I am no arbiter of marital accord, or how to achieve it. Your mother and I had a difficult go of things. Not just because her depression was so deep, but the fact is I was a lousy farmer and I had a lot of guilt over skipping out on a country at war, and from marrying a woman who never loved me. She sure tried. She was just never mine for the having. Tooey was her love long before I was graced by her ride. But I am daily grateful for her generosity in marrying this almost soldier, who would have died from cowardice over there before a bullet could have grazed me. She gave me two girls I

281

can't love any more than I do, who've blessed me with more than I know I deserve. Fact is, she never wanted to come back to the farm, let alone stay. But because of my predicament, and the fact that I saddled her with a new baby right off, she felt forced to. I long have urged both of you to let go of any responsibility you two may have felt toward your mother's death. But a part of me lives that believes she left like she did because of me. It's the part I try to whittle down daily, but it pops up in times like this. I suspect it grows in Beth too. We forget, she may have been only eight then, but she was no dupe. When I look at how aware Sam is of any kind of discord, compared to the way Jake just kinda rolls with things, I can't help but remind myself you two were roughly the same age as the boys during those treacherous days.

I know you want an update on how Beth's faring in the role of temporary caregiver. She's no you, Peachy, but she has an endearing knack for the boys, probably, as she jokes, because she's about their mental age. Somewhere in the middle. She puts it at seven and I don't argue.

Yesterday was busy for Beth, and a little confusing for the boys. They asked why she was here still and not with you in New York, and she said, "Because I love your mother and I want you guys to still be my friends." Sam asked her why you were mad at Beth, and she said, "Because I did something very wrong and your mother is very right to be mad at me." And when he asked her what she did, she said, "The worst possible thing to the people I love the very most." Then Jake asked if she felt sorry, and Beth said she did and would for the rest of her life.

That seemed satisfactory to them. The boys seemed to regard Beth with a kind of wary affection because they know you left in anger and that Beth had something to do with it. Sam had a small and uneventful episode; it came and went in under seventeen minutes. I was here, so there was nothing to worry about. Beth was out with

Jake and Scoots at the pond. Beau's been doing a lot of weekend work at the shop. He doesn't want to be around, and that's understandable. But he was home to tuck them in. Will be tonight too.

I know you don't want to hear this, but as a man who's done some awful things too, I worry for Beau. He's done big damage, but mostly what he's guilty of is seeking selfish comfort in a place that had no business giving it to him, not the least reason being there was none to give. People like Beth can be powerful vortexes when they're holding on to the bottom rung, as I believe Beth's been doing for some time. I've often trotted out that old hippy saying of "living in the moment." Smarter people than me say it's the definition of happiness. But sometimes I think Beth lives too much in the moment, especially when she drinks. She's become completely unaware of the consequences. I also believe that she's letting go of that ladder.

You know she drinks. You know my policy on preaching. What I'm saying is that if this be her bottom, *we have to ensure a hard landing pad. This time I can't catch her. I told her that and she cried like a child. I cried too. Later, in private. These have been hard days for me, because to know there is hatred and betrayal between your children is an awful kind of parental cancer.*

Peachy, you once wanted to be a social worker. You wanted to help sick and damaged people. And because you are a natural saint I know you will proceed with your graces intact, which you probably feel have abandoned you. They haven't. They're just dormant.

From your loving father . . .

No doubt Lou hoped to have a palliative effect on me. He wanted to use his words to build a buffer between me and Beth, between me and any actions I had planned on taking against her. But instead of a pause, instead of a reconsideration, his note left me feeling inflamed and, frankly, bereft. I kept my reply brief, knowing Beau or Beth would probably read it before handing it off to Lou.

Thanks for your note. I hope when I screw up you'll be equally eloquent in

285

making my case to my loved ones. I will see you at the airport tomorrow. Kiss and hug the kids for me. Tell them I'll be home after lunch. Tell them they only have to go to sleep and wake up one more time. I hope Beau is comfortable down at the trailer. And I hope Beth kisses the farm goodbye. I'll be taking my better graces out for dinner and drinks tonight. Perhaps that'll revive them.

As usual, I got ready too early, but even with the air-conditioning, I felt too hot to pace the apartment. I was a hurry-up-and-wait-type person, for the boys at school, for Beth at the airport, for Beau after work. I was the really early bird who waited for the worm to surface. I heated up food I had cooked too soon. I drove around the block to avoid being the first to a party or a shower. I ordered another while I waited, and waited, the serial killer of time. But after catching a glimpse of my face in the mirror, I realized applying makeup passed time rather dangerously. A solid layer needed to be troweled off, which carved a necessary fifteen minutes from my potential "wandering the block" time.

I did look nice in that dress, the skirt cutting across the part of my legs that were thinnest, the firm fabric draping over my ass like a heavy flap.

The slit provided the perfect amount of sexiness. I grabbed the folding map and checked my route to the restaurant. In these shoes anything was walking distance, I decided, and stepped out of the elevator into the lobby.

Jonathan looked up and then covered his eyes and then uncovered them.

"My, my, my," he said. "You look wonderful."

"Why, thank you," I said, spinning around like a goof.

"And what occasion could warrant such a dress?"

An occasion informed by fraud and vengeance, I wanted to say. With a dollop of sexual danger thrown in.

"I'm meeting a friend for dinner. In Greenwich Village," I said, feeling entitled to those words.

"Where are you meeting your lucky friend?"

I told him, and he gave me directions that matched the lines and arrows I had drawn on my own map. Despite the motives behind meeting my so-called "lucky" friend, I felt terribly proud of myself.

"Thank you," I said, smiling, winking, flirting. I was flirting. I was good at it.

When she was in love, I could see how this city could feel like Beth's costar, her cohort, her coconspirator. I could see why flowers in buckets that she might normally pass with little appreciation could suddenly turn into tiny Ziegfeld girls in this city, marking a path with a theatrical tilt of their heavy heads. That's the way I saw things walking to Greenwich Village in my dress. Even the garbage men seemed romantic here, hinging themselves out from the side of their churning white trucks, looking more like regal jousters than portable janitors. I was feeling floaty and foolish, remembering that Beth once told me that the best thing about New York is that the city itself cared about who you were and what you wore.

"And that's a good thing?" I asked.

"No, Peach. That's a great thing," she said. "Why do you think talented Canadians leave Canada for New York?"

"For American money?"

"No," she said. "It's because talented people tend to be weird and weird people tend to be iconoclasts and Canada has no idea what to do with people like that."

"But you're not a weird iconoclast, Beth."

"Not yet," she said. "But I'm working on it."

I passed an old cookbook shop, marveling that a shop specializing in old cookbooks could be a viable business anywhere. Who shopped there? Who urgently needed to buy a used cookbook? I walked up Bleecker Street and past all the gay shops and people, trying not to gawk at flamboyance. I turned onto Hudson, nauseous with worry, even though Marcus was meeting Georgia, not married Peachy whose husband had recently been caught cheating. He was meeting a horse-riding, private-school-going girl named Georgia, not a university dropout and current housewife with a brain-stormy son who peed his bed and fainted in malls. He was meeting Italian-speaking Georgia, a chick with a bright future and a yellow racing bike, not Peachy, who still lives with her father in the same house and town in which she was born. Georgia was single, arty, and original, the type of woman who would never even give Beau Laliberté the time of day, let alone sleep with him, marry him, and give him a couple of sons.

My stomach was getting busier as I got closer to the restaurant. God, I thought, Beth put herself through these painful procedures all the time. All those first dates she'd told me about, the assessments, the acceptances, the dismissals. It couldn't be good for the health or digestion, let alone the human spirit. The mere potential for mortification that evening felt so corrosive, I could only imagine that serial rejection could ruin a person forever.

Where Hudson met Eighth Avenue, I strolled to a stop at a small park and lit a cigarette. I watched women blow by me, leaving a lot of different sounds and smells in their wake. Some were yakking into the space in front of them, like zombie models, their phones hooked around their ears. Like Beth, they seemed to wear a wall of purposefulness around them, like an invisible, expensive force field. I watched a specter of a woman poke through the middle of a slow-moving crowd. She was a wisp really, clacking her staccato stilettos toward me, bouncy hair bracketing her shoulders, a mouth like a punch, eyes angry, breasts rising and falling a beat behind the rest of her body. Without breaking stride or looking at me, she careened around my body like she was an avatar from one of the boys' computer games, controlled by a celestial joystick. I was not this, I thought. I could never be this. I was too fleshy, too earthbound.

Just ahead I could see the restaurant's sign dangling above the street. I threw my cigarette in the gutter and smelled my breath. I couldn't remember if we had said that Georgia was a smoker. I looked at the time on the cell phone, feeling a little disappointed that I was still ten minutes early. Beth always said she arrived late for everything, so people had a chance to feel anxious to see her. "Huh," I had said, my stock answer to all her odd rituals. I had noticed earlier that the cell's battery was nearly depleted, so I shut it off for the day to save up enough juice to squeeze in one more call to the boys.

Beth answered on the first ring.

"Put one of the boys on, please," I said.

"Sam's not here. He went with Lou to town. Jake is though. I was just going to call you. Where are you?"

"Jake then, please. My cell doesn't have a lot of battery power left. I forgot to grab my charger. So if I can't be reached for the next couple of hours, that's why. But call me at your place if there's an emergency, and only if there's an emergency. I'll phone from the airport in the morning. Also, please tell Dad that he's going to have to get over his no-coming-to-America thing, because he has to pick me up. I don't want to see Beau's face either."

"Jesus, Peachy," she whispered.

"I mean it."

"Peachy, please talk to me. I am worried about you there."

"Not now, I'm running late and I just want to talk to my son."

In the silence between us I tried to picture her face. It was likely makeupless and looking drawn. Saturdays are long when you have children. Some mornings the empty hours seemed impossible to fill, but by the end of the day everything you'd planned invariably took longer than you thought. That's what Sundays were for, to complete the stuff you had started the day before under the misconception that you had nothing to do and too much time on your hands.

I could hear her yell for Jake and then his little feet on the wood floor running to the phone. "Mom! Where are you?"

"Hi, buddy!" His voice was food to me. I wanted to eat it, chew on it, savor it. "I'm still in New York. Just one more day. I'll be home this time tomorrow! But guess what? I went shopping!"

"What did you get me?"

"You'll see," I said, stunned I had forgotten to buy them anything, a first among firsts for me that weekend.

"It is a truck or maybe candy?"

"I can't tell you. It's a surprise. How's Sam? Where's your brother?"

"Grandpa and Dad took him to get movies for tonight. He had a spell this morning and peed on the kitchen floor. He hit his head, but Auntie Beth said no stitches!"

My whole body buckled. His seizures were commonplace irregularities to all of us, but I could count on one hand how often he had seized while I was more than ten miles, or ten minutes, away. Four times, exactly, and each seizure felt more portentous than the one before.

"Honey, I miss you so much and I will see you tomorrow. Could you put Auntie Beth on please and stay good. I know you're being so good. I love you."

"Okay," he said.

"Hey," she said.

"What the hell happened with Sam this morning?"

"I wanted to tell you, Peachy, it was crazy. I can't believe you do that every day!"

"Just—is he okay?" I started to feel that awful strangulation of the parental heart.

"Totally, Peachy. No. He's fine. It was me I was more worried about."

"How surprising," I said. My hands were shaking with worry and regret. What the hell was I thinking staying away for three days? Surely there was a special corner of hell reserved for selfish mothers like me.

"Don't, Peachy. That's not what I meant. I'm just saying it scared the shit out of me."

"Tell me what the hell happened. Everything."

She told me she was alone, she had woken early and was making coffee, when Sam entered the kitchen muttering raggedy dream details, something about a moat, something about elephants coming toward the house at great speeds, then their huge legs churning and stopping in the mud, clothing and money in the mix.

"He seemed a little weirded out that I was there. That you and Beau weren't. But not upset.

"On the other hand," Beth said, "Jake would have made a champion orphan." Apparently he bounded down to the kitchen and took in Beth's news of his parents' absence with his patented blitheness, a trait I hoped would accompany him throughout his life.

"Jake goes, *'If they're gone, then we can have Lucky Charms.'* "

"She said Lou got up off the couch where he had fallen asleep the night before, splashed his face in the kitchen tap, and took Jake into town to buy a box of that forbidden tooth rot.

Though my feelings about Beth were still steeped in awful ire, I was sorry to hear she was alone when Sam's eyes rolled up and back and away. She told me he dropped to his knees by the dog bowl, spilling Scoots's food all over the Mexican tiles we were meaning to replace with carpet for that reason. She didn't know he was falling into a fit, so picking up the damn kibble had temporarily distracted her, therefore preventing her from catching his head. Beth tried not to panic, she said, as she sat next to my almost-gone boy, inching closer to him, but afraid. She watched his body fight the current running through him before he finally succumbed. She pulled his head onto her lap and started wiping the blood off his forehead.

"Honestly, it's a little tiny cut. He doesn't need stitches. And Lou agreed. I'm so sorry, Peachy. I didn't catch his head. I fucking hate myself," she said.

"It happens," I said coldly, not mentioning all of the times I'd settle him down into a spell and go back to finishing the dishes. I pictured their little kitchen pietà, worried over what could have happened, but ashamed of the ownership I suddenly felt over his seizures. They happened to Sam, but they had always been my moments to manage and contain. I clutched the side of the bench.

"I kept saying, 'It's okay, it's okay,' " she said, describing how she rubbed Sam's twitching arms, trying to move some stillness into them, while reciting to herself the rules governing the next several minutes of his life.

Sam's pee had reached up under Beth's legs. She had tried to make a dam with her hands but couldn't stop it from soaking her pajama bottoms. For a second she said she thought it was her own pee, her own blood, and I almost laughed to myself thinking that she must have been totally petrified of adding Sam's death to the map of carnage she had already charted through our home. When Scoots started to lazily lick at the pee, Beth pushed his head away with a purposeful shove. After several minutes passed, each one less difficult than the one before, Sam's slippers finally slowed to their blessed twelve o'clock stop.

"Then I said, 'Come back, Sam. You can come home now, guy,' like you always say. And then his eyes opened and he opened and shut his fists and rubbed his jaw and the first thing he said was, 'Mom,' and I said, 'No honey, it's me. Auntie Beth.' "

By then I was sniffling audibly. Beth was oblivious, describing how it seemed like Sam was embarrassed while lifting his bum from the wetness.

"I told him there was a little blood because he smacked the tiles. And I told him I was sorry I didn't catch his head. And you know what? *He* apologized, Peachy, for peeing his pants. Poor kid. So I told him the pee was probably mine," she said, nervously laughing, adding she wasn't altogether sure it was untrue, she'd been that scared. She said her legs were so numb they felt welded to the tiles. She described how she had folded my son forward, keeping her hand on his wet back for a second while he took in his surroundings. Even after Beth added several minutes to the clock on the microwave, only remembering to time it out as Sam was coming to, it still sounded like one of his shorter spells.

"When I was firing up the shower, I asked him, 'How'd I do?' And he goes, 'Okay, I guess. Not as good as my mom. She never lets me hit my head.' So I told him that I sometimes wish your mother would let me hit *my* head more often," she said, leaving a bit of silence dangling at the end of the sentence.

"You seem to manage doing that all on your own."

The pride in her voice was hard to hear. I imagined her in her pee-soaked shorts, moving the soapy water around in circles on the floor, her heart calming down a little with every swirl.

"God. It must feel heroic to always be so *necessary*," she said, exhaling.

I ignored the statement, but I wanted to say, to tell her, that the horror of always being so necessary is the worst part about being a mother, something no one tells you about until you have children.

"That's good," I said. "I'm relieved to know that your guilt didn't interfere with helping my child get through his seizure."

"Peachy. That's not what I meant. I'm trying here."

"Trying what?"

"To be good," she said. "I'm trying to tell you that I think you're a fucking hero for what you do every day. I'm trying to tell you how sorry I am for what I did, for how I hurt you. I'm trying to show you I can be a good person."

Beth had a knack for walking down the brightly lit corridors of other people's dramas, dropping their most interesting hurts into her grocery cart.

"Beth. Thanks, okay? But the only hero here is Sam. And I'm glad you were there, but what do you want, a medal? That's just what has to be done. That's life. That's what it looks like."

"I know. I'm aware of that. I've been made aware of that, among other things," she said in a voice so meek it was barely recognizable as Beth's. "Where are you? Are you going to meet Marcus? You know I almost stopped in town to check the email. I was going to send him one, telling him everything about what I did, but I didn't even have a minute. Not even one fucking minute today. It was kind of great."

"Yeah, well, Saturdays with kids are like that. I gotta go, Beth. I'll be home around noon tomorrow. And I don't want you to be there when I get home."

"Peachy, please. We have to—we can't not talk about what happened."

I hung up just as the battery was signaling its near death knell, and just in time to prevent Sam's dilemma from giving Beth an opening back into my heart. Too often Beth had left me feeling like all those police officers in all those superhero movies, relegated to moving people along. "Nothing to see here," they'd say, while awestruck cleanup crews dealt with the upturned trains and toppled buildings the hero left in his wake. I wanted to tell her there were no capes in my closet. Sam's spells had nothing to instruct, nothing to show us. These were stupid and unruly events, I wanted to tell her. They came with almost no warning, and our powers merely consisted of the casual clichés of parenting;

cushion the fall, soften the blow, do what you can, hope for the best, apologize if necessary, but when someone goes down, you have to try to catch their goddamn head.

chapter fifteen

The bar part of the restaurant was front-loaded with attractive people, men the same size as the other men, all in dark suits and white shirts, the women the same size as each other, each looking vaguely related. I felt like I'd walked into a family reunion for which I was the sole adoptee. I craned around, suddenly panicked that I couldn't remember what Marcus looked like. I can see why Beth says that it's possible that even people who are supposed to meet still don't find each other in these homogenous crowds of people trying so hard to look so different from one another that they all end up looking the same. The women seated at, or standing near, the bar seemed to possess Beth's anxious energy and shoulder-length hair, expensive-looking and clean, hanging unnaturally straight and giving off an unnatural golden glow. Their heads were bent up toward the men they were talking to like so many chatty, skinny flowers. And the men's booming voices barking back down at them seemed to be the heavy beat that underpinned this social symphony. Just then, a tall man in a dark suit leaned away from the crowd of talkers to touch my elbow.

"Georgia?"

"Georgia," I repeated.

"I mean, I'm . . . you're Georgia, right?" The man squinted into my eyes, which then traveled from my forehead and down the length of my body to my new shoes, just beginning to pinch my toes.

"Yes. Of course! That's me," I said, shaking his hand with so much aggressive delight I think I frightened him at first. Marcus's hair was not as red as it appeared in his picture, and he was taller than I expected. He stooped over to take in my face, giving me the impression that he was studying it a little. What saved him from being considered a gawky redhead was the way he stood with his hands in his pockets, flashing a ridiculously great grin—the wide kind—that confident people tend to sport. I grinned back, thrilled to see the features from his photograph finally moving. I was also stunned that the prank had worked. In me was the feeling that I had successfully built something complicated from a set of dubious instructions, like a gas barbecue or a small airplane.

"I'm Marcus."

"Yes," I said, wittily adding, "I know."

"And you are Georgia," he said, sounding like a teacher introducing a foreign-exchange student to a silent classroom. I couldn't tell if his eyes were green or blue.

"Yes. That's who I am!" I said, slapping the side of my thigh and trying hard to keep my smile undisturbed by the pain the rest of my body was in. Lying hurts, I realized, its clean execution almost impossible for the amateur. Then, sounding an awful lot like Nana Beecher, I said, "Gosh, it's really crowded, eh?"

"Yes, it's Saturday night, so—"

"You're very tall. And you're much better looking than in your picture too," I quickly added.

He thanked me, then looked around to see if anyone had heard.

"Seriously. And your shirt's really nice, too. And those shoes," I said.

"Okay. Thanks," he said. He pulled his lips into a stiff grin and held a hand up as though to deflect further compliments into the crowd. "Let's sit down before my head gets so big it falls over on you, shall we? We're back here."

He steered me quickly to the restaurant part of the bar where he had reserved a tippy table. I felt like he'd taken a rolled-up newspaper, slapped me on the nose, then led me by a leash to the doghouse.

"So you've been here before, I imagine," Marcus said, pulling my chair out for me and glancing around again. I couldn't tell if he was hiding from someone or was fully expecting the room to burst into "Happy Birthday."

"Um. No. But I didn't have any trouble finding it," I said.

"That's right, you live in Park Slope."

"Yes, that's right," I said, burying my face in the menu.

"Good. Well," he said, sitting down. "I'm not in love with this restaurant, but they do a nice osso buco. And their wines aren't ridiculously marked up." He cracked his knuckles and erected his menu between us and began lobbing questions over the top of our laminated divide.

"Do you do a lot of Internet dating, Georgia?"

"Oh. No. I don't. You?"

"Ahhh, no. Can't say I have. I find it all too easy to misrepresent oneself."

"I can imagine," I muttered, taking a sudden and superkeen interest in the specials insert. But the words were playing wacky tricks with my eyes. *Veal ravioli* was becoming *real vile liar.* *Beet salad* looked a lot like *silly bitch. Poached tilapia* became *pathetic twit. Marinated flank steak* reminded me that I was *married with two kids* while *grilled radicchio* told me that this was *totally ridiculous.*

"You know, I don't even know what half of

this stuff is," I said, shrugging, trying to sound charming, but coming off exactly like Beth's hick replacement. I knew there was a chance this could begin as badly as it was likely to end, but I wasn't prepared to haggle over my feelings about it. Traitorous tears seemed to sting the corners of my eyes, and my mind desperately tried to locate the part of my brain that controlled the ducts. Close. Shut them now. Batten down the hatches, or hatten down the batches. What the hell am I doing? I thought. I have a husband, albeit a cruddy one, and two young boys who needed their mother at home, not wandering New York in an expensive dress, sitting across from a snooty lawyer who likely thought my ass too fat to merit further investigation into my personality, if indeed he imagined I had one.

"So. Let me see. You speak Italian, Georgia. Maybe you can tell me what some of these items on the menu mean," Marcus said.

He knew. I didn't know exactly what he knew, but I knew he knew something. I froze with a kind of hiker's terror, when stumbling upon a bored bear in the woods.

"Would you excuse me for a second," I said, standing up. Marcus casually pointed out the general direction of the washrooms, and I left him sitting at the table. And if he wasn't gone when I returned, he'd leave in an acid hurry after I told him the truth of things. Because I was going to. I was going to pee and pray and tell him everything.

I negotiated around the Beth clones lining their lips in the mirror and talking to each other about the Marcus clones waiting for them at the bar upstairs.

"He needs it for work. I understand that. But why he brings his fucking BlackBerry to dinner is what I don't get."

"He's addicted to that fucking thing. It's the same as any drug," another one said. "Those things are turning people into human rats. Send, send, send. Receive, receive, receive. Gimme, gimme, gimme. More, more, more."

"You know what I hate? I can be sitting right next to him and he can be typing something to someone he's *fucking* and I wouldn't even know it. He could be all, *It's work, it's a work thing.* And I wouldn't even know it. It's not like email. I can check his email. But that thing . . ." A cell phone went off and the girl talk tone shifted immediately into professional barking.

"Hi. It's okay. [pause] Click on Gemfile. On the desktop. [pause] What does it say? No. Yeah. That one. Read me the third clause. [pause] Yeah, but we were talking aggregates. [long pause] I don't care what his client says. Just— you know what? We don't have to deal with this right now. [pause] Make sure you put it in rough billing. Yup. First thing. Okay. Bye."

"Fucking hell," one of them said.

"Can't even have a fucking bite to eat," came the reply.

I listened with growing sadness. Boy talk and work talk. Beth talk. I wanted to yell over the stall that I wanted a career too, once. I wanted clients and appointments. I wanted a different kind of busy than being a mother. I wanted to fill out forms and make decisions. I wanted things to talk about too, bosses and wages and hours and commutes. I wanted other people's stories to be my airplane small talk, not my own. No wonder I invented a woman with attributes so foreign to me that pretending to be her required a completely different language. I just wanted a night off, a bit of time away from being Peachy Archer Laliberté, to try on a bit of being more like Beth. But while Beth seemed to find a kind of pride in mastering what it was like to be me, I couldn't pull off the art of being Beth. I was so much myself and so suited to the task of being me, I wearied of resisting it anymore. I didn't even bother to wash my hands before heading back to the table.

I was not at all surprised to find that me and my newfound truth, the one I felt ready to burst with, would now be dining alone. Marcus's side of the table was empty. Vanity is a strange thing when it finds you among strangers. Why should I care what people in the restaurant thought about the empty chair across from me? Blame it on being the mother of two young sons, but I instinctively bent to look under the tablecloth.

"No fair! You said you were going to count to twenty!"

It was Marcus holding two sweaty wine glasses.

"Oh, I wasn't—I—frankly, I thought you'd left," I said.

"No. I would never—I just went to the bar to get you a drink. I think our waitress was abducted. Hope white's okay."

He seemed hurt by my comment, my final cue to end the charade. This whole thing was meant to hurt Beth, but now I was doing damage to someone whose only crime was to rid himself of a damaged woman.

"Marcus. Listen. My name's not Georgia," I said. "Well, it is Georgia. But I don't speak Italian. I speak only English, even though I'm Canadian. I mean, I should know more French, I guess, but I don't. And I didn't go to a fancy school. And I don't live in Brooklyn. In fact, I'm only visiting for the weekend. And there's more, but it doesn't matter now. All I want to do is to apologize for all of this," I said, sweeping my hand to indicate I had included the entire room, and perhaps the block and city too. "And then I'm going to leave. How much do I owe you for the wine."

He rested his chin on a fist, his eyes misty from thinking.

"I figured something was up," he said.

"What was your first clue?"

"Probably when you said 'eh.' "

"It was never meant to hurt you, or to make you feel bad. I can't tell you how sorry I am. This whole thing was between me and my— who—God—I can imagine how creepy this all —so 'eh,' huh? I hardly ever say 'eh.' "

The word now dangled in the air like a gaudy bauble.

"Yes, 'eh,' " he said. His hand mostly covered his mouth, so I couldn't tell if he was angry or bemused.

"I apologize. Really I do. And um, so . . . why don't you just tell me how much I owe you for the wine and then I will get lost, okay?"

"A hundred and fifty dollars," he said, leaning back in his chair. I nearly spit the sip I had just taken into my mouth back into the glass. Between the dress and the wine, I had blown the family "extras" budget for the entire year.

"Holy shit!"

He started to laugh.

"You *are* naïve. Wow," he said. His insult sounded more like a compliment, but I wasn't trying to be cute. If the dress could cost half of Beau's weekly paycheck, why wouldn't I believe a glass of wine would cost as much as Jake's soccer registration?

"Well, I'm glad you find it amusing," I said with kindness. "But you've earned the right to make jokes at my expense. I don't blame you. But I will pay for my wine at the bar and then I will get the hell out of here. Goodbye. It was nice meeting you. Sorry it couldn't be under less criminal circumstances."

"Wait! Wait, wait, wait," he yelled, trapping one of my hands under one of his and winding down his giggles. A few faces turned to face us. "I have a confession to make too, Georgia, or, Peachy. Um, *Nadia* called me. You know Nadia? Your *sister's* friend. Your sister *Beth?* That would be my ex-girlfriend, and, it would seem, your little Internet partner in crime."

"I think I know who you mean," I said, scanning the room for the exit. Do all Americans have guns? I wondered. Can they carry guns on their person, or was that just in Westerns?

"Seems your lovely sister, *Beth,* told Kate what you two had been up to, and, of course, Kate told Nadia this afternoon. Because Kate can't keep anything to herself. And, well, *Nadia,* being crazy about you, apparently, wasn't impressed. She said she tried to call you but your phone was off. But Nadia being Nadia didn't want to see you do anything stupid. In fact, she asked me *not* to come, but, as you can imagine, I was pretty angry about

308

you and your sister's sick little stunt. And, frankly, also pretty intrigued to meet someone related to Miss Beth Ann Archer. Especially a sister. Especially someone with a name like Peachy."

I stared at the white tablecloth, replaying my entrance in my head. Nadia knew too? I felt devastated by that because I loved Nadia, and I didn't want Nadia to think I was anything like Beth. My sadness was slowly replaced by anger. Beth had done it again, however inadvertently. By telling Kate, she had robbed me of the opportunity of getting her back. Even if revenge was an option I might never have exercised, its possibility was comforting.

"But wait, there's more!" Marcus said. "Any minute now, Kate is going to *coincidentally* find herself here. In case I don't show up. So she can take you by the hand and bring you home. Or in case I *do* show up, and turn into a raging asshole, which I have delayed by opting for the white wine," he said, draining his drink and smacking it on the table. " 'Cause when I got here, I planned on ordering the red. Red wine leaves awful stains. Then I thought throwing a drink on you would be very ungentlemanly of me. And I am nothing if not a gentleman. Then you had to show up in *that* dress, and I didn't have the heart. It's a hell of a dress."

I blinked. Tears had been alerted and were on standby.

"Okay. I better go. Again, I'm sorry. I didn't mean any harm. I just—you know what I wanted?" I said, blessed laughter busting through the absurdity. "I just wanted to go on a goddamn date. Do you realize I've never been on one? I didn't either until very, very recently. But that's not really your concern. So I'll just go now. Again, I apologize from the bottom of my shitty heart. I really do."

I stood up and inched away from the table. Marcus stood up too, and I braced for a possible white wine shower after all. But as afraid as I was of his ire, I was more afraid of Kate's yammering. The standby army of tears allowed a few watery soldiers through. I felt them running down my cheeks. The thought that came to me was one I used to comfort the boys: I only had to go to sleep and wake up one more time and all this would be over.

"Wait. Don't turn around. If you want to avoid Kate, who I *think* I see coming into the bar—"

"Fuck."

He wiped his mouth with his napkin and threw it on the table. He used a hand to nudge me to the back of the restaurant toward the kitchen. I'm not sure why I let him shove me past the bustling wait staff, past tall pots of boiling water and the stunned-looking dishwashers, and the cooks manning grills the size of desks, mildly scolding us that we weren't supposed to be back there, asking, hey, where you going? *Home,* I wanted to scream. *I am going home where I belong. Because I don't belong here. I belong to two boys who I should be tucking in at this moment, and to a Texan hairdresser happily stranded in a world so opposite to the one I'm visiting, if I emerged from the restaurant suddenly speaking in tongues, it wouldn't surprise me. And though my husband may have thrown himself down a dark marital well, the paper we signed says I still belonged to him, too.*

Marcus hauled open a vaultlike door, and we found ourselves gasping for air in a cool Manhattan alley, his demeanor suggesting that he still planned to beat me to death up against the sweaty bricks.

"Thank you, Marcus. And again. I am sorry. Now if you could just show me where to get a cab, you will never see me again."

"What if I said no?"

"Well, then . . . I . . . I can find one," I said, slowly backing away from him, making my way toward the street.

"Hold up!" he yelled. I froze. I had no Mace, no gun, and no idea it would be this easy for a madman to overcome me. "What I mean is, you said you wanted to go on a date, so let me *take* you on a fucking date." And with that he grabbed my hand and pulled me fast down the alley toward the lights of a busy street.

• • •

What I remember most about my first real date was the money; Marcus rained money on everyone who came near us, talked to us, drove us, fed us, opened and shut doors for us, who brought us drinks and took the empty glasses away from us. Money to the cabs we hopped into and out of. Money to the man at the door of a dark club we ducked into for a drink, sitting at a bar lit from below in a way that made my face look moody and intelligent in the mirror across from us. He gave money to the woman who brought us tiny scallops stabbed with metal sticks. To the man who dropped two pink drinks in front of our arms, and to the lady who later brought us two fancy coffees bundled in napkins and sprinkled with chocolate. Then more money to another driver who took us to a different part of the city where Marcus ordered food so foreign to me (Soft-shell crabs! Foie gras! Ceviche!) it was a supreme act of trust just to stuff my face. Then money to the ice-cream guy, money to the homeless kid, money to a person selling books on a towel after I cooed over a hard copy of *Little Women*, a book Beth and I both loved and one I lamented that the boys would never read because of its feminine title. And I let him, because there was nothing else for my face to do but to eat and drink and listen to Marcus talk about things I never knew

312

about Beth; why he loved her, why he didn't, and why, in the end, he ended things the way he did.

Their relationship was hatched in the heady space between nine-to-five power flirting and last call at happy hour at the pub below the building in which Beth housed her company. When she hired Marcus to do the season's contracts, he knew she might be trouble. But he thought it might be the sexy kind of trouble that sometimes resulted in vertical sex in the hallways, followed by those long bashful brunches where you pretend you're reading the newspaper but you're really just planning your next move, "You know what I mean, Peachy?"

"Ahh . . . no."

He laughed. I was making him laugh a lot that night, and it felt nice to finally get the hang of the type of laughter that came from laughing at me, and what it sounded like when he was kind of with me on something.

"Anyway. I liked her a lot. And right away too," he said. We were sharing a cigarette with the rest of the smokers clogging the club's sidewalk. "Pardon me for saying, but she's fucking hot. My friends all thought so too. Not that that's important."

"But . . . it's important."

"Exactly," he said, laughing the "with me" laugh. "So, at first it was great. Crazy great. But then she started to show up late for things already a little drunk. Which, whatever, I didn't think anything of it at first. But at the end of the night, she didn't want to shut it off. She had to keep going. So, you know, little blow here and there, no big deal. I don't partake myself, but my friends sometimes do. But then it was a little more if we were going to a party and she had too much to drink and didn't want to go home. I mean, I like my cocktails like the next guy, but she was really starting to scare me a little. And I was getting sick of being her fucking babysitter: *Where's my coat, where's my keys, where are we, take me home, I don't want to go home, what time is it, it's early, it's late, let's go here, let's go there.* And on and on. A person starts to feel pulled. And stupid frankly."

I was sick at the thought of Beth snorting coke in the bathroom of some fancy restaurant, or some seedy bar she'd frequent to seem cool and edgy, where she wouldn't have the benefit of knowing the bartender because she hung out with him in high school.

"I know she likes to party," I said. "But I didn't know about the blow. She's never done it around me. God, she'd never risk bringing it over the border. At least I like to think she'd never."

"*Likes* to party? No. Peachy, your sister lives to party. And she wouldn't listen to me. I just cut my losses. And okay, I was cruel about it, but I wanted out."

After the night she attacked the bouncer, he said he knew it was time to walk. He called her up and left a message on her cell number telling her in so many words to lose his number. When he tried to get out of his contract, she threatened to sue. When he found a good replacement to finish the season, she resumed her efforts to seduce him. He told me he had only posted the online ad to prove to her that he was done, because the more he tried to extricate himself from Beth, the more she promised to change, to behave, to be good. I thought of our phone call. I didn't think the boys would be in any danger in her care, unless you counted near brain damage from Sam hitting the tile floor. Besides, she was being supervised by Lou and Beau.

"Look," he said. "She's a fucking workhorse, and she's highly functional. She's not going to lose her company anytime soon. She's careful during the week, and then she dries out every few weeks at her place in Michigan. But if the shit she pulled with your husband isn't a wake-up call, then I don't know what is."

"Yeah, well. About that place in Michigan . . ." I said, cocking an eyebrow.

"Yeah, I can imagine," he said.

"How come she never invited you to her *weekend* place in Grosse Pointe?"

"You know, I asked. She said it was undergoing major renovations and that this summer she'd definitely bring me. Definitely, definitely. Fucking delusional. But by the time I was ready to pack my sunscreen, I was over her, you know?"

"Renovations. She's probably not wrong about that. Because there's gonna be a big doghouse under construction as soon as I get home," I said, plucking the smoke from his fingers.

"That's a tough one, Peachy, but I would caution you to be cautious. Men are pigs, for sure. If it's in the trough, it's dinner. But Beau doesn't sound like a pig. He sounds like a guy who made a stupid, stupid mistake."

"No, he's a pig."

"Is he a nice pig at least?"

I thought for a second. "He's a handy pig."

"Well, that's something. You could *build* on that. Ice cream?"

"Yes," I said, feeling flattened under all this new information. I thought of the Chinese boxes and ceramic holders decorating Beth's apartment. I decided to scour her apartment when I got back, and if I found her stash, I would flush it.

"It's nice, you know. Doing things with you Beth never wanted to do. Not that this is a *date* date, right?"

"Right."

• • •

It was only eleven-thirty when Marcus and I finally reached Beth's place after a quick stop near Washington Square Park for ice cream. My cone had almost made a clean exit into my mouth when I noticed chocolate staining two of my fingers. Whatever I had on usually substituted as a repository for my boys' messes, so it was no surprise that my automatic response was to look for a place on my beautiful dress to wipe them. Marcus stopped my hand and carefully examined the chocolate. Then he did what I had often done with the boys' own delicious fingers. He put mine in his mouth to clean them. I felt that familiar tornado stir just behind my belly button, the one that kicked up when Beau did this with my fingers. I looked around for Jonathan. I wasn't sure if Beth's doorman knew I was married, but I needed to look into a familiar face to remind me that I was.

"My feet are killing me. I thought these shoes were my friends," I said, trying to change the subject and to get my mind off of what was happening to my middle.

He plucked my fingers from his mouth and said, "Take them off. I'll stick your toes in my mouth too."

I regarded him, his face, his gingery hair, his nice forearms, his wide mouth.

"Pretty hot what I just did, don't you think?"

317

"Yes."

"Beth has air-conditioning, doesn't she? I can't remember now. We mostly dated in the winter months."

"She does. But—"

"No, no. Yeah, yeah. Just wondering. It's a valid question. I can ask questions."

I exhaled, thinking that though I didn't want my night to end, I didn't want to end my night in bed with Marcus. Bad enough I married the first man Beth had sex with; I didn't feel like capping off my weekend with the last man she'd been with too.

"So, you aren't going to invite me up into the air-conditioning, I gather? What if I told you I'd *looove* to see pictures of your kids?"

"No," I said. "I can't. I mean, I *could*. But I can't."

"Dammit. And I spent all that *money* on you!" He pretended to stomp around like a toddler in a tantrum. "Not fair."

"Oh. Is that how dates work?"

"Yes, Peachy, no one told you? That's how a date works. When a boy spends a lot of money on you on a date, it's incumbent upon you to sleep with said boy. A blowjob or a hand job is sometimes okay too. Or you can just make out with him on the couch and let the boy play with your boobies or something. There are various options. And we could discuss them *all* if you would just"—he was using his index finger to indicate up—"let me come in for a minute. Or thirty. Thirty tops. Thirty and then I'll go."

"Seriously?" I said. "You want to come up?"

He nodded so quickly his face went blurry. It was a different kind of sexy knowing that I was standing opposite a man who wanted me but didn't need me one bit. And though getting to this point in the evening had been exciting, as well as expensive, I had the feeling of being sated enough to end things there. To do more than kiss Marcus once and full on the lips wouldn't have been criminal. In fact, it would have been completely understandable. But it would have left me feeling greedy. I would have carried home that glassy look the kids sometimes had after they'd gorged themselves to the gills at a birthday party.

"I had a lovely time, Marcus Edward Street."

"I have to pee?"

"And I can't thank you enough for spending lots of money on me and showing me around the city. I loved every minute of my date."

"You know what? I need to make a phone call. My cell's dead too. See?" he said, shaking it. "Totally dead. Broken."

"Beth lost a great guy. But maybe if she gets her shit together, you guys could try again?"

"Can't."

"Why not?"

"Because. What if, you know, God forbid, and I do hope He completely forbids it, that Beth and I end up getting married. I can't go around coveting my sister-in-law for the rest of my life. That would be fucking hell. Oh my God! Look! Is that smoke coming from Beth's window? We better go see if Beth's apartment's on fire!"

"Thank you," I said.

"Don't thank me," he said, smiling an impossibly white smile and placing his hands on the sides of my arms. "I mean, *make out* with me. Sure. Sleep with me, yes. But don't thank me."

He was handsome. He was funny. He smelled clean and industrious. His hands were big enough to encircle my upper arms. He held them firm. I bet he bit. I bet he slapped and lasted. I was young and owed this, so far beyond reproach that I couldn't imagine St. Peter himself would keep me standing long outside the gates of whatever heaven I'd be sent to. And still, and still . . .

"Good night, Marcus."

"No."

"Good night, Marcus."

"Why not?"

"Because I can't."

"You should."

"I know. But I can't. I'm sorry."

"You should be," he grinned.

"Good night, Marcus."

"Good night, Peachy."

With that he pushed a long, firm kiss into the middle of my forehead. When he pulled away, he kept his lips puckered and one eye tightly closed. I rotated him easily, steadied him from behind, and launched Marcus gently back into the Manhattan night.

I slowly passed by Jonathan, who had probably seen a bit of my goodbye on the security camera. I was heartened that he kept his feet up on the kiosk. Without looking up from his TV, he sleepily asked, "Have a nice time, Peachy?"

"Such a nice time, Jonathan," I said, pushing the UP button.

"That's good, Peachy."

"Good night, Jonathan."

"Good night, Peachy."

Marcus's pleas had made me damp, and my legs felt floppy from exhaustion. I kicked off my shoes into the dark of Beth's apartment, not caring what they hit. While I waited for the computer to power up, I fished out my soggy sandals and threw on a pair of shorts and a T-shirt. Then I went on a digital rampage, killing Almost Me's profile and email account. Mapless and unafraid, I went back downstairs, passing Jonathan's darkened kiosk. I headed toward the Hudson River, a few blocks west of Beth's condo. My hair hung limp in the boggy heat. There were people out everywhere. A lovely hum and chatter echoed out of the restaurants and bars I passed, and through some low-slung windows you could see crowded parties happening inside. Along the Hudson River park, I merged with the wall of foot traffic, watching for Rollerbladers and even a couple of carriages pushed by couples taking a stroll while a baby slept inside. I stopped to watch some lithe and daring trapeze artists perform a midnight show for the small crowd below. It started to feel normal to me, the idea of walking at night alone, of casually stumbling upon a brightly lit cage of circus people, flying and spinning and laughing and falling. Beth had mentioned there was a trapeze school, had said she wanted to try it, had been meaning to try it, and even at Earl's just two nights earlier, she vowed she'd do it if I promised to watch.

"It's something I've been meaning to do," she said, sensing the wave of nausea that came over me at the idea of Beth aloft, Beth falling.

"Yeah, I can see how breaking your neck could be high on your to-do list. Yeah."

"Don't try and talk me out of it, Peachy."

"Go ahead. Break your neck. I don't care. In fact, when I tell you *not* to do something, you do it all the more."

"Not true."

"True."

"No-oh."

"Yea-ess."

"Like when?"

"Like . . . oh, everything. It must be so exhausting to be a constant contrarian."

"You know something? It is. And I'll tell you another thing I've been meaning to do. See that sign?" She closed one eye and pointed her finger like a gun at the Starlite Variety sign across the street. "I'm going to go over there and tell those fuckers that it's about time they spelled 'starlight' right. Doesn't that drive you crazy? You have two kids who are going to grow up thinking that that's how 'starlight' is spelled, Peach. I mean, that would make me crazy. It's making me crazy right now."

"Well, go tell them, Beth," I said, my voice filled with mock encouragement. "You just go tell them it's wrong. I dare you."

The words had barely left my mouth before Beth tamped out her cigarette, leapt off the stool, and tipsily made her way across the street without watching for cars.

"I was kidding," I said to Stu, and we watched as Beth finally exited the store trailed by a startled cashier, the youngest son of the Korean family that had long ago bought the store. They had kept up the same stock of weird-looking dolls and greying birthday cards, but added an impressive selection of ramen noodles. She pointed to the "Starlite" part of the sign.

"What is she doing," I mumbled to Stu.

"She's being Beth."

But it was all for show, this stunt another in a long repertoire that comprised the Story of Beth. It didn't matter whether it was "Starlite" or "Starlight." What mattered was how I told the story of how Beth had the temerity to tell the owner's son that "Starlite" was incorrect and how funny it was when she got up from the bar and crossed the street to tell that poor Korean kid his sign was wrong. And that's when I felt done. It was hours before she had had sex with my husband, hours before I left the farm in a fury, but I was done telling the Story of Beth.

We were mostly quiet on the ride home except when Beth reiterated her desire to take to the trapeze that weekend. Instead of daring her or fighting her, instead of finding flaws with her plans, I shrugged and said, "Should be fun."

She had never inquired if it was something I'd consider doing, because it was always understood I'd remain below, her precious watcher, her vigilant observer, her constant cheerleader. And why would she think otherwise? Until that night I always thought I was among the Stus and Marcuses, the Nadias, Kates, and Jebs, looking in amazement and sometimes disgust while Beth performed her daring feats, secretly tsking her, expecting, possibly hoping, to see what would happen if she failed or fell. But the truth was, I had never stood with the gawkers and the cheerleaders. Instead, I'd always been her stalwart net—slightly frayed and bowed—but I had always, until now, kept my sister from hitting the unforgiving pavement.

chapter sixteen

Two and a half days was not a long time to be away. The weather did nothing new to the sky above us. Nobody in town moved or died. The boys hadn't grown, my father hadn't aged. As far as I could tell by scanning two city skylines from a fast-moving car, no new buildings were completed, no old ones torn down. The trees and flowers remained at their ripe, midsummer stage. A few stubborn acres of brush and soy still prevented the spreading subdivisions from swallowing up our town. Our garden had a bit of bedhead, nothing ten minutes of weeding couldn't tame. The house was clean, too clean, really, the beneficiary of a sleepless and dry Beth, who apparently kept busy bleaching counters and organizing the pots and pans until well past both midnights. Lou told me this on our drive back from the airport, during which I couldn't stop searching the boys' faces, checking and rechecking for evidence of my absence, to seek out whether it had had any effect on them. There had been that unsettling tide of tears I unleashed at the sight of their faces in the crowd at Arrivals, but that couldn't be helped. I saw them through the glass before they saw me, a gift really, because I was able to watch the way love moved from the heart to the face, when the object of affection (me!) came into view. I had probably seen them brighten up like that before, their smiles splitting wide open, arms and legs doing that goofy, kinetic dance. But not since each of their births had I appreciated what a painful effect their faces could have on my heart. You could die from this, I thought. It is entirely possible.

"Boys!" I screamed, pushing through a clot of bovine travelers heading toward the turnstiles. "Here! Over here! Jake! Sam!"

It was all so animal, how their ears seemed to pick up the timbre of my voice, and how their eyes scanned the crowd, eliminating everyone who wasn't me until they landed on their target, and how I pulled past the awful people keeping me from my kids a few seconds longer, and how I got on my knees—not to pray—but I should have thanked someone for this, and how they nearly knocked me over with their wet kisses and their messy heads and their sticky hands coated with the remnants of whatever treat Lou had used to pacify them during the wait.

"Mom, mom, mom," Jake sang, while Sam asked, "What did you buy us?"

I used an open palm to wipe the tears off my cheeks, the other to shove a plastic bag full of stupid souvenirs, snow globes, tea towels, erasers, an "I Love NY" mug meant for Lou, not Beau, expensive and useless things I had picked up on the LaGuardia side of the trip. But to see the boys express such gratitude for the idiot trinkets, that was when I realized this was the love affair of my life, this thing with them.

I pressed a finger near the nick on Sam's forehead.

"Does it hurt?"

"No. No stitches, either," he said.

"Well, you got a strong head, Sam."

When I looked at Lou, more tears sprung from my eyes, and he hugged me to him while the boys busied themselves with the bag of goodies. After a few tight seconds I broke away to breathe.

"Dad, thanks for coming to get me. I know what it meant."

"Ack. It was nothing," he said. "Shoulda crossed the border a long time ago. I'm actually ashamed for waiting all these years."

"Where's Beth?" Half of me hoped she'd be sitting alone in a plastic chair watching all of this joy.

"We brought her here a couple hours ago for a morning flight. Then we just killed some time."

"How does she seem?" I asked, distracted by the boys' hair. I assumed Beth had done the grooming because their hair was parted where it didn't normally part.

"She doesn't seem anything, Peach. She *is* feeling awful. But, fingers crossed, she gets it. Things gotta change with her, and they will."

At the airport, in the parking lot, on the drive through Detroit and Windsor, then all along the county roads, I hadn't asked about Beau. Instead, I told Lou about Beth's doorman, and how nice he was to me, and how, when I said goodbye to him, he had chucked me under the chin the way Lou did when we were little.

The chatter from the back seat was ceaseless and musical, the boys filling me in on how Auntie Beth had forgotten a load of laundry in the dryer, and how when she drove back to town, it had been neatly folded by a kind stranger. And how she had made a rhubarb pie from scratch.

"Did you like it, Jake?" I asked.

"Yeah. It was okay," he said, shaking his snow globe with phony enthusiasm. "My mouth hurt from it though. Maybe I could go visit Auntie Beth sometime."

"Maybe," I said. "Because you really have to see New York for yourself."

"Did you ever get lost?"

"Not once. Not even a little bit."

"Were you scared?" Sam asked.

"Sometimes. Not of New York though."

"Of what then?"

"Oh, I don't know. Of how much a person could miss her people."

Jake pulled a crumpled pack of cigarettes out of my purse.

"Nasty! You shouldn't smoke, Momma."

"I know, baby. I'm stopping." I made a mental note to send some flowers to Nadia, to thank her for the party and the dress.

"And I don't think you should go away from us ever again, either," Sam said.

"Yeah! Never!" Jake screamed.

"Deal," I said, uttering the first of many lies I'd tell them over the next few years, because now that I'd been away, I'd go away again, never too far or for too long, and never under the same kind of dramatic circumstances. But the seal around the farm had been broken. It wouldn't take long, a few months maybe, before I'd begin to leave them on a regular basis: three nights a week to finish the degree; after that, two days and every Saturday to study for my master's. And though I had wanted to, had fully intended to make a living helping people help themselves, I'd one night find myself chatting with Sam's high school principal in the frozen food section of the grocery store. She had just fired the guidance counselor over a scandal involving steroids and a star athlete, and she wondered if I'd consider dropping my old plans for new ones—part-time at first, full-time later—once I passed the requisite probation. I said yes, even though Sam didn't need much catching by high school, or much of anything else for that matter. And though Jake would eventually require the nets and grips we had long stopped using to catch Beth, as he careened from lawyers to prayers and back again, he'd get through. And though we'd owe Beth big during those fraught days and nights, it would take months after that weekend away before I'd speak to her again. She'd try and fail several times to get sober, nothing taking until she sold her company and moved to West Hollywood to work as a wardrobe consultant for feature films, and where she'd find A.A. meetings as ubiquitous as Starbucks, and where she'd surround herself with people as flaky as she'd become. But it would take more than a year after that weekend before she'd be allowed back on the farm, and it was only upon Lou's insistence that both his daughters be at the wedding, and upon his lovely bride's that we be wearing the same godawful dress, in which I could not avoid meeting Beth's eyes, both of us desperate not to fall apart during the somber ceremony.

"You actually look fat in it," I whispered.

"That's the nicest thing you've said to me in a long time."

Lou always said things happen for a reason, and for the longest time I was loath to attribute anything good coming from that weekend— least of all anything like love. But it did. And though Lou held tight to the fact that banishing Beth from the farm was too harsh a penalty, from it sprung the oddest, most brilliant of blessings. Because to spend time with his wounded oldest, he had to go to her, a reluctant journey that quickly turned monthly after he finally caved to my pleadings to have an innocent coffee with an authentic widow named Lee from Long Island, who was kind to me in my time of need and had remained so by email. In a nondescript diner in Midtown Manhattan, my father fell in love again, later sharing long phone calls with Lee, then long road trips to Vermont, Quebec, Maine, then a flight to Paris, a city they'd both been meaning to see before they, or anyone else they loved, suddenly died. And because her country had broken her heart, Lee had no trouble leaving it for the farm, Lou reminding everyone during his toast that happy endings are really the results of sad people trying to do the next right thing.

But those days were still ahead of us. Pulling up the driveway, I only remember noticing that the farm had lost much of its shabby menace; the grass had been cut, the laundry lines were empty, the junk stacked against the carport had been put away. Inside, the rooms sparkled with more than my customary spit and polish. Bills, flyers, and magazines weren't merely spanked into neater piles, they were gone. Even the often-ignored toaster glowed with muscular attention.

Lou carried my suitcase upstairs and tossed it on the bed. The boys started pulling my things out, pausing to take in the new dress that Jake named the Goodbye dress.

It was dusk by the time Beau came home. The boys scrambled downstairs, yelling, "Mom's back, Dad. Look what she bought us, go see her, she's here, she's home!" I could hear Beau asking, "What time did you guys get in? Where's Grandpa? Are you hungry? Is your mother upstairs? I don't want to wake her up if she's sleeping." But he knew I wasn't sleeping. He knew I was already waiting for him to make the trip back upstairs, a journey that wouldn't be completed for months and months but one that would start that evening with a slow ascent, a soft knock at the door, a muttered welcome back, and a choice of chicken or steak, and whether I wanted him to eat with me and the kids, or down at the trailer, to which I replied, "Chicken and the trailer, for now," to which he replied, "Yes, okay, no, I understand, and I'm happy you're back, I truly am," and then he shut the door.

I fell back on the bed listening to the boys and men banging around in the kitchen, while I thought out my inventory: I am a pretty good mother. Beau is a pretty good man. The boys are perfect. I will let Lou do the job of loving Beth. The house is sturdier than our marriage, for now, but that's okay because when the driveway's paved, the dormers done, we could make a mint. If we sell. Which we never will. And if a storm knocks out the power, we have a backup generator, and if the well runs dry, we have a barrel on the roof to catch the rain.

Reading Group Guide
The Almost Archer Sisters

SUMMARY

Georgia "Peachy" Archer Laliberte has almost gotten her life under control. Peachy, her husband, Beau, and their two rambunctious sons live on the family farm in a small town in Canada, just across the border from the United States. Their closest neighbor is Peachy's draft-dodging hairdresser father, Lou, who lives in a trailer on their land. Although her son Sam has epilepsy, Peachy, Beau, and Lou have worked out a successful system to care for him and maintain as normal a family life as possible, and Peachy's status as a superhuman caregiver has its own rewards.

When her life on the farm isn't quite enough, Peachy can always live vicariously through her glamorous, New York City–dwelling sister, Beth. Thin, successful, and passionate, Beth has clawed her way to the top, stepping on anyone it takes to get there—including, every so often, her younger sister. Still, Peachy and Beth are close, and they support each other through crises of all kinds.

They support each other, that is, until Beth decides to sleep with Peachy's husband, Beau—who just happens to be Beth's ex-boyfriend. Furious, Peachy decides to go to New York City —alone—and leaves Beth home to care for her family. As she spends a terrified, exciting weekend alone in the middle of Beth's life, Peachy must confront questions of love, loyalty, and family to find her way back home.

Group Discussion Questions

1. *The Almost Archer Sisters* is written entirely in Peachy's first-person perspective. Do you trust Peachy's narration of the events in the novel? Are there specific events that you question? For example, how might Beth have told the story of the abortion differently? Of the discovery of Nell's suicide?
2. On the first page of the novel, Peachy describes herself as "unremarkable," "kind," and, perhaps most significantly, as a "stayer." What do you think are the benefits of being a "stayer" like Peachy, or a "leaver" like Beth? What did you think about Peachy's perception of herself in the novel overall? Does she like herself? Do you like her? Why or why not?
3. When Peachy is telling the story of Beth's teenage years, she observes, "I had experienced adolescence largely through Beth, much the way I like to think she'd later experience adulthood through me." (50) In fact, Peachy repeatedly emphasizes her own "adulthood" and Beth's "adolescence" in the novel. Do you agree that Peachy is the most

"adult" character in the novel? What aspects of Peachy's character are more "adolescent" than Beth's?

4. In a particularly dramatic moment in the novel, Peachy has an argument at the U.S.–Canadian border with her father, Lou, about Beth's adultery. Peachy, furious with her father for defending Beth, tells him, "I didn't take my sadness out on the whole fucking planet." Lou responds, "That's right, Peachy. You don't. You're lucky. But because Beth does, we have to try to love her more." (174) Do you agree with Lou? Do you think Lou is a good father? Does the novel offer a definitive judgment on good and bad parenting? If so, what is it?

5. On page 93, Peachy says, "I've never envied my prettier, smarter, funnier, skinnier, richer sister. Her uncertainty drained even me." Despite this observation, several of Peachy's thoughts and actions seem dominated by her sense of competition with her sister; perhaps the most vivid example is on page 140, when Peachy considers making love with her husband: "Once he had it in his mind, he was like a snowplow in his single-minded pursuit of sex. . . . I had wanted Beth to overhear a variation of this later that night. . . . I wanted her to know that, despite my complaints, I had made all the right deci-

sions about my life . . ." Do you think Peachy's portrayal of Beth's judgment of her choice is fair, or is it merely a projection of her own doubts? Were you sympathetic to Peachy's insecurity about what Beth thinks, or frustrated by it? Why?

6. On page 90–91, Peachy says about her marriage to Beau: "I know now we had just begun the mysterious process of growing apart, something that used to baffle me about other couples. I used to wonder how, after seven, eight years together do you possibly 'grow apart'? And please can you show me how to do it?" What do you think of Beau and Peachy's marriage? Do you think Peachy bears any responsibility for Beau's cheating with Beth? What do you think happens to the marriage after the novel ends?

7. Sam's epilepsy is a major controlling force in Peachy's life. On page 30, she declares, "Life was all Sam. . . . It was hard to think of anything but his ceaseless metabolism." In what ways did dealing with Sam's epilepsy affect Peachy's understanding of Beth? Of herself?

8. When Peachy decides not to pursue a career in social work, ostensibly to take care of Sam, she says, "Because I believed I was needed at home, Beau and Lou believed it, too. But no matter how I couched my excuse,

Beth wasn't buying any of it." (40) Two-thirds of the way through the novel, Peachy describes Beth as "a woman who never, ever dropped her guard for anyone, except for maybe me." (220) Are Peachy and Beth the closest characters in the novel? Do they know each other best?

9. The novel often focuses on the theme of outsider and insider status—who belongs and who doesn't belong in a certain place or time. For example, when Peachy returns home with her boys the morning after finding Beth and Beau having sex, she has a sudden vision of Beth as Beau's wife, and reflects: "Maybe this was all a big misunderstanding, I thought. Maybe they were the ones who had gotten married all those years ago and I was the one *just stopping by*." (157) What are some other examples in the novel of Peachy feeling like an outsider in her own life? Do you think she creates that feeling for herself, or is it a result of her circumstances? Does she overcome that feeling by the end of the novel?

10. When Peachy decides to go to New York without Beth, she calls her and goes into an astonishing, climactic litany of her duties as a wife and mother: "Before you leave for Detroit, make a lunch for Beau. No meat. The fridge is broken at the shop. His thermos

is in the dishwasher. Washer's still broken. There's four loads of laundry already separated in the basement. Throw them in the trunk." (The entire speech can be found on pages 165–168.) In many ways, this is Peachy's first true moment of self-assertion in the novel. Do you find it pathetic, as Peachy herself does ("Jesus, it sounds like my life sucks") or triumphant? What did you think of the novel's portrayal of the life of a stay-at-home mother?

11. Upon her arrival in New York City, Peachy says, "I felt young and dumb, and suddenly I wanted a mother, any mother, to wrap me in a shock blanket and take me home." Where else does the theme of the absent mother appear in the novel? (A particularly beautiful passage where Peachy describes the effect of her mother's suicide can be found on page 163: "And they can't shake it off.") How does Nell's death affect Peachy's own motherhood? How do you think it affects Beth's interaction with her nephews?

12. While spending time with Jake and Sam at the park, Peachy observes Jake's behavior and says, "I suddenly caught a glimpse of what a little asshole he might become at twenty or thirty, when he was grown up and hopefully some nice woman's problem." (154) Did you find Peachy's periodic matter-

of-fact assessment of her children jarring or realistic? Did it make you more or less sympathetic to her as a character? Why?

13. Although Peachy is tempted, she ultimately decides not to invite Marcus up to the apartment after their date. Were you disappointed or relieved by her decision? Do you think Marcus's attraction to Peachy was feigned or genuine?

14. Did you like the way the novel ended, with brief snapshots of the future, or would you have preferred to be left in the dark? Why?

Reading Group Activities

1. Using inspiration from Peachy's date with Marcus, make the meeting an indulgent and slightly fancier affair than usual. Ask all of your guests to wear their favorite dresses (like Peachy's Diane von Furstenberg wrap dress) to the meeting; serve posh hors d'oeuvres and white wine for refreshments. You can even dim the lights of your living room to create the "moody and intelligent" lighting that Peachy notices in the club with Marcus.

2. Before she became pregnant with Sam, Peachy dreamt of becoming a social worker. Your group can live a day in the missed life of Peachy by organizing a day of volunteering at a local charity, such as a soup kitchen or, like Peachy, with special-needs children. You can find volunteering opportunities in your area at the Web site http://redcross.volunteermatch.org/.

About the Author

LISA GABRIELE is also the author of *Tempting Faith DiNapoli.* Her writing has appeared in the *New York Times Magazine, Vice, Glamour,* and *Nerve,* as well as various anthologies, including *The Best American Nonrequired Reading* series. She lives in Toronto.

Center Point Publishing
600 Brooks Road ● PO Box 1
Thorndike ME 04986-0001 USA

(207) 568-3717

US & Canada:
1 800 929-9108
www.centerpointlargeprint.com